A FRANKENSTEIN'S VOW

At the top of the stairs, Ian stopped. "Miss Frankenstein, you do realize that the vampire is only a creature of legend?" He held his hand up when she tried to argue. "In spite of what your Uncle Tieck wrote, in spite of your Uncle Victor's paranormal research, there are no such creatures as vampires. Do I make myself clear?"

Clair smiled. "I'm sorry, but I beg to differ with you. My studies into the arcane world indicate, rather emphatically I might add, that there *are* such creatures. You, my lord, are one of them. And I will prove it with or without your help!"

The Remarkable Miss Frankenstein

Minda Webber

LOVE SPELL

NEW YORK CITY

*To my son, Jakob, for being the wonderful
person he is and for keeping me laughing over
the years with his great sense of humor.*

LOVE SPELL®

July 2005

Published by

Dorchester Publishing Co., Inc.
200 Madison Avenue
New York, NY 10016

ISBN 0-505-52637-9

The name "Love Spell" and its logo are trademarks of Dorchester
Publishing Co., Inc.

Printed in the United States of America.

Visit us on the web at www.dorchesterpub.com.

ACKNOWLEDGMENTS

To my sister, Marilyn, and my mother, Maxine, for their help and support. Also, my editor, Chris, and my agent, Helen, for believing in this book and appreciating the humor. Karri and Karen for being good friends over the years. My bookstore family: Yolanda, Flo, Terry, Marilyn, Sue and Connie for all their good wishes, Cyndi for reading the book before it was a book and Karla for giving me the clothes off her back.

The Remarkable
Miss Frankenstein

AUTHOR'S NOTE

I have taken certain liberties with many historical facts and literary characters, making this definitely all fiction. Please forgive me, but I couldn't resist.

To twist Mark Twain's famous quote on his *The Adventures of Huckleberry Finn*:

Persons attempting to find sense in this narrative will be prosecuted; persons attempting to find a moral in it will be banished; persons attempting to find historical accuracy in it will be shot.

A Bat in Hand is
Worth Two in the Coffin

The trouble with Clair Frankenstein was that she was a Frankenstein. Her ancestral name required living up to feats such as creating life and forging new frontiers in scientific discovery, no matter whose toes one stepped upon or whose grave one walked over—or in her famous uncle's case, whose grave one robbed. In general Clair felt all her Frankenstein relations were a royal pain in the neck, their creations included. And tonight was no exception as she made her way cautiously down the steep, stone staircase in the direction of the Huntsley family vaults.

"I must have bats in the belfry," she muttered to herself, feeling a malevolent quality to the dense air surrounding her. Suddenly she broke out in goosebumps, overwhelmed by a sense of gloomy urgency, as if destiny were stalking her with tiny catlike steps. She shook the feeling off.

Her movements were silent as she descended into the pitch blackness of the stairwell. The utter darkness encircled her, surrounded her, impenetrable and infinite. The only light came from her flickering candle, which cast gold highlights in her tawny hair and ghostly shadows on the thick limestone walls. Yet Clair could scarcely contain her excitement, for soon she would enter the room where the object of her quest was kept. Finally she would be able to put her theory to practice, to prove beyond a reasonable doubt that which was both improbable and impossible. She, a mere woman, though a Frankenstein, was about to prove a shocking supernatural fact: Vampires were living and feasting in London. Skeptical scientists had laughed at her theory. They believed that few vampires existed and these all lived in Russia or Prussia. Clair disagreed. Vampires were in London. And she, Clair Frankenstein, was going to prove it by accosting one of these elusive London vampires in its own home.

Well, Clair mused, a half smile on her face, she was not actually going to accost the vampire himself yet, but she was going to view and study his coffin. If she was feeling a slight case of nerves at the idea of the blood-craving fiend that inhabited the coffin, who could blame her? After all, she was as sensible as any lady in 1828 London, including her nemesis, Lady Delia Channey, daughter of the Earl of Lon. Just because Clair didn't faint at a drop of blood or the closing of a coffin lid didn't mean she was any less refined.

Clair pictured Lady Delia, with her cupid-bow mouth and mincing mannerisms, the one lady of the *ton* who had made Clair's life a misery ever since Clair was a young girl in pigtails. Regrettably, Clair's childhood foe had never let an opportunity pass to politely mock her. Lady Delia was always chastising her for the many long hours she had dedicated to the advancement of the research of scientific phenomena. It was all done in Lady Delia's most ladylike manner, of course, and always before a most amused audience, causing Clair to wish that she had developed the skin of a rhinoceros.

Ah well, Clair reflected, if wishes were horses, then beggars would ride and Lady Delia would grow warts on her pert nose.

Yes, sometimes she felt as if she carried the weight of the world on her small shoulders. But Clair knew that in reality it was only the very invisible but very great weight of the Frankenstein family fame—or infamy, depending upon with whom she was speaking at the time. After all, when your uncle created a new bachelor from dead body parts, people were either extolling his virtues in scientific journals or up in arms with torches. That's how people felt about her uncle's creation, the monster Frederick.

How anyone could be upset about Frederick, whom her uncle Victor had legally adopted, was beyond Clair. Frederick, the Frankenstein monster, was like a brother to her. Frederick wouldn't hurt a fly, although he occasionally ate them. And he had a heart of gold. Well, not actually gold, since Uncle Victor had tried that scientific route and it had failed dismally. But her uncle had never been one to let failure defeat him, and he had adapted his theory of creation and replaced the heart of gold with the heart of one Mr. Thaddeus Applebee.

Orphaned at an early age, Clair had been raised by her uncle. He and his sister, the Lady Mary Frankenstein, had raised Clair with love, and the freedom to think, to create and to discover whatever could be learned about the unknown world. And while her playmates and peers were being read the fairy tales of the brothers Grimm, Clair's uncle Victor was creating his own grim tales, crossing thresholds no man had crossed before and making his name a household word. He'd shared that strange but exciting world with Clair.

Clair certainly had big shoes to fill—not only her uncle Victor's but Frederick's as well, and Frederick's boot size was an unheard-of sixteen. That was why a very determined Clair had decided she must make good on this new supernatural research project with which she was involved. She wanted to make her family proud, to make her mark in the Frankensteins' annals of achievement.

And now she had the perfect chance. *The Journal of Scientific Discovery* was going to publish a book on the Scientific Discovery of the Decade, along with honoring the chosen scientist with the Scientific Discovery of the Decade Award. This award was what every scientist in the world aspired to own.

For Clair, though the prestige of being classed a top-ranking scientist—a feat no woman had yet achieved—was remarkable, she had a greater goal. She wanted her theories to be published so badly she could taste it. But Clair well knew she had some stiff competition. Dr. Jekyll, a rather two-faced medical man who dealt in odd new chemical compounds, evolution and brain activity, had recently been keeping his cards close to his chest. Of course, Clair reasoned that was like Dr. Jekyll—always hiding something.

Durlock Homes, a well-known sleuth and scientist, was another contender for the prestigious award. Homes was a friend of Clair's uncle Victor, and so she knew he was going to present a paper on something called the "Hound of Hell." Which was all well and good, but if Clair found a live vampire—well, as alive as a vampire could be after being dead for three or four centuries— she would top Homes's and Jekyll's discoveries. A century earlier, Dracula had made his nefarious home in London, but townspeople had gathered together and purged London of all its supernatural creatures at that time. Most of Society didn't even believe in shapeshifters and the un- dead anymore. But Clair knew better.

She would show them all. Besides, Clair thought, flushing with excitement, by the time she was done she would not only have unearthed a vampire in London but a werewolf as well. And anyone worth his scientific salt would recognize that a pair—that is, a vampire and a werewolf—beat some devilish dog any day of the week.

After her disastrous pig misadventure and her impru- dent foray into that demon hunt, Clair found herself having a devil of a time getting anyone to take her work into the otherworldly as serious. Her pride was sorely pricked. But winning the prestigious Scientific Discov- ery of the Decade Award would validate her existence and career. She would make her family proud, even if it killed her, such as by having her blood sucked dry.

Sometimes it was so hard to be a Frankenstein. Yet in spite of it all—the tremendous pressure and desire to succeed, the sacrifices she had made for her research— Clair recognized that she wouldn't trade her name for any other in the entire world. For when she was delving into her science, she was a whole person. She never felt more alive in her cells and in her inspiration than when she was probing and investigating the unusual and unknown, expanding the boundaries of human knowledge to their very outer limits. Her uncle Victor had taught her that.

Other women might find it tedious to spend their daylight hours with heads bent over dusty tomes, but never Clair. Her happiness was at its peak when her mind was revolving around the mysteries of the universe. Though she rarely went to balls or routs, Clair had no qualms about that social sacrifice. And it had never seemed more worth it than tonight, Clair thought, her features animated. For this moment in time was pivotal in the proving of her scientific theorems. This night was to be the pinnacle of her career and was a point of no return. She was about to make an important scientific discovery, perhaps even a life-and-death discovery to a vampire victim or two.

None of it had been easy, she acknowledged. It had all been quite difficult, in fact, Clair mused as she stumbled on an uneven stone step. But gracefully correcting the balance of her trim but curvy figure, she descended downward.

Clair frowned at both the smell of damp mustiness, like very old leaves rotting, and the thought of the difficulty she'd had in bribing Baron Huntsley's footman. The footman hadn't wanted to give her the information she needed to prove her conclusions—which meant the baron's staff was either extremely loyal or extremely terrified. Clair would bet on the latter. And she was not a person prone to betting, except for charity, or on an occasional hand of whist with her aunts. Or every now and then a horse or two.

Clair pursed her pouty lips, thinking. Here she was, a solitary female alone in the house of a supposed vampire. Maybe she was a bit more of a gambler than she'd thought.

Glancing cautiously about her, Clair felt the strongest sense of menace yet. She almost shuddered at what lay ahead of her, and the frightening possibility that the coffin might spring open, the vampire popping up with fangs bared like a rabid jack-in-the-box.

"Quit trying to scare yourself silly!" she scolded the shadows. "You have your theory to prove beyond a shadow of a doubt. No matter the danger from the undead. You have your research to publish," she said. "You can't let a little thing like a bloodsucking monster stop you. You are first and foremost a Frankenstein."

She often talked to herself, discussing her conclusions and her strategies. "No Frankenstein has ever gone unpublished," she continued. Then, wrinkling her brow, she realized that wasn't quite true. Her great-uncle Aaron had remained unknown. Of course, he had believed he was a ghost. He often regaled Clair with the exploits of his hauntings, but also used being a ghost as an excuse for not publishing. He would tell Clair that everyone knew ghosts could not be expected to write anything visible to the human eye. Then she and her great-uncle would have quite the debate, which would always end when she perversely brought up the fact that everyone had heard of ghost writers.

The sudden sound of bells clanging in the far distance overloaded Clair's senses. Heart palpitating rapidly, she shivered. It was midnight. The witching hour.

" 'Ask not for whom the bell tolls,' " she quoted, whispering to herself and tasting fear. She had not realized that the taste of fear was metallic.

Quickly she scanned the darkness, sensing something she could not define. Cold air stirred in currents around her. The darkness felt oppressive, like a great dank weight resting upon her chest. She felt as if Fate crouched nearby, watching with jaundiced eyes, waiting for her to make a mistake.

Moving her candle in a clockwise circle, Clair once again searched the shadows. There was nothing, yet she couldn't help feeling as if something wicked this way came—and right at her! But only dark silence met her fears. She was alone, wasn't she?

Biting her lower lip, Clair nervously squared her shoulders and continued her descent. She couldn't quit now; she had put too much time into her research. Her meticulousness had unearthed the unearthly living and feeding in London.

Yes, Clair in fact believed that a whole nest of vampires were in hiding here, though no deaths had been attributed thus far to such creatures. However, her assurance in her theories and her eventual scientific jackpot made Clair's journey into the unknown much more palatable. She knew that many *Nosferatu* hid among the English aristocracy's *ton*, in the perpetual dark of night and the perpetual motion of the affluent. For what better place to be than among those who seldom went to bed before dawn? Vampires couldn't select a more perfect place to thrive than among the upper crust of English society, who so loved the night, its decadence and lechery.

"Yes," Clair muttered. "London is the perfect place for the bloodthirsty fiends. Like it or not, Baron Huntsley, here I come."

Clair had never met the baron face to face. Her interest in him had been stirred to frenzy when she met a stranger on the train, both of them staring out the rear window, watching the night flash by. The younger woman, a Miss Hitchcock, had served the Huntsleys for several years as a maid. And on the train the maid regaled Clair with the baron's exploits. Some Clair had heard before. She'd known the baron was handsome and wealthy, his cunning for making money almost magical. He owned estates in the north of England and several also in northwestern Wales—rather a north by northwest arrangement of land holdings. A notorious womanizer, the baron was said to love the hunt better than the actual conquest. It was, however, the other tales the maid confided that kept Clair spellbound and aroused her suspicions.

Now, a year after that fateful train trip, Clair had gathered enough background information to warrant a scouting expedition into the baron's estate, though she'd decided to move when he wasn't in residence. And that piece of information had been delivered two nights before, after her great-aunt Abby's predictions with tarot cards. It had accompanied the icing on her suspicions' proverbial cake, when Clair's great-aunt had dramatically stated that the ominous Baron Huntsley was a creature of the night. And so the last damning piece of evidence had fallen at Clair's feet—or, to be precise, on the card table—at the same time Clair discovered her opportunity: the *ton* believed Huntsley would be attending the Amberton Ball, an affair to last until dawn.

Clair grinned, wanting to pat herself on the back. "While the vampire's away, the scientist will play," she whispered as she reached the bottom of the stone steps.

A heavy wooden door loomed to her left. Cautiously, Clair inched it open. The bottom scraped against the hard stone floor and the sound echoed off the walls. Her heartbeat did a staccato dance in her chest.

9

"You can do this," she said. "Be the brave Frankenstein I know you sometimes are." Gathering her courage like a warm coat against brutal wind, she prepared to enter the room which she believed held Baron Huntsley's coffin.

She knew she must be brave and must loose caution to the winds in the search for truth. No matter the danger or the hardship, she must march onward and prevail. "The truth at all costs," she reminded herself. It was the Frankenstein family motto, and mottoes must be upheld—else why have them, she reasoned quietly.

Still, sneaking about in the dark in the minutes just past midnight, the witching hour, looking for the coffin of a vampire, might be throwing a bit more than caution to the winds. In fact, some people might just call it pressing her luck. She knew her aunt Mary felt that way. Unlike her great-aunt Abby, who, eccentric and mad as a hatter, was always remarking, "Off with their heads." Of course, Abby was Queen Elizabeth this week, and that was one of her favorite Queen Elizabeth lines.

Clair entered the room, thinking to herself, "I shall prevail."

Scanning the looming blackness, she nervously sucked on her lower lip, moving her candle to her left hand while her right hand grasped the rather large silver cross around her neck. A bit of wax dropped on her skin and she gasped slightly at the pain as she moved slowly into the eerie room. Candlelight danced across the damp stone walls, highlighting the large marble crypt in the corner.

"Aha! I have it!" she announced joyfully, her eyes dancing with both pride and excitement. The vault room was exactly as she had pictured in her overactive imagination: dark, dank, gloomy, with a hidden treasure . . . her treasure! Some might consider it hideous, but not Clair. She found the coffin absolutely, magnificently marvelous. She was a genius. But then that was never in doubt, with her Frankenstein genes, she thought cheerfully.

Clair grinned. It felt like Christmas morning and she could hardly wait to open her gifts. Except this time her gift was in the form of a marble crypt.

"Eureka! You're mine, all mine," she cried.

But the best-laid plans of mice and women sometimes come crashing to a grinding halt. Unfortunately for Clair, this was one of those times. A deeply compelling voice interrupted her self-congratulation.

"Beg your pardon, but just what is yours?"

Clair spun around, almost losing her balance. Stunned, she took careful stock of the owner of the voice. He was holding a five-stemmed candelabrum, the candles' dancing flames revealing a strong, formidable face. His cheekbones were high and well-defined, as was his nose, indicative of his Welsh heritage. Clair noted that his brows and hair were so dark as to blend in with the night, and his hair was long, the edges curling several inches past his collar. The intruder was tall and sturdy, with wide, muscular shoulders filling his broadcoat. His cravat was loosely tied, and he was attired entirely in black and gray. In essence, he was a study in shadow.

Wide and sensuous, his lips gave the parody of a smile, with gleaming white teeth. Big white teeth, Clair thought, gasping, which stood out in sharp contrast to the darkness surrounding them.

From somewhere deep within her a scream rose, but Clair managed to swallow it. She was standing face-to-face with a real, live vampire.

Well, perhaps not live, she reminded herself.

11

Dr. Frankenstein, I Presume

"Hmmm?" Now *that* was an answer, she noted dismally. She was finally rendered speechless. Uncle Victor would be stunned. Somewhere in the back of her mind, Clair knew she should be running for her life. But no, that was too melodramatic. Instead, she stood her ground like one of the Elgin statues all London was agog over.

Should she apologize for dropping in unannounced at his bedtime, or should she pretend to faint? No, fainting was too dangerous. The sly baron might decide a midnight snack was in order, and she would be the main aperitif.

Peeking up at him from beneath her eyelashes, Clair felt her adrenaline surge. Her morbid curiosity seemed to be overcoming the worst of her fears. Her mind, a steel trap–like device, was already compartmentalizing facts. She was in the presence of a vampire. He could be centuries old. Who knew what secrets he had learned over the years? It was utterly terrifying, utterly illuminating, and utterly bloody remarkable. Clair was spellbound. Her host had a powerful, predatory air, a wild energy about him that was almost primitive. If he was centuries old, he was well preserved. Hmm, *very* well preserved.

"Madame, and I use the term loosely, I am waiting for an answer!" Baron Harold Ian Huntsley's voice was clipped, the evident rage enough to release her from her bemusement.

As nonchalantly as possible in the presence of the Baron and his very predatory glare, Clair took a tiny step back—an infinitesimal step. When the attractive aristocrat remained absolutely still, she took another step backward, putting as much distance as possible between herself and the threat of danger.

Clair had the strangest sensation that the baron was stalking her, even though he hadn't moved a muscle. "So this is what a mouse feels like," she muttered.

"I beg pardon," he asked arrogantly, watching her with blazing eyes

Clair blinked. The man radiated hostility, and most of it she feared was directed at her. "This isn't what it looks like. Not at all. This is a mission of science," she explained.

"Science?" Baron Huntsley snarled, once again revealing sharp white teeth. He studied her with a hard glint in his eyes. "You look as though you are standing in my basement uninvited."

"Well, I am. I mean, I obviously am here in your basement uninvited. If I weren't here, we wouldn't be having this conversation. Not at all," she protested, biting her lower lip nervously, wishing she were in India right now, or even the London stews, that hotbed of thieves, murderers, and prostitutes. She wished she were anywhere but here. Baron Huntsley would be a frightening figure even if he were not part of the supernatural world. Quickly she recited to herself again, "The truth at all costs."

Ian, Baron Huntsley, stared at the woman who had dared interrupt his solitude. He asked, his tone icy, "So, why have you broken into my basement?" He didn't know her game, but he would find it out. No one stole from him. Still, this five-foot-three-inch bit of bluster and bravado didn't look like a thief. Actually, he surmised as he studied her, with her fraying black cape, she looked like a reject from the London stews.

Clair dramatically waved her hands in the air. Baron Huntsley was truly formidable. "Broken in? Appearances can be deceiving," she said with a false smile.

Slyly examining him from top to bottom, Clair began compiling scientific facts, wondering if the devastatingly handsome baron could turn into a bat. She wondered too why he was back so early from the party. She wondered if he was going to bite her neck, and if he did, would she mind terribly? He was a rather handsome dog for a vampire. And he had such broad, strong shoulders. His legs were very long, his thighs heavily muscled. She wondered if he ever got cramped in his crypt.

"With what were you planning to make away? Just what in my basement would interest a thief?" the baron asked.

"I was not stealing anything. I could never be a thief. It just isn't in my genetic makeup," Clair answered honestly. She hesitated a moment, then added, "With the exception of a corpse or two." Although Clair really didn't consider it thievery to rob graves—at least of their bodies. The dead were generally dead—unless they were the undead or her uncle Victor had gotten hold of them.

The baron raised a brow, his aristocratic features sharply delineated by the flickering candlelight.

"Medical purposes . . . the corpses," she explained.

She's insane, Ian thought sadly. Such a beauty. She didn't look like a lunatic.

Staring right at her, he thought of another reason she might have come. He asked, "Are you here to compromise me, then?"

Clair was shocked. "No! What a ludicrous thought. I value my blood and my bloodline too much to do such an unladylike thing as that. No, I am here to compromise your coffin. But since you seem rather in a hurry and appear to be in a bleak mood, I think I'll just take my leave now," she went on in a convoluted manner, hoping to dazzle the wily baron with a profusion of words, allowing her to slip away unnoticed. She took a step around him.

Ian blocked the woman's route with his muscular body, his eyes widening in surprise. He was momentarily speechless, a first for him. He had seen and done many things in his jaded lifetime, some things he would carry to his grave as scars upon his soul. But he had never seen anything like this small Amazon standing quite proudly, although quite stupidly, in front of him.

In spite of his shock, he couldn't help but notice how pretty she was, what with her tawny gold-brown hair and her huge eyes. They were gray, the color of the rain-streaked skies over his beloved Welsh mountains.

"My coffin?" He finally processed what she'd said. "What coffin?"

"Baron Huntsley," Clair started, then stopped. "I assume you are Baron Ian Huntsley of Yorkshire and Balmoria in Wales?" He nodded, so she continued. "That dog won't hunt, Baron Huntsley. You are *not* going to play that old game."

When he remained silent, she scowled. It was so like a man to play the innocent when he was guilty of hiding secrets. But this secret couldn't be hidden. It was staring them both in the face: his crypt.

Her Frankenstein curiosity taking over, Clair forgot most of her fear. Yes, this was the baron's crypt. This was where he probably slept the day away, dreaming of ill-gotten gains of blood and who knew what else a creature of the night like himself might dare to dream in the depths of sleep.

"What game are you speaking about?" Ian was fascinated in spite of himself. He should call the Bow Street runners, he thought. He should call his staff and have her thrown out, but he'd rather have his staff throw her into his bed. She was a petite beauty and she was in his territory now, right where she'd put herself.

He drew closer, nostrils flaring slightly as he breathed in her scent. She smelled of winter, fresh and frosty. He found it remarkably stimulating.

Dramatically, the woman pointed and chastised him. "How about that great big stone coffin in the corner? My lord, you are deliberately trying to draw my attention away from it."

"Oh, *that* coffin," Ian replied stiffly, questions flooding his mind. He wondered if any of the enemies he had made spying for the British government had something to do with this. He wondered if she was playing a game, and if so, what were the rules? He wondered if the woman was mad as a hatter. Then he wondered if he himself was mad as a hatter for listening to her demented ramblings in his basement on a Tuesday night. Surely he was. But though curiosity had killed many a cat, he was as curious as any cat—and not as easily killed . . . nine lives or not.

Clair smiled smugly, her fright easing. The baron had not rushed her. He had not attacked her, leading her to believe that he probably wouldn't. She felt fairly safe—as safe as one could feel in the presence of a crusty, mad vampire. And though he was a handsome devil, he would still have to get up pretty early in the morning to fool a Frankenstein. And he went to bed in the mornings.

"Yes, that coffin." She pointed primly to the massive stone monument. "*Your* coffin."

"Actually, that's my ancestor, the second Baron Huntsley's coffin."

She snorted.

The unladylike noise from the woman caught Ian unaware and had him staring at her transfixed. He arched a brow as he observed the way the candlelight highlighted the golden strands of her hair. Parts of it had become undone from her braid, giving her a wild, tousled look, as though she had just stepped from a lover's bed. He wanted to be that lover, although he couldn't tell much about her figure with that grotesque cape she was wearing. Still, that didn't stop the flow of blood to his groin.

She actually gave a little laugh then, the sound chiming in the darkness like the brisk bells of St. Matthew's

Chapel. "Baron Huntsley, somehow I knew you would say that."

Ian cocked his head to study her. "If you knew the coffin was my great-great-grandfather's, why pretend it's mine?"

Again she snorted. "No, I know it is yours. Your coffin. Although I do find it odd that you are returning to it so soon, after only leaving it a few hours ago."

He'd been right. She was mad. What a pity. Such a beautiful woman to be raving. "Returning to it? Do I look like a corpse to you?"

"Not now." She stopped, groping in her pocket and pulling out a watch. "But in six hours you will be."

"I will be what?" Ian asked with the barest modicum of civility, wondering why he was still standing there arguing with a Bedlamite.

"You will be a corpse."

Ian smiled. It was a smile devoid of all warmth and humor. "I do so love challenges. Are you planning on killing me?"

He should be concerned, he supposed, but instead he was simply intrigued. It had been a long time since he had felt this way. Life had become a blur of days and nights, blending into one stark shade of gray. Nothing was special anymore, or remarkable; all was mundane.

Lately he had wondered if something essential in life had passed him by some afternoon when he was hunting or playing cards. For the past five years, the joys of his life had faded into the vague nothingness of memories. That is, until tonight, when he had been alerted by the sound of footsteps making their way to his basement and he had silently followed. Suddenly the night had seemed more alive than it had in years, as if a fresh stiff breeze were blowing away the cobwebs in his mind. Unfortunately, it appeared his savior was a loon.

She stared at his mouth. "Do you plan on biting me?" she asked.

Ian looked her up and down. "I can't tell in that awful cape. Are you good enough to eat?"

Clair cocked her head, glaring at him. "No." The baron really was too saucy for his own good. But then, she reasoned, vampires were masters of manipulation and seduction. Still, she would be no one's puppet, even if this vampire did make her heart almost stop with his rich, husky voice and his attractive features.

"Then why would I bite you?" he asked.

She gave him a look which named him stupid. "You're a vampire, of course."

Ian Huntsley, fifth Baron of Huntsley, threw back his head and laughed. Long and hard.

"I see no humor in this remarkable and riveting discovery," Clair said haughtily. "After all, it took great skill and courage to track you to your lair."

He chuckled. "My lair . . . ?" Suddenly the chuckles faded and he growled, "Madame, I do believe you have a screw loose. Maybe more than one."

Clair glared at him. "How dare you presume to say such a thing? I, sirrah, am a scientist!"

Ian eyed the woman, a scowl darkening his features. "That makes little sense. No sane person I know, a scientist especially, would enter the . . . what did you call it? Ah yes, the lair of a vampire alone, at night, with no protection!"

She could be killed pulling such stunts as this, he knew. London was a dangerous place, especially at night. All kinds of creatures were lurking about. And this small woman was out seeking bloodsucking demons and God knew what else. In addition, as bad luck would have it, she was seeking them in his home. The group of men with which he sometimes did business, would not be pleased if they found out about this night's adventure.

"I am not just anyone," the woman stated dramatically, her nose stuck proudly in the air. "I am Clair Elizabeth Frankenstein, niece to Dr. Victor Frankenstein and niece also to Dr. Johann Tieck."

"Oh, good Lord," Ian groaned. "You are niece to both a quack and a deranged writer."

Until that point, Clair had been cautiously keeping her distance between the devil and the deep blue sea, mainly this baron of vampires. But hearing the unkind remarks the man made about her uncles, Clair threw caution to the wind. Dashing forward, she closed the distance and slapped Ian smartly across the face.

"How dare you demean my uncles? They are great men, worthy of the Frankenstein name!"

Ian looked down at the furious spitting kitten and had to clench his teeth to stop from grinning. "I am sorry, Miss Frankenstein. I lost my good manners at the surprise of your illustrious family heritage."

She eyed him suspiciously. He was staring at her neck and he had all those white teeth. Those big white teeth. THOSE BIG WHITE TEETH!

"Stop staring at my neck," she demanded bravely, feeling far from courageous, wondering how those big white teeth would feel in her neck. She bet they would hurt tremendously. Then her mind spun down other scientific avenues. Would she like sleeping underground . . . so far, far underground? If she became one of the undead, would the dastardly baron let her have a nightlight in her coffin so that she could continue her research after-hours? She would insist upon it. After all, if she were to become immortal, she would certainly take advantage of some fringe benefits.

"My lord, I would appreciate it if you would leave off eyeing my neck. You make me feel rather like a lush roast pig."

"Your neck? I am staring at your breasts," Ian corrected devilishly, his eyes devouring how her cloak draped open and revealed the pale expanse of the upper slopes of her generous bosom. Lush was the right word indeed for what he could see of her figure. He licked his lips. He did so delight in large-chested women; there was so much more to nip and suck.

Clair gasped, closing her cloak. "You, my lord, are a bounder. I heard you were a rake beyond reason. I see the rumors are correct."

"I thought you heard I was a vampire?" Ian reminded her, grinning and enjoying her chagrin.

"Are they mutually exclusive?"

"Probably not," he retorted. "But, more to the point, who is spreading such rumors, compromising my good name?" Ian asked the question nonchalantly, but it was anything but casual. Whoever was telling such tales must be taken care of, and quickly. All Huntsleys demanded loyalty first and foremost; lives depended upon it. Betrayal was not a laughing matter, and certainly not one Ian took lightly.

Gracing Clair with a look that had scared grown men, he waited impatiently. The stubborn wench remained silent. Ian knew she was afraid—he could smell the fear on her—yet she held her ground like a Spartan.

"Come, who has been telling tales about me?" Ian questioned.

"Who would dare?"

"You are being evasive."

"You are being elusive."

"You are prevaricating," Ian growled, arms crossed tightly against his chest.

"You are posturing." Clair grinned.

Ian snorted. "Possibly, but then you are staking your life on it, aren't you? Creeping down my basement stairs, all alone . . ." He narrowed his gaze, studying her again, fresh anger spurting though his veins and pounding through his body. He had been betrayed, slandered, his sanctuary had been invaded, and worst of all, this beautiful woman had placed herself at risk.

"Staked my life on it? Well, that's better than being staked," she hedged. She didn't like the gleam in his eyes. He looked hungry for something other than her blood. She fanned herself.

He took a step closer. She took a step back. She was no fool. She recognized danger when she saw it; it didn't have to jump up and bite her on the neck.

"You are a dangerous man," she admitted, more to herself than to Ian.

"Let me show you just how dangerous. . . ." He trailed off suggestively.

Her mind was a mass of swirling convictions, warnings, and yearnings as she peered up at him from beneath thick brown lashes. Suddenly, she slapped her head with her palm. "You are doing it again!"

"What?"

"Trying to draw my attention away from your coffin."

"My great-great-grandfather's coffin," he corrected.

Clair scanned his body quickly, then glanced over at the coffin. "It looks as if it would fit you perfectly."

"That's ridiculous. One size fits all in coffins," he snapped, wondering what it would be like to taste her. Probably heaven—or, more likely, hell. Getting involved with a Frankenstein would be like standing up to an avalanche: downhill all the way.

"In a pig's eye, they do." The way she said it caused the baron to break into laughter again.

Without thought Clair took two steps forward and kicked him in the shin, her eyes flashing fire. "I don't like being laughed at."

Realizing what she had done, Clair bit back a groan. She had bearded the lion in his den and then attacked him. Her aunt Mary was right. Her temper was going to get her into serious trouble. And it looked as though tonight was the night, for an enraged vampire could only spell trouble with a big, fat capital T.

Ian noted the variety of expressions crossing Clair's face. First there was anger, then chagrin, then fear, then remorse, and finally terror. Although Ian generally preferred people to maintain a healthy fear of him, he didn't like it from this small powder keg. So, before she could run screaming into the night, he pulled her into his arms and kissed her.

She tasted like the first snow of winter—soft, wet, and invigorating. She tasted special, creating in him an addiction that would not soon be satisfied. He felt the blood rushing to his groin, making him as stiff as a poker. This Clair Frankenstein felt just right in his arms, neither too tall nor too short. She made him hunger. She tasted so good that he had to taste her again.

Clair felt the air whoosh out of her lungs as the soft heat of Baron Huntsley's lips pressed against her and his arms enclosed her tightly. How dare he be so forward? How dare he try and seduce her with his vampire tricks? Her mind screamed these things, but a small voice was whispering how delicious and decadent it all was.

Wanting to push him away, her arms instead ended up wrapping around his neck. She could feel the luxuriant thickness of his hair where it lay over his collar. It was as soft as silk.

And his body felt wonderful. In the back of her mind, Clair decided to put the inertia principal into practice, to take the path of least resistance and just stay in his arms for a bit longer.

A lick of fire shot like a comet from her stomach to her lips, tingles spurting from her toes to other regions. The sensation was astounding. She had never felt the like before. No wonder vampires were the lovers of choice in those gothic stories if they could kiss like this, she mused. Why, it made her blood rush to her head! Her heart beat giddily faster, pumping more of her hot red blood. . . .

Blood! That was the key word, her mind inserted loudly. Her blood was hot and she was hot and he was a vampire hungering for her life's fluid, wanting to steal it from her! While she on the other hand was rather fond of it and definitely wanted to keep every last drop.

Regaining her somewhat bemused wits, Clair shoved against his chest. Reluctantly Ian released her.

Clair hastily and rather belatedly grabbed her cross, shoving it into his face. Inching away, she warned, "Stay back! I am not afraid to use this."

Ian merely yawned.

"So much for the cross," she muttered. Undaunted,

she quickly groped beneath her large black cape. "Aha," she added triumphantly as she pulled out a stick.

Ian had to bite his lip to keep from laughing. She held a small stick not much bigger than his index finger, about four inches long with no sharpened end.

"I take it that is a stake?" he said.

Clair looked at what she held in her hand. "Well, actually no. It's what I used to pry your window open upstairs." She dropped the stick and fished around inside her cape again, coming up with a garlic clove.

He sniffed, then shook his head. "Try again."

Frustrated, she dropped the garlic.

Ian shook his head. If she wasn't so deliciously scary, she would be dangerous. She gave him a haughty look.

Arms crossed on his chest, he watched her fumble around inside her cloak again and wished it was his hands roaming her body. "I could help." He smiled, a rakish smile that had lifted a thousand skirts. The effect it had on Clair, however, was somewhat different from what Ian anticipated.

"You have awfully big teeth," she said suspiciously.

He couldn't help himself. "The better to eat you with, my dear." His grin was pure wolf.

"My lord, this is no joking matter! I am human and you are . . ." She paused. "Well, you *aren't*. Control yourself, sir."

If you only knew, Ian mused. His control was perfect, all he wanted to do right now was lay Clair Frankenstein across that coffin and ravish her thoroughly until she screamed with pleasure again and again and again.

"I would say I am exhibiting remarkable control," he told her. "After all, I haven't had you arrested for breaking and entering. What would society say? What would your uncles say?"

"Nothing, for neither rain nor snow nor sleet," Clair began, then ad-libbed ingeniously, "nor vampires can stop a Frankenstein's quest for truth. Besides, my lord, no one will ever know I was here."

"And why is that?"

"If you told them we were here alone, then I would be compromised by you and—"

Ian interrupted. "*You* compromised *me*."

Ignoring his remark Clair continued, "You would either have to marry me, leave me to be ruined, or tell them I was here searching for your daytime hiding place. And I am positive that you don't want anyone to know where your resting place really is. After all, I assume that is a vampire's cardinal rule. And if you ruined me, I could reveal your daytime sleeping quarters. So you would be forced to marry me . . . if you were to tell anyone I was here."

Ian shook his head. "Ah, a fate worse than death to be sure."

Clair frowned, wondering what he meant: others finding out about his coffin, or marrying her?

He took two steps toward her, a roguish gleam in his eye. "I could just have my wicked way with you and make you my vampire queen," he suggested.

Clair didn't find that amusing. "I would make a terrible queen, and besides I detest the color red. It looks ghastly on me."

He couldn't help himself. He had to ask. "Red?"

"Hmmm?" Clair murmured, once again hunting through her big black cape. "Yes, well, all vampire queens wear red."

Ian turned his back to her, hiding another grin. "Did you happen to notice what color I am wearing?"

"Black. But I mean at nighttime. You know—bedtime, I mean. Sleeping garments. Vampires wear red to go to bed. I mean, to go to their coffins. Or when eating."

Ian turned back around, staring in fascination. "And how did you arrive at this conclusion?"

"It was my uncle Victor's theory. Less wear and tear on the clothes with all the bloodstains. My uncle is so brilliant, he simply astounds me at times. I am very fortunate to have him for my relative. When other children were being told about sugarplum fairies, my uncle was discussing with me how electrical impulses can regenerate dead flesh."

Ian shook his head. This tiny, possibly batty female astounded him. "And your uncle Victor came up with the red-clothing theory?"

Clair nodded.

"I rather thought vampires retired without their clothes, au naturel," Ian said slyly, watching her rummage through her cloak. He had always enjoyed cloak-and-dagger stuff before, but tonight he was positively thrilled at the prospect of discovering just what lay beneath the cloak.

Clair chose not to hear him. "Aha!" she said. This time she pulled out a fairly decent-looking stake, approximately ten inches in length, oak and very sharp.

One of Van Helsing's models, Ian noted, if he was not mistaken.

"I knew I had it somewhere," Clair added brightly.

"Now, what do you intend to do with it?" Ian asked.

"Why, win my way free of you, of course."

"You are going to stake me?"

Clair shook her head. "No, only frighten you." She didn't really think she could stake the handsome baron, no matter how much time went by. He was much too good-looking. And then there had been that kiss, a kiss which made her think of red clothing and and love bites and bedtime in vampire-land. That kiss had not been just a kiss, on that she could rely. She sighed.

Holding the vampire stake upright in her hand as though she were holding a candelabrum, she motioned the baron forward. She was very proud of herself. She had been face-to-face with a master vampire and survived. Clair hoped her aunt Mary was still awake, for she had a tale or two to tell of the crypt tonight.

"Please, my lord, would you lead the way out of here?"

Ian nodded, thinking she was either the bravest woman he had ever known or the craziest. He gallantly did as she requested.

At the top of the stairs, he stopped. "Miss Frankenstein, you do realize that the vampire is only a creature of legend?" He held his hand up when she tried to argue. "In spite of what your uncle Tieck wrote, in spite of your uncle Victor's paranormal research, there are no such creatures as vampires. Do I make myself clear?"

"I'm sorry, but I beg to differ with you. My studies into the arcane world indicate—rather emphatically I might add—that there are such creatures. You, my lord, are one of them. And I will prove it with or without your help," she sallied. She pushed open a heavy door leading into a long hallway behind the main stairs of the main foyer. Stepping through, she and Ian startled a serving maid walking by with linens in her arms.

"I am sorry, I didn't mean to frighten you," Clair

apologized. The young Welsh serving maid's eyes went round, her mouth a perfect O as she gaped at the stake Clair held in her hand.

"Rats," Clair temporized. "Big rats." The maid scurried away as fast as her feet would take her.

Ian sighed as he watched the maid go. It looked as if he would have to find a replacement. "Keep this up, Miss Frankenstein, and you will find that you have bitten off more than you can chew," he warned.

"I rather thought that was my line," she said haughtily. Then, with a swish of her skirts, she stormed regally off. It would have been a great exit, Clair later commiserated with her aunt Mary, if she hadn't dropped another piece of garlic on her way out the door.

Early to Rise and
No Vampire Ashes

"The rumors of my being undead have been greatly exaggerated," Ian stated formally, his green eyes glinting with mischief.

"It's impossible," Clair said, clasping a hand to her breast. "You are not a vampire!" Stunned, she stared at Baron Huntsley, who stood in her morning room alive and well and certainly not bursting into flames. Not even one ash was upon the fool man. Didn't he know the rules of vampiredom? A vampire burned to a crisp in broad daylight.

"When my butler, Brooks, announced you, I thought he had misheard," she said to herself. Drat the blasted reprobate. She fumed, feeling like her friend Alice, who had fallen down a rabbit hole. How was the impossible

possible? She was hallucinating, perhaps due to burning the midnight oil once too often.

She blinked. No, Baron Huntsley was still there. She glanced outside the bay window, scarcely noticing how the bright sunlight lit the evergreens. Yes, it was indeed morning. She glanced at her pocket watch, noting the time: two hours until noon, a time when all good vampires were home in bed and sleeping the sleep of the dead. Yet all evidence to the contrary, vampire Huntsley stood firm and handsome before her, a mocking grin on his aristocratic face as he watched the thoughts tumbling through her mind.

Clair shook her head in disbelief. "How is it possible? Do you have a twin? Am I dreaming?" She quickly pinched herself. *Ouch.* No, she wasn't dreaming.

"How could I be wrong?" she contemplated pettishly. "Such diligent, brilliant research. So very much time and effort wasted . . . wasted!"

The family butler stood nearby, the epitome of the well bred English butler. He was in his early fifties, though sometimes looked like he was sixty, and was a slight figure of a man with dark brown hair. One silver streak ran through his thinning tresses. He had learned early on in his life with the Frankensteins to never act unduly surprised. Nowadays in particular, he never revealed his high anxiety, especially over Clair's blazing escapades.

"Perhaps the baron would care for some refreshment?" he asked stoically, a long-suffering look on his face. He knew his mistress's moods and quirks too well, and right now she was in her "I can't believe I've wasted all my time for nothing" mode.

Clair glanced at Brooks, nodding at the suggestion, then zeroed in on the baron. "Sir, you are no gentleman. How could you let me believe that you were a vampire? It was not well done of you at all. I was up half the night recording our meeting in my notebook."

Ian raised a dark eyebrow. "I never claimed to be a vampire, Miss Frankenstein, if you will only recall." He shook his head slightly. What a little minx! She was miffed because he wasn't a bloodsucker. Yet if he had been one of the undead, her life expectancy would have been greatly reduced that night.

She sniffed daintily as Ian studied her from the top of her burnished head to her rather small feet. She was dressed in a gown of apricot silk, with lace around the bodice and puffed sleeves. Her glorious golden hair was caught up in an elaborate twist with a few curls dangling about her cheeks. A ribbon of the same color as her dress was entwined in her coiffure.

In broad daylight and with that awful cape gone, Ian could view her figure to his heart's content. And what a figure it was, from her tiny waist to her plump breasts. Since Ian was definitely a breast man, he was doubly impressed. He had visions of burying his head between those full globes and sucking sweetly.

He lifted his eyes, hoping his perusal had gone unnoticed. It had. Miss Frankenstein once again had her head in the inexplicable and cloudy academic realms she frequented. He watched her chewing on her bottom lip.

In actuality, while Ian was studying Clair, Clair was readjusting her scientific schedule. This would put her back a day or two. It frustrated her to no end. She truly hated wasting time, but it was not the baron's fault, she finally conceded. She knew she had been taught better manners than to blame others for her mistakes. Her aunt Mary would have a fit.

"Forgive me, my lord. You are correct. It was my research and my mistake. Please accept my apology."

She was still upset that all her work had led her to the wrong man. But what a man, she admitted silently. He really was ruggedly handsome, the morning light shining on his raven locks, bringing out the bluish highlights. His dark green eyes reminded her of the rebirth of spring, of hope after a long winter vigil. They were really quite remarkable eyes, she reflected, so filled with fire and heat.

"Research?" Ian asked, wanting to know more, *having* to know more.

"Hmmm . . . yes. My research into the habits and nature of supernatural creatures," she answered. "In other words, I have done an intense study on things that go bump and bite in the night. All things supernatural, that is."

Fascinating, he thought. And frightening. Most ladies would be terrified to admit such creatures existed. None, he knew, would try to research the subject to do just that.

"Is that truly why you were snooping about my house last night?" Ian knew all about sneaking and spying, having been employed by the government.

"I wasn't snooping," she responded hotly. "I was intending to conduct important scientific studies, and your name topped my list of subjects."

Clair silently seethed. He thought her to be one of those people who was always going about indiscriminately sticking their noses into someone else's business—like that Homes fellow, who was a friend of her uncle Victor and aunt Mary.

"Very important scientific studies. You know, extremely important inquiries into the realm of the arcane."

"I see," Ian said, thinking how cute she looked with her deep gray eyes shooting sparks at him. "I should have realized that any niece of Victor Frankenstein would be interested in the more unusual roads of scientific inquiry."

"You mentioned my uncle last night . . . albeit mistakenly. Do you perhaps know him?" Clair asked.

"Who could not know the great Dr. Victor Frankenstein? I attended several of his lectures during my university days in Vienna. I was quite impressed with some of his suppositions. Although some of those theories do trip into the realm of the extremely bizarre."

"Such as?"

"The cloning of people."

"Ah yes. One of his favorite theories. Uncle Victor believes that someday scientists will clone many things. Perhaps a goat or a sheep or even people. He also believes doctors will be able to harvest organs from dying patients and place them in people who have weak hearts or kidneys."

Ian arched a skeptical brow.

"It is a beautiful hope for the future."

"Hope springs eternal."

"True. Hope and good old-fashioned hard work and research. Research my uncle is on the cutting edge of," Clair added proudly. "Uncle Victor is quite brilliant. Perhaps the most brilliant of all scientists alive."

Ian nodded politely, amused. Victor Frankenstein was brilliant, but he was also a card-carrying lunatic. He was most famous for his forays into animating dead flesh—

queer work which had created widespread controversy, not to mention chaos when his creation escaped and roamed the countryside, eating up blind men's food and setting fire to the Ritz after a particularly bohemian display of dancing.

Ian couldn't help cringing when he remembered that fated night. He and some of his cronics had gone to see the dancing monster the night the Ritz had gone up in flames.

Ian sighed, admitting to himself that Victor and the monster had danced a mean soft-shoe. But who else but a card-carrying lunatic would introduce a monster to the Countess of Deville and expect all to go well?

The countess was well known for her love of big men and their larger-than-life attributes, and one couldn't get much bigger than Victor's monster. The countess was also known to be rather randy and grabby. She had grabbed the monster by his assets and squeezed.

The monster, taken by surprise, had backed into the Earl of Kent, who in turn fell on the Marquis of Stoker, who in turn landed on Major Van Helsing, who knocked over both Mr. Bear and his wife, etcetera and etcetera, until the stage lights had been knocked over and the stage curtains had caught fire. It had been a typical Frankenstein fiasco. Still, Ian didn't want to hurt Clair's familial feelings.

"Yes, your uncle is brilliant. By the way, how is the monster faring?"

Clair frowned. How rude! "We don't call him the monster. His name is Frederick Frankenstein. My uncle adopted him, you know. And he is doing quite fine, thank you."

She crossed her fingers behind her back. She had recently gotten a letter from her uncle Victor. Silently she sent a prayer upward: *Frederick, please come home.* Frederick had wandered away again, and the villagers were in an uproar. Sometimes, she thought, Frederick was worse than a mischievous pup—although in his favor, Frederick was house-trained.

"You know, Frederick has really had quite a hard life, growing up as he did," she told Baron Huntsley.

"You mean, being pieced together from different human body parts?" Ian asked.

Clair shot him a quick glance to see if Ian was mocking her, then motioned for Brooks to enter with the tea tray. "I mean he is lonely. After all, he is the only one of his kind. It sometimes makes him rather melancholy. I used to give him pets. Once I gave him several lizards for company, when he first came to live with us." Clair stopped suddenly, a strange look on her face.

Brooks set the tray on the table. Seeing the sad look on his mistress's face, he tried consoling her in his stiff-necked, formal way. "Now, Miss Clair, you couldn't have known that Frederick would eat those iguanas or the fish."

Ian coughed, trying to cover his laughter. "Fish?" he finally managed to inquire with a straight face.

Clair nodded, pouring the tea. "Goldfish." Again, she shook her head. "It seems they are a favorite delicacy of Frederick's."

Holding up the tray, she asked, "Cream or sugar?" Ian shook his head, taking the cup as Brooks left the room. Clair sighed, watching the butler depart. "Well, I guess not everyone is a pet lover," she mused sadly.

"Quite," Ian agreed, taking a sip of tea. It was spicy. He commended himself on his excellent ability not to howl with laughter at her downcast face and outrageous statements. She was a mixture of refreshing innocence, bulldog determination, and the most outrageous habit of saying whatever came into her mind.

Still, he needed to grab hold of himself. Enough admiring of this madcap female, he had information to ferret out!

Observing that her butler had left the room, Ian went on the attack. "Miss Frankenstein, can you tell me why you thought I was a vampire?"

She glanced up from stirring cream into her tea. "Well, of course, Baron Huntsley."

Ian waited with bated breath. This was one of the main reasons he had dropped by the Frankenstein house on Pelham Square, aside from getting another chance to view the delectable Miss Frankenstein.

Clair took a sip of her tea, then spoke. "My investigations revealed that you were known to be seen only at night. You have an allergy to silver, you only wear gold jewelry on your person, and you . . ." She hesitated, seeming embarrassed.

"Yes?" he prodded.

"You . . . umm. You are reported to be a remarkable lover. In fact, a few of the women say they . . . umm." Clair paused, her cheeks pink. Ian thought the color became her immensely. "You are a lothario of the first order. Women say that they swoon from pleasure when you make love to them. These interviews, I felt, supported my hypothesis."

"And your hypothesis would be . . . ?" he prodded, enjoying her discomfiture. He was a man for all seasons—well read, well fed, well bred and well bedded. He was a virile man who exuded confidence and sexuality, the latter ensuring legions of willing women gracing his bed. He was a man whom other men looked up to and whom women found irresistible.

"That you were draining their blood as you made love to them. That they fainted from loss of blood, not your great talent at inspiring all-consuming passion."

She is an open book, Ian thought as he viewed the expressions passing rapidly across Clair's fair face. He was amused to note that they ranged from thoughtful to studious to awestruck to embarrassed—then to thoughtful interest.

"So that was your hypothesis. Now what do you think, now that you see me here this morning—in the flesh, so to speak?" He couldn't resist the tiny jab.

Clair glanced at the floor, not wanting to meet his eyes. "Well, I guess it is possible that your lovemaking is so wild and abandoned that these women do lose consciousness. Although without scientific proof . . ." She trailed off, apparently lost in some conundrum of scientific bent, her mind clearly in a state of perpetual motion.

Unwittingly she spoke her thoughts out loud. "I wonder if a scientific study would be possible? Although one would most likely have to be a master on the subject to judge it accurately."

Ian choked on his tea. "I would be happy to apply as your lab rat," he said, grinning wolfishly. His nostrils twitched slightly as he breathed in her scent. Clair Frankenstein made him hunger in a fundamental way. She made him want to snatch her up and carry her off like a primitive man would, to teach her the meaning of the passion that was buried beneath her logical mind. Yes, he concluded, still waters did run deep. And with

Clair Frankenstein, you might just drown if you didn't watch your step.

Clair's eyes grew round at the thought of the baron as her specimen. Oh, the charts and angles she would have to inspect, and the body of scientific evidence—the very large, very manly body of Baron Huntsley . . . ! The techniques she could use would be invigorating and insightful and . . . She shifted in her chair, feeling an uncomfortable heat between her legs.

The research would not only be highly informative, she feared, but highly enflaming as well. Too enflaming, she mused, remembering the kiss of the previous night. She was treading in dangerous waters. She was becoming wild, uninhibited, wicked, wanton. Not a scientist. Who knew what she might do next? She might end up reading that scandalous Henry Fielding novel or dancing naked around her bedroom. She might start saying "legs" in public instead of "limbs."

Although Lady Delia had often remarked that Clair didn't have a romantic bone in her body, Clair knew herself better. Sometimes, late at night, she would dream of that one man who was made specially for her, like a gift for her birthday. He would love her mind, her body, and her pilgrim soul. He was a man who would cherish her and yet let her be her true self. He was a man to inspire her curiosity and enflame her senses. And when she went into his arms, it would be like coming home.

Licking her lips slightly, she faced facts. She was a closet romantic in an era when well-bred young ladies had two options: they either waited on the shelf for Prince Charming to ride up and take them down—even if they were almost twenty-five years of age—or they leapt off the shelf and made their own life. Of course, Clair's great-aunt Abby in her more lucid moments was fond of saying that the leapfrog ladies ended up getting warts and too many little tadpoles, since they weren't often content to sit on one lily pad but had to hop around the whole pond.

"I thank you for your sincere application, but I fear I am studying supernatural creatures, not super-sexual escapades."

This time, the laugh did escape Ian. Here was a sad romp. "So again I ask, why me? I would have thought that it would be next to impossible to be a vampire and the holder of an ancestral title. It would be too dashed difficult to remain undetected."

"Balderdash. Years ago, perhaps. But no longer," Clair argued. "My uncle Tieck actually wrote the very first vampire novel ever published in England. He was fortunate in finding a real, live vampire. Some years later he befriended the vampire of whom he wrote. They became cronies, until the vampire's death five years ago in a raging fire."

Ian nodded. Yes, that would do it. Fire worked as well on a vampire as a stake through the heart.

Noting Ian's nod, Clair continued with her explanation. "The vampire was a French count and a melancholy fellow, for every quarter century he would have to leave his estates and travel to far-off lands for another quarter century. He would leave so that people wouldn't notice that he didn't age. He stayed away so people would forget how he looked. After a few decades or more, he would come back, pretending to be a son or a cousin, and that would explain the family resemblance."

"Yes, that is precisely what I meant when I spoke

about vampires and titles," Ian remarked. "And I certainly have not done this twenty-five-year thing. I have been in and out of London since I was in my early twenties."

Clair held up a hand. "Precisely. You've come and gone. Also, most of the aristocracy goes to schools like Eton. You stayed at your estate in Wales, unseen. Then, like Athena, you sprang forth as an adult."

"Easily explained. My ancestry is Welsh and English. My mother wished me to stay home to go to school. My father obliged her," Ian said. Yet a bleak look came into his eyes. "My father died when I was fourteen, leaving me to grow up extremely fast. I had a barony to run. Unlike other young bucks, I had my duty to my estates and my heritage as well as my mother and my sister to take care of. Didn't your research reveal these things?"

Ian schooled his expression. He had wandered lost in a vast world, struggling at a young age to understand who he was, what he was, and what he was to become, to preserve his heritage. Although his youth had been lost, a bitter cup to drink, the burdens he suffered had made him who he was today. And that was something he wouldn't trade for all the tea in China.

Observing the way his face tightened, Clair knew there was much more to Ian Huntsley than met the eye. He reminded her of a great fortress, invulnerable and extremely well guarded.

"My findings revealed that until five years ago, you had a townhouse here in London which was so rarely used that it was considered a ghost house. Prior to these past five years, your forays into town were almost nonexistent."

"Yes. And now you know why. My father's death kept me tied up for many years."

Minda Webber

Clair winced inwardly. "I thought you were your father. I thought the so-called son, Ian Huntsley, was actually a paid servant, while you were in reality Blaidd Huntsley. Then you, Blaidd, 'died,' and you sent the servant away to America so you could assume the role of Ian Huntsley."

Ian snorted, both amused and indignant at such elaborate imaginings. "What a ruse that would be. But your timing is off, and though I bear a strong family resemblance to my father, we are not the same. His nose was much longer than mine and his cheekbones much more pronounced. Anyone knowing either of us would never take us as the same person. Your theory falls flat on its face."

Lowering her head and studying Ian, Clair nodded. Then she confided, "Differences in appearance can now be manufactured. Recall, I told you about the French vampire count and my uncle Tieck? Well, Uncle Tieck introduced the count to Uncle Victor, who discovered a way to reconstruct parts of the face. For instance, to shorten a nose, raise a hairline, or add a cleft to a chin. You do know vampires heal quickly?"

"I daresay it wasn't in my storehouse of knowledge," Ian responded dryly. "But do go on. I haven't been so entertained in years." He added the last so sincerely that Clair could not take offense.

"Well, do you know how vampires react to silver?"

"I do believe that I heard somewhere that it burns their skin, rather like acid," Ian replied cautiously. He knew exactly what silver did to a vampire, and it wasn't a pretty sight.

Clair nodded enthusiastically. Ian was as intelligent as

42

he was darkly handsome. "Yes. Vampires are extremely sensitive to silver. It can actually kill them in large and prolonged doses. But it is perfect for certain surgeries, if the dose is minuscule. Since vampires heal too quickly for any type of facial surgery to be permanent, my Uncle Victor developed a technique called silver surgery. He implants tiny particles of silver—not enough to damage a vampire or kill him, of course—in whatever facial area he is reconstructing. That way, a shortened nose stays shortened, unable to grow back to its original length due to the implants. Thus a vampire could return to his ancestral home immediately after surgery."

"And I fit this profile," Ian remarked, understanding so much more than he had. "I suppose, in a strange way, your theory makes sense. You thought I was a vampire pretending to be my human father, who later pretended to be me, myself."

"In a word, yes."

"That is so insane that it is absolutely brilliant."

She nodded her thanks, her pretty cheeks pinkening at the praise.

Tapping his fingers on the armrest of his chair, Ian couldn't seem to relieve his worry. "This subject you've chosen, the undead, is a grave one. Not to mention dangerous. Why pick this particular subject? There are other important scientific spheres to study. Why the *Nosferatu*?"

"All Frankensteins study what is difficult. And all Frankensteins are published. Our great name is revered in the hallowed halls of academia. I can do no less but try to follow in my forebears' footsteps. I am who I am. After working with my uncle for a number of years and seeing his interest in animating flesh, I admit to having become quite interested in the dead and the living dead. Hence any interest in the vampire."

Ian didn't like her answer. It didn't fit with his plans. "But it could be extremely dangerous to research that particular subject. Besides, there are no such things as vampires."

"You are kind to warn me. I know the dangers of my research. Even Uncle Victor tried to put his foot down."

"I see that it did little good," Ian noted gruffly.

"How could it, with Frederick's foot right beside his?" she teased. "Uncle Victor may be many things, but a hypocrite he is not. So instead of hindering me, he gave me my first sharpened stick."

"Stake," Ian corrected, wishing he could get his hands on old uncle Victor.

Clair nodded. "He also told me about the garlic and holy water."

"Yes . . . the garlic." Ian sighed, reached into the coat of his pocket, then held out his hand. It was filled with garlic. "You forgot this last night."

Clair took the cloves, laying them on the table. "You must think me a complete nodcock. First, I break into your home, although for a good purpose. I accost you with garlic, then with a stake. Then, to top it all off, I accuse you of being a vampire and flee, dropping garlic in my wake."

She shook her head, sending her tawny curls flying. "Is that why you dropped by today? You wanted to return my garlic? We do have more in the kitchen, you know. Still, I thank you."

She hated to admit it to herself, but she was rather

disappointed to note that the baron had only been interested in her left-behind spices.

Ian took her small hand in his. "No, Miss Frankenstein, I do not think you are a nodcock. I think you are an original. And besides returning your property, I wanted to see you again and invite you to go riding in the park with me this afternoon."

It took less than two seconds for Clair to decide. She had much to do today with her studies, especially since Baron Huntsley had turned out not to be the leader of the London nest. And he was a mere mortal. Still, he was a fascinating man and only the second man she had ever kissed. An hour or two shouldn't hurt her project. "That would be lovely."

Not as lovely as you, he mused. "At four, my lady." Then Ian left the room, his long strides taking him down the hallway.

On the way out, a commotion by the stairway caught his attention. Three ladies dressed all in black were marching in what looked like a funeral possession down the corridor. It was a scene straight out of *Macbeth*, with old crones murmuring chants. Two more ladies joined the procession. The fourth was small and plump with the same tawny hair as Clair, but with a hint of silver at her temples. The fifth was very tall and very thin. Even though she wore a black veil, Ian could tell she was crying copiously.

The plump lady held the veiled woman's arm, trying to gently comfort her, while the first three women fluttered about the room in high anxiety. Before Ian had the chance to retreat, the plump lady glanced up at him. She had a quiet serenity, a graceful beauty that time's march would not mar. He judged her to be somewhere in her forties. She also had Clair's eyes. It had to be Clair's aunt Mary.

He spoke quietly. "I am sorry. I am intruding at a bad time. I take it you are leaving for a funeral?"

Clair's aunt gracefully raised her hand and pointed to a small brown coffin. "This *is* the funeral. We are doing the march. Clair was busy, or else we would have had her playing Mozart's Funeral March. She is quite talented on the piano," the woman boasted. She knew exactly who had come to call, and her little matchmaking heart was beating a furious rhythm.

Ian stared at the tiny coffin, trying to decide what on earth would fit in it, but in this asylum, anything was possible.

"You must be Baron Huntsley. I am Clair's aunt, Lady Mary Frankenstein. And this is Mrs. Heston." Mary nodded toward the gaunt, grief-stricken woman.

"I am pleased to make your acquaintance and only sorry it is at such a trying time," Ian said politely, glancing again at the tiny coffin. Beside Mary, Mrs. Heston had suddenly snatched the tiny casket, hugging it to herself. Her shrieks filled the hallway.

"Polly, my sweet dear Polly! How can I go on?" The old lady's voice broke as Mary enfolded her in her arms.

"There, there, Mrs. Heston. It will be all right. Just think, Polly is in heaven and probably has loads of those crackers she likes so well."

Appearing in the hallway, Clair took Ian's arm, gently pulling him away. As they walked to the door, he glanced back once. "I didn't mean to intrude upon a funeral. Who is Polly? Is she a relative of yours?"

Brooks, his face solemn, glanced down the hall at the

last of the procession as he opened the front door for them. He said nothing.

"She's a parrot," Clair explained.

"A parrot?" Ian asked, confused, as he took his hat and gloves from Brooks. The butler was bearing up quite stoically in this cuckoo's nest he occupied.

One of the old ladies was adjusting her large black ostrich fan hat, covering both her ears. Another was crying into a black handkerchief, hiding her eyes. Still a third covered her mouth, hiding her sobbing.

"A parrot?" Ian asked again, trying to wade through the confusion of Frankenstein logic.

"Yes."

"Uh . . . did you know this parrot well?"

"Never saw her before in my life. Although I did hear she had paranoid tendencies. Afraid of people stealing her crackers, you know."

Ian shook his head, a strange expression filling his green eyes. "Then why is the funeral at your home?"

Clair smiled as the baran stood in the doorway, hat in hand. "Aunt Mary does pet funerals. That is her specialty. Last week we had a funeral for Charleston the monkey."

Ian bowed at once and left, escaping into the cool light of lucid day. Pet funerals! He had heard it all now. He grimaced. He was on the planet Frankenstein, and it was a madhouse.

To Be, or Not to Be, a Frankenstein

Later that afternoon, Clair studied the tall, brooding figure of Baron Huntsley. He was a commanding presence, tooling his flashy green high-perch phaeton toward Hyde Park. The horses' hooves made a smart rapping on the cobblestones. They arrived a little before the fashionable hour—the fashionable hour being a time for promenading every type of conceivable carriage with teams of matching horses all decked out in their Sunday best, and the occupants of every carriage dressed in finery, wanting to see and be seen as they made slow progress along the countrylike lanes.

The brisk wind whipping about, Clair adjusted her bonnet, glad that Baron Huntsley had picked her up early. She enjoyed having the man to herself. He was such an intriguing specimen, even if he wasn't a vampire.

This afternoon, the baron was dressed in the height of fashion, in a tailored riding coat of dark gray superfine which only enhanced his very broad shoulders and slender waist. With a hungry glint in her eyes, Clair observed how he filled his doeskin breeches to perfection. He was very muscular, and the breeches were very tight.

Clair bit her lip, beginning to feel like a Peeping Tom or a trollop. She had never noticed things like this before the darkly intriguing baron. Normally breeches were breeches and men were men, unless those men were werewolves or vampires. But the baron made her sit up and take notice. He made her feel distinctly feminine.

Slyly, she studied him. His ebony hair was tousled by the wind, and his cheeks were red. There was a nervous energy about him that she quite liked. He was brimming with life and with something wild that reminded her of primeval forests in the dead of night. She could easily see how she had made her mistake in thinking that the baron was one of the seductive *Nosferatu*.

"I can see why I thought you were a vampire." She spoke her thought aloud. "It is a shame. You would make a most distinguished one. You are so dark and . . . I don't know. There is something wild in your bearing. And you have such big white teeth."

Ian slowed his matching team of chestnut bays, thinking how pretty she was in her blue velvet pelisse with dark gold braiding on the collar and cuffs. Clair was also wearing a saucy poke bonnet in the same blue hue. The white feathers fluttered in the breeze. The clothes deepened the color of Clair's gray eyes, making them appear a smoky blue, and gazing into them, Ian could feel himself getting lost.

"You have mentioned the teeth before." He grinned, showing them off. "All the Huntsleys have them— broad, strong teeth, that is."

He would have loved to tell her what else he had that was overly large, but figured that would pop her cork. In spite of her scientific bent, which appeared to lead the little imp into areas other ladies feared to tread, Clair Frankenstein was still an innocent.

For personal safety, it had been a long time since Ian had wooed a virgin. He was considered a prime catch on the marriage mart, which was a fact overanxious mamas and drooling debutantes reminded him of often. That had kept Ian away from innocence untried, for if he took a lady's virginity, he would be at the wedding chapel at the drop of a hat as honor and society demanded.

"So your teeth are a family trait, like a large nose or thin limbs?" she teased.

"Something like that." He glanced back to the road leading to the park. "Are you terribly disappointed I am not a creature of the night, drinking blood and sleeping in coffins?"

Clair laughed. "Last night I was devastated. Today I am more resigned. After all, if you were a vampire, then we would not be having this drive in the park. I think I shall count my blessings."

"Yes, the bright light of day does often bring sanity. And logic and most certainly reality."

A beetle landed near his boots, and he glanced around. To his left a blackbird took flight to here, there, and everywhere. A few noted Corinthians on horseback pranced in the Norwegian Wood just off the park. Four brightly colored curricles filled with couples drove slowly down the long and winding path nicknamed

Penny Lane. Their laughter was often false and forced, he noted. So many nowhere men with the world at their command, each human life touching no life but his own.

Strangely, Ian felt a stirring of pity for all the lonely people. Where did they all belong? Yesterday he might have been one of them, until he saw Clair standing there, like a taste of honey. He reached for her hand, wanting to hold it.

"Miss Frankenstein, the reality is that I have questions." In spite of his growing attraction to Clair, they didn't call him the spymaster for nothing. Ian would uncover her secrets—and uncover them quickly.

Clair's heartbeat picked up as she stared down at her hand in his. She had to admit it looked altogether perfect. His hand was hot and comforting.

There was something in the way he moved and something in his smile that touched her.

He made her skin tingle. He made her nervous. He made her think of things behind closed doors. She was afraid she was quickly becoming a woman of loose morals, thirsty for things she didn't understand. Yet her body at the cellular level was primed and ready to go. Her hormones were on the hunt. "Yes?"

"Who told you that I hid during the day?" He had to know who in his employ or acquaintance had noted his recent odd habits.

"Please, let it be."

"I can't."

"No one in particular," she lied.

"This is important, or I wouldn't ask you to betray a confidence. But a man like myself has many enemies, and secrets can hurt me." His tone was grim, his look stern. "Please. It is a word I don't often use." Truer words were never spoken. Ian Huntsley was a formidable man of many talents, some deeply hidden. He did not suffer thwarting lightly.

Yes, he was a complex man, loving few things. But those things he loved, he loved deeply and forever. Life had made him both strong and self-reliant. No matter how many times he got knocked down, he would always jump back up, swinging. And the perpetrator would end up being much, much the worse for wear.

Clair turned her attention back to the road in front of the carriage, watching how the bays moved in perfect tandem. They were an exquisite pair, with sleek coats and sooty-trimmed manes flying in the wind. She could see why the baron owned them. Even his mistresses were prime specimens, women most beautiful and accomplished. And thinking of mistresses, Clair recalled their words extolling the baron's lovemaking techniques.

She blushed. She was becoming a lascivious, licentious, lusty, and lewd lady. Hmm. She hadn't realized so many negative words began with the letter *l*. This won't do, she mused, concentrating on scientific *l*-words, like laboratory, lithosphere, the Luckenback Principle and lubrication. Oh dear, wrong *l*-word. She was already feeling a bit of moisture between her thighs. She certainly didn't need to be reminding herself of lubrication.

Ian interrupted her thoughts. "It's truly important to me, Miss Frankenstein. I must know who has been gossiping."

Frowning, she debated with herself, hating to break a source's confidence, but at the same time understanding the baron's need to know. "I did a study, a thorough investigation of your habits and life. For instance, I spoke with a tailor who said he came to your house only at night. Your retired man of business, Mr. Bell, also said you chose the night to do your estate work and other business. The second-to-last mistress you employed—I believe her name was Miss Trixie Delight—said she saw you only at night. Your last mistress, a Mrs. Joy N. Morning, also confirmed the fact."

At the mention of the word "mistress," Ian lifted an eyebrow. Well-bred young ladies never mentioned the *m*-word. They politely pretended the demimonde had only existed in biblical days and certainly not here in the mother country.

"I put two and two together and . . ."

Ian interrupted grimly. "And came up with five." He flicked his wrist, giving the bays more room to roam on the path. He would deal gravely with the men who'd betrayed him. His business was his own, and he liked no one gossiping about him. He dealt in too many different arenas, in both his personal and business life, to have his actions questioned.

Clair laughed. "I guess so. But you can see where I got my numbers."

Ian shrugged. "Not really. Many men prefer to work and play at night, then sleep during the day. That doesn't make them vampires. Especially since such creatures don't exist."

Clair shook her head, rolling her eyes, and her bonnet feathers shook. "So you say. However, my family feel quite differently about the subject."

He really had to change her mind about studying the secrets of the supernatural world, which was shrouded

Minda Webber

in peril. Blood oaths had been taken, which made the whole situation even more dangerous. However, Ian doubted he could change Clair's mind.

At the most basic level, it was a woman's prerogative to change her mind—almost a passage of youth from pigtails to pearls. Ian understood that. And it was a prerogative which women practiced consistently, in his view. But Clair was not most females. She was a Frankenstein, and Frankensteins seemed to be made up of an entirely different and altogether less predictable mettle. (And if you happened to be one of their creations, then you could be made of any old assortment of odd body parts as well.)

"Vampires are a myth, a legend of ignorant peasants and fodder for writers," he said again.

Clair cocked a brow, studying him. "Baron, this is 1828. We are at the dawn of new scientific discoveries both in the natural and supernatural world. Take Babbage's difference engine, Oersted's theory on magnetic effects, and Brewster's kaleidoscope, for example. You'd be surprised how many of those men believe in the supernatural and the *v*-word."

"The *v*-word?"

"Vampire," she clarified, leaning closer. "You, my lord, should really keep an open mind. Expand your horizons."

Glancing at two of Clair's most prominent assets, he tightened his jaw, feeling some expansion in his nether regions. The woman was a threat to everything he stood for, to his sanity—and worse, to his willpower. With a little more encouragement from Clair, his staff would be at full mast, flying high in the wind.

Stealing a glance at her face, he was very relieved that

she couldn't read his mind. He wanted to expand his horizons all right. Right down to taking off her lacy drawers and having his wicked way with her all week, each day and each night. A marathon of sexual hijinks both vertical and horizontal. Horizons, indeed. "I will keep that in mind," he commented drolly.

"Science never advances when thoughts are stagnant. We must go forth and search, knowing that science has no boundaries and that possibilities are endless and infinite. Why be limited to known reality when there is obviously so much more?"

Ian grimaced, wondering to himself when the name "Frankenstein" and reality had ever not been mutually exclusive. Setting his bays at a brisk pace, he found his carriage passing more curricles of all sizes and colors as the fashionable hour drew near.

He and Clair nodded at a passing acquaintance or two. But Ian was in no mood for talk at the moment, pondering as he was his dilemma. Miss Frankenstein was not going to cease and desist. It was not in her nature. He had to stop her research and investigations into the otherworldly. He had thought long and hard on the problem the previous night and come up with a solution. He was male and she was female. It would be the oldest trick in the book. He would call it Plan A, *The Seduction of Clair Frankenstein*. Although he wouldn't actually seduce her to the point of taking her maidenhead, he would keep her distracted enough to forego her investigation. It was a dastardly task, but he was just the right man for the job.

After several minutes of their carriage's brisk pace, Clair touched his arm. "I have another confession to make."

"You are looking for goblins too?" he teased, his manner lightening.

"Don't be silly. Goblins don't exist."

"You don't believe in goblins, but you do in vampires? An interesting conundrum."

"You are being a boor."

"My dear Miss Frankenstein, I am never anything so mundane."

She smiled. "True. In fact, you are actually so imposing that I thought you the leader of the vampire nest."

"Ah. I guess I am flattered that you see me as a *leader* of monsters," he teased. Then he probed for more information. "Did you say 'nest'?"

"Yes. I don't know if you are aware or not, but many vampires live in nests of sorts. You know, birds of a feather and all that rubbish. Sometimes their familiars live with them." Clair and her friend Jane Van Helsing had discussed Clair's theories, with Jane giving pointers on vampire rules and regulations. And Jane should know, being a member of the Van Helsing clan, notorious vampire hunters as well as manufacturers and marketers of a fine line of quality oaken stakes.

Ian urged the horses forward as his mind raced. Just what did Clair know? Or, rather, what did she think she knew? "Familiars?"

"Yes. Familiars can consist of a warlock or witch mixed in with the vampires. They give the vampires guidance with their magic. And wolves. Well, not actually wolves, but werewolves. Vampires can call warewolves. Of course, if they want them in wolf form, they must wait until the full moon, so the shapeshifter can shift to animal form."

Ian cursed silently. He had to forge ahead carefully.

Clair Frankenstein was digging up a whole can of worms that would wriggle around and bite her most shapely little arse if she didn't back off. "Werewolves? I thought the vampires would be able to call bats."

"Those too," she answered, uncertain if he was teasing her. "Vampires are powerful and can call more than one animal to them."

Ian winced. "So you intend to go around chasing these monsters down and then writing about them so you can publish your discoveries?" His expression was grim.

"Yes. It is my most heartfelt wish. I wish to win the prestigious Scientific Discovery of the Decade Award."

"Dead women don't win awards."

"I am being careful. Didn't I have my garlic and stakes with me last night at your home?"

Ian glanced toward the heavens, thinking that it would take a small miracle to keep Clair Frankenstein from being eaten alive by her research projects. "How does your aunt Mary feel about this?"

Clair shrugged. "She is resigned to it. However, my great-aunt Abby, who is Uncle Victor's aunt, is very excited. She has always believed in otherworldly creatures."

Ian pulled the carriage over on the side of the path. "Miss Frankenstein, if there are such creatures about, don't you think that they might not want to be brought to the public eye?"

"I imagine they won't be thrilled."

Ian shook his head slightly. He responded, his voice thick with irony, "No, I don't imagine they would be. Do you think they might dislike it enough to get violent?"

"Well," she hedged, "their natures are violent. But I did most thorough research. No one has died of loss of blood due to a wound in the neck for over five years."

Ian snorted. "A vampire is supposedly a most villainous creature. I have read some of the stories written about them. They enjoy torture. Every one is a predator. Someone is bound to get eaten. What do you think they will do to a human who dares expose them?" His bays moved restlessly, and Ian tightened his grip on their reins and got them moving again.

Clair looked everywhere except at his vibrant green eyes. "I imagine they might be a tad irritated."

"A tad irritated," Ian echoed sardonically, wanting to yank her into his arms and shake some sense into her. He wanted to take her in his arms and kiss her senseless. She was many things, but he had to admit faint of heart was not one of them. "I would say it might just be a bloodbath. *Yours!*"

Clair paled, pulling her cape tightly around herself. "True scholars of the sciences must go forward. We can't stand back because we are afraid, and let the truth be buried. Besides, you don't believe in such nonsense."

Ignoring her words, Ian reached over and touched her cheek. "I don't want to see *you* buried, Miss Frankenstein."

His touch was tender, sending a shiver of excitement through her. "Clair. Please call me Clair."

"And name is Ian."

"It is a fine name." Then she laughed. "But not much of a name for a vampire."

Ian shook his head and grinned tiredly. "No, I don't think I have heard of a single vampire called Ian."

Clair released his arm. Gazing into his eyes she said, "I thought you said you didn't believe in vampires."

Ian's patience snapped. "Clair, if there is a possibility of supernatural beings living in London, a slight possibility, I don't want to see you hurt by trying to discover who they are and where they are. I can't stress this enough!"

Clair looked down at her hands in her lap. "Thank you, Ian. I appreciate your concern. But I cannot stop my scientific studies. It would be cowardly and wrong. What would happen to the world if we gave up when the going got difficult? What would happen to man's spirit if he let his dreams die?"

She gazed at him steadily, trying to help him see. "Thoreau wrote, 'If you consistently advance in the directions of your dreams and endeavor to live the life which you have imagined, you will meet with success in common hours. If you have built castles in the air, your work need not be lost. That's where it should be. Now put the foundation under them.'" She glanced away, emotion stark on her face. Her dreams and goals were who she was and what she lived for.

Ian was deeply moved. For too long he had lived in a gray area between dusk and dawn. He had lost his youth, his father, and almost his mother to her morose grief. Yet he had gone on, anticipating neither the journey or the journey's end. "I have heard Thoreau read before, but never have I heard words put so beautifully and to such purpose."

Clair blushed. "So you understand this is my destiny, to follow the star that only I can see?"

"Ah . . . a believer in the Fates."

She laughed. "You have to be if you're of Frankenstein ancestry. Uncle Victor always says there's no escaping destiny. It's like a runaway train, hurtling us to our unknown destination. We can get off the train for a bit, but ultimately we must always reboard or be left behind in obscurity."

"You will continue on this path you've set yourself, even if you know it will get you killed?"

Clair wanted to make him understand. It was important to her to know that he accepted who and what she was. "How can I do less than the legions of Frankensteins before me? Uncle Tieck was laughed out of university for his novel on vampires. And look at Uncle Victor. The villagers tarred and feathered him for creating Frederick. But their travails never stopped my uncles from their scientific or artistic quests. How can I give up? How can I be less than I was raised to be? It is who I am, *a Frankenstein*," she finished modestly.

Scowling, he knew he was going to have to do some serious thinking to try and change her mind. She was a woman of strong convictions. Even worse, she had a quest. "I don't suppose you are interested in the Holy Grail?" he said.

"Why, Ian, what a strange question." Clair chuckled.

"Forget it. It was only a passing thought," he replied glumly. "Well, I'll be deuced! I thought he was still in the Highlands."

"Who?"

"See that giant coming toward us? The one in the dark green riding jacket?"

She nodded, studying the figure who was approaching at a fast clip. The man was large, not heavy but stocky. And he appeared to be very tall and wide of shoulder like Ian.

"My cousin, Galen McBain, my father's sister's son. Someday he'll be laird of the McBains."

Ian pulled his bays over and onto the unbeaten path,

out of the way of the promenading curricles, as Galen McBain arrived on his tall roan mount. He dismounted lithely for such a big man. He stood holding the reins of his steed, a friendly smile on his face.

Galen studied the enchanting woman with his cousin, while Ian made the introductions from where he sat. Although Clair Frankenstein was a lovely lass, Galen couldn't help but be curious, since she was in a far different league from his cousin's usual *chères amies*, who mainly consisted of widows, opera singers, or courtesans, with a bawd or two thrown in for good effect. But this was a Frankenstein, and Frankensteins were trouble, with their manic ideas and unshakable curiosity.

Clair was delighted by the unexpected meeting of a relative of Ian's; however Galen McBain was a little intimidating. When Ian was tall, Galen was well over six feet by at least four inches. He had arms the size of small tree trunks and his shoulders were formidable. His hair was a pale wheat color, his eyes a stormy dark blue. They reminded Clair of dusk, after the oranges and pinks of the sky made their appearance and signaled night fall.

Soon she forgot his size and concentrated on what the two cousins were saying. She could tell by their attitudes and tone of voice that they were close.

The conversation flowed easily, since each had a sharp wit, but Clair made a blunder which took the conversation to a more somber tone. Mistakenly she inquired if Ian's mother had remarried. Ian's features seemed to contort as he told her most emphatically his mother had not and would never remarry.

"My mother almost died of grief when my father was

61

killed in a freak fire. If not for my sister and myself, I believe my mother would not be alive today. She loved my father dearly. Theirs was a great love story and, as with all great love stories, it ended quite tragically."

"I am so sorry. I lost both my parents when I was quite young also. I do understand the sense of loss and aloneness," Clair responded. She leaned over and tenderly patted Ian's arm.

It was a move which did not go unnoticed by Galen. The man wasn't sure how he felt about the attraction between Clair and his cousin. Ian was a hard man, but even hard men had been known to break, especially when a lovely lass was involved.

Clair's sympathy touched Ian. He squeezed her hand. "Thank you. It has been a long time."

"Grief knows no hourglass," Clair added.

Galen broke the spell by saying they were all growing maudlin, and he began regaling Clair with a few stories of he and Ian growing up. She learned that Ian had been quite the mischiefmaker, slow to learn a lesson and passionate in his pleasures. One of the best stories was of questing for honey after seeking the bees' nest for two days.

Galen's eyes sparkled with mirth as he related the tale. "Both Ian's parents had warned him repeatedly not to attempt to rob the bees. But Ian knew best. He conceived a plan to distract the bees so he could gather the honey. He wore a bee disguise that he had created with false wings, and painted his shirt yellow and black."

Clair started giggling. She could almost see Ian in his striped shirt. "What happened?"

"The bees didn't recognize his kinship. Ian returned

home empty-handed with a swollen nose. However, his adventure did have a moral."

Clair was laughing hard, tears running down her cheeks. "What?"

"A fool and his honey are soon parted!" Galen howled with laughter.

Ian took offense, his dignity wounded. "Don't you have someplace to be, Galen? Someone to pester besides myself?" He stood in the carriage, staring down in the perfect picture of the aloof aristocrat. "Or do you intend to follow us to Miss Frankenstein's home?"

Galen took the hint. Cantering off, he decided to reserve judgment on the Frankenstein and Huntsley union. He left, his husky laughter in his wake.

Sitting back down, Ian flicked a wrist and his bays leaped forward, eager to be on the go after their lengthy immobility. Clair wiped her eyes, deciding wisely to keep her amusement to herself. Men could be so touchy when teased.

As the phaeton lurched forward at a fast clip, Clair clutched the railing with one hand and her bonnet with the other. After they drove in silence for some minutes, she commented on how much she liked his cousin.

"Just don't like him too much," Ian warned lightly, wondering as he spoke where that remark came from. He didn't get jealous. Women were generally possessive of him. He also knew that his cousin was less handsome than himself. Yet that had never halted most females of the species from falling at Galen's feet. Ian knew most assuredly that he wouldn't like it one bit if Clair joined their fawning ranks.

"You're teasing," Clair said, blushing, looking at Ian

and hoping that he wasn't. No one had ever been jealous of her before. It was a remarkably stimulating feeling.

Ian shrugged. "I don't think I am." And with those telling words, he turned his attention back to his driving. He was mostly silent after that, a dark look marring his arrogant yet handsome features.

Clair beamed. She could hardly wait to tell her dear friend Arlene, and to write Jane Van Helsing with her inspiring news. She did so later that night:

Dear Jane,

Despite the infamous pig incident at the cemetery, which no one has let me forget, I am continuing toward my goal of achieving the prestigious Scientific Discovery of the Decade Award. My supernatural studies that we have previously discussed led me to believe that Baron Ian Huntsley was a vampire. Unfortunately—but fortunately for me—I made a slight miscalculation.

Yes, the rumors of Baron Huntsley's undeath were greatly exaggerated. He is not dead, and in fact is quite handsome. However, I shall prevail. I have leads on another vampire subject, who this time I just know is a vampire. Soon I will watch him feed. As your father, Major Van Helsing, always says, "A vampire tooth in hand is worth two in your neck."

I hope all is well with you, and I look forward to your return from the country. Take good care of yourself and I shall let you know how my research turns out. More on Baron Huntsley to come. Be sure to tell Major Van Helsing, if he asks, that Baron Huntsley IS NOT A VAMPIRE. I wouldn't want the baron to be mistakenly staked, especially if the mistake were made by me in the form of mistaken identity. There's too much at stake. Did I tell

*you that the baron took me riding in his carriage this af-
ternoon? He really is quite handsome for a man I believed to be a bloodsucker pretending to be human.*

With sincere affection,
Clair Frankenstein

Love at First Bite

The huge chandeliers glittered like diamonds, casting a soft glow over the brightly colored assemblage. The women were dressed in their most vivid colors, flitting about the room like butterflies in the wind. The men, not to be outdone in attire, also glided this way and that, leading their partners in dance. On the edges of the ballroom floor, members of the *ton*—the upper, upper crust of British society—stood talking and waiting for scandal to erupt.

Ian took it all in stride, searching for Clair as he entered the throng. She had mentioned the day before on their ride home from the park that she would be attending this, the Faltisek Ball, the next night.

As he strode past a large marble column, Ian was halted with a touch on the arm by the Honorable Christopher Wilder. "Huntsley, good to see you," the blond, curly-haired man commented, his brown eyes narrowed.

Ian nodded warily. Christopher Wilder was a force unto himself. His affections were all reputedly feigned, his eyes cruel, his debauches legend. "Wilder," Ian acknowledged coolly.

"I heard you were escorting the younger Frankenstein female yesterday."

Ian scowled, recognizing that the only thing in London more pathetic than the *ton's* affinity for gossip was its limited attention span and even more limited ability to tell truth from fiction. "This concerns you how?" he growled.

Wilder's smile was anything but friendly. "What maggot's in your head? It was only an innocent comment. I had just remarked upon it because she's not your usual fare."

The man glanced over to where Ian saw Clair holding court with two elderly gentleman, one slender and silver-haired, the other balding and plump of both pocket and figure. Ian also noted that Clair was dressed in a dark green gown, so dark it almost appeared black, over a tawny golden slip. Tiny puffed sleeves decorated in gold were attached to a décolletage which showed off bare shoulders and much of her pale breasts. Too much of her breasts for a public place, Ian noted darkly.

Watching Ian watch Clair, Wilder commented slyly, "Although she is a delicious piece of womanhood."

"I've killed men for less," Ian snapped, his fists clenched, his eyes flashing green fire.

"My, my, how territorial you've become, and in so short a time. Cupid's arrow must be sharp indeed."

Bowing, Wilder turned and blended back into the rapacious crowd, a sneer twisting his lips.

A scowl marred Ian's austere features. He didn't want Clair conversing with just anyone, not with that neckline cut practically down to her navel. Peevishly, he began making his way through the thickening crowd to where she conversed with the two men, a false smile plastered on her face.

Clair didn't much care for places where the general conversation was insipid and uninspired; she still remembered her years as a debutante, where the most common focal point of conversations had been the chance of rain. She had been a radical, turning the talk to explanations of condensation and transpiration in the rain cycle. She had added the carbon cycles as well. The memory caused her to grin. Yes, she had been a true rebel, so much so that the younger men of the *ton* remembered to this day, and were even now leaving her alone. The pig incident of eight months before hadn't helped much either. She was now a social pariah to most of the *ton*.

Viscount Evans interrupted her musings. "My dear Miss Frankenstein, is it true what they say about the monster?"

The viscount reminded her of a fat owl, Clair decided, cocking her head and regarding him intently. But he was certainly not wise. She was irritated by his reference to her cousin as "the monster." "His name is Frederick," she chided gently.

Lord Price and Viscount Evans both raised their brows. Still, Clair continued trying to explain the unexplainable. "We do not think of him as a monster. He is much like any man, with a tad more stuffing than *most*."

Clair couldn't resist glancing at Viscount Evans's paunchy waistline.

"But that is just the point, my dear," Lord Price laughed.

The laugh caused goosebumps on her arms. Clair had always wondered how such a thin, harmless man could have such a haunting laugh. But, then, Lord Vince Price's laugh was rather his signature, in a town where signatures were worth their weight in gold, if one could be designated a nonpareil or an original.

"He is not just a man. Why, I heard that he is rather . . . well endowed in some aspects," Viscount Evans finished with a speculative leer to his eye.

Clair blushed, knowing exactly to what he was referring. It was true that Frederick was rather massive in all areas. And knowing Uncle Victor, it was possible, just possible, that a nip and snip here and there . . . She blushed even brighter as she remembered the rumored affair with the Countess of Deville, and that her own favorite stallion Pegasus had become a gelding after the great electrical storm of 1819 and Frederick's creation.

"By the deuce, Evans!" Lord Price admonished. "What a rum-cursed thing to say to this lovely young lady. You forget yourself."

"Indeed you do," Ian broke in with a clipped, icy tone, which matched his frigid countenance. "Miss Frankenstein is a lady in the strictest sense."

Viscount Evans's face was pale. He stammered, "I-I meant no disrespect. I know Miss Frankenstein is . . . a lady of the . . . ut-utmost quality, but she is also a lady of science. Ladies of scientific study enjoy a bit m-more freedom in both speech and thinking."

Ian stepped closer to Clair, partially blocking her.

But Clair knew the truth when she heard it; Evans had meant no harm. She had been given much free rein while growing up, in a day and age where other young ladies were put on pedestals and left there to mold. She lived in a time when to have a brain was manly, and absurd for a woman. Yet Clair not only used her intelligence, she spoke earnestly and brightly about subjects upon which many men were less than informed. Older men found that fascinating. Younger ones found her daunting, while women found her peculiar.

Gracefully, Clair placed a restraining arm on Ian's wrist. "I know the viscount meant no offense. He and I have discussed matters of scientific import before. He has an inquiring mind." Then she added for Ian's ears only, "I sometimes fear it overrules his tongue and brain."

Ian narrowed his gaze on Viscount Evans. "I don't think this particular question has much to do with science, but more to do with a morbid curiosity of the titillating."

The viscount bowed to Clair. "Again, I . . . I beg pardon," he squeaked. The viscount knew better than to pull the tail of a tiger. Baron Huntsley was infamous for being dangerous and easily provoked.

"I accept your gracious apology." Clair didn't particularly care for the viscount, but every once in a great while he did contribute something to her knowledge of the natural world. Upon her absolution, he scurried away, Lord Price following in his wake, both men glancing nervously over their shoulders.

Ian leaned over and whispered, "I must admit he has aroused my curiosity as well."

Clair glanced up, a question in her eyes.

"*Is* Frederick hung like a stallion?" Ian's eyes twinkled with mischief.

"And to think I thought you were a knight in shining armor riding to my rescue." She tapped him soundly on the arm with her fan. "You are a scoundrel."

"Alas, my lady, my steed is as black as my deeds."

"And I see you have left both your armor and your lance at home."

Ian snorted. If the little innocent only realized what she did to him. His lance was fair to bursting with need and he had hardly left it at home. He had been in torment from the moment he noticed Clair's display of her rather abundant charms. Charms which he and every gentleman in the kingdom were getting a chance to gawk at.

"Is your aunt Mary here tonight?" he asked, his tone curt.

Clair nodded, trying to reason out why he was suddenly in a bad mood. He was a most curious man. He fascinated her thoroughly, more so than any man she had ever met. He was certainly of a different mettle, a man among boys, making her insides go all shivery and liquid. Her reaction was a dilemma to be systematically evaluated. She hoped the process took years.

Thoughtful, Clair subconsciously bit her lip, a nervous habit she'd had since she was small. She was suddenly wondering how she had ever managed to hide her licentious nature for twenty-five years, especially from herself. She was becoming a wanton. Who would have ever guessed that underneath her guise of devoted scientist, she'd harbored such a penchant for lurid matters of the flesh? Especially when they were not matters for the microscope in her uncle Victor's lab.

Distracted from his thoughts, Ian was mesmerized by Clair's cleavage, so amply displayed in her form-fitting bodice. She must be freezing, he thought sourly. He had visions of warming her, carting her off to have his wicked way. He had visions of other men seeing what should not be seen by eyes other than his own. "Does your aunt approve of this gown?"

Clair glanced down at herself, embarrassed and stung. She had dressed carefully, hoping Ian would notice and think her one of the loveliest ladies at the ball. In fact, the only reason she had come to this dratted ball was to see him. And he had the nerve to complain? "You don't like my gown?"

Before Ian could answer, Lady Mary Frankenstein approached, almost bouncing along, curls jiggling atop her head. She was decked out in a deep blue gown with silver trimming on the sleeves and bodice. A striking set of sapphires hung around her neck.

"Baron Huntsley, how nice to see you again," Lady Mary said, her smile warm as she held up her hand for Ian to kiss. "How handsome you look tonight." Shooting a quick glance at her niece, she added, "Clair, don't you agree?"

"Most assuredly," Clair responded, thinking Ian did look divine. His starched cravat was tied neatly, and he was dressed all in black, his elegant evening clothes fitting him like a glove. Fitting him exceptionally well everywhere, showing off his broad shoulders and strong thighs. Suddenly she had the most urgent need to run her hands up and down the baron's rock-solid legs. She wanted to feel those muscular appendages for herself.

Quickly she glanced away, hoping her aunt hadn't noticed her ogling the baron and her rapid descent down the road to perdition. Milton was right. Paradise would indeed be lost if all gentlemen looked like Ian in their evening clothes.

Watching the interaction of the two young people, Lady Mary's eyes twinkled with mirth. She was not one to let the grass grow under her feet. She knew when two people were physically attracted to one another, and it was glaringly obvious that her niece and the baron's desires were screaming like harridans to be indulged. She smiled a secret smile. Another baron in the family was just what the Frankenstein family needed. She would wear blue to the wedding—nothing too fancy, but of elegant design. Perhaps Belgian lace would decorate her décolletage, with a tiny smattering of seed pearls.

"I was wondering, my lord, if you would care to dine with us tomorrow night. Nothing formal, just some family friends," Lady Mary said coyly.

"What an intriguing suggestion," Ian managed to say with a straight face. The old bat was playing matchmaker, he would bet a monkey. He grinned. He was too old to be ensnared by such a flimsy plot, but he wasn't too old to enjoy the challenge of skimming its edges. Besides, it fit perfectly well with his Plan A, *The Seduction of Clair Frankenstein*. "I would be delighted."

Before Lady Mary could say more, Lady Delia Channey, in a pink confection of a gown, maneuvered her way into their midst, her eyes devouring Ian. "Lady Mary, Miss Frankenstein, how nice to see you here," she commented, her voice breathy as she turned her big brown eyes on the Baron.

Clair grimaced. Lady Delia reminded of her a toothy shark, just waiting in the depths to rise up and snatch whatever she wanted. Unfortunately for Clair, Ian was a prime catch in the marriage mart. Still, manners demanded she introduce the little schemer—but that didn't mean Clair had to like it.

Stiffly, she made the introductions, her eyes narrowing as Lady Delia batted her eyelashes at Ian. Before she could stop herself, Clair blurted, "Lady Delia, do you have something in your eye? Perhaps I can help?"

Ian coughed into his hand to cover a snicker. It appeared that Clair was jealous! A good sign for his Plan A.

Ian coughed again as Lady Delia gave Clair a look that would have melted iron. "I am fine, Clair. And you? I have not seen you in many weeks. I take it you have been doing your usual manly deliberations in and outside of your dusty lab?" Her voice was sugar-sweet, her fan batting in a mating signal at Ian.

It was a classic Delia move, this opening gambit, the game being to embarrass Clair before a fresh audience. Clair responded coldly. "Yes. You know my work keeps me extremely busy."

"I am always so impressed with your studies. But they are beyond me. I can't imagine researching what you do. I have always heard that science is a field for gentleman scholars, not delicate females. Why, I can't imagine little old me knowing what to do in those laboratory places." She spoke the word "laboratory" as if it were a den of iniquity.

Yes, Clair surmised, Delia was in her prime. "I'm surprised to find that you even know the word 'scientific,'" she responded archly. Check! she thought proudly; she had countered with a bold move.

"Oh dear," Delia mused. "I fear my association with you must be rubbing off. Whatever shall I do? I don't want to be a bluestocking like you who never lets anything keep her from her research. People talk about how unladylike it is. But then, everyone knows you are a lady." Her eyes were fixed on Clair, a slight smile on her lips as she finished, "At least I think they do. They did before that unfortunate pig incident."

Damn! Checkmate. She was going to have to concede the game, Clair thought bitterly, a taste like ashes in her mouth. Clair blushed, both embarrassed and angry at the same time. How like Lady Delia to bring up that little unfortunate misunderstanding in front of Ian!

"That was much ado about nothing." Her reply was firm, her bearing haughty. She would show Delia. She had been mocked by the best and the worst, Delia being both.

Ian, amused, watched the battle raging between the two titans. *What pig incident?* He knew without being told that the tale would be a whopper.

Observing Clair and her aunt, Ian recognized immediately that neither wanted to talk of it. Clair was staring with desperate interest at the Venetian chandeliers high above. Her aunt Mary had joined her in wonder at the lights. Ian wondered what mischief Clair had gotten into. His curiosity barely contained, he raised a questioning brow at Lady Delia.

With great relish, in her breathy little voice, Lady Delia spoke. "Why, our dear Clair was researching the ghostly disturbances at Murray Manor. It appeared that the cemetery had ghosts residing there. Clair went to investigate the apparitions."

Clair wanted desperately to sew Lady Delia's mouth shut, and Clair did so hate sewing. Lady Delia certainly wasn't her dear anything. This was war!

Glaring at the woman's smug expression, Clair reminded herself that Delia, the daughter of the Earl of Lon, was a woman of a thousand faces, all of them false. Drawing herself up to her full five foot three, Clair engaged in battle. She could still try to save her king.

"I was requested by the marquis himself to help stop the nightly visitations," she said. "The marquis was concerned because his guests had been complaining for quite some time about the noises in the cemetery." She said each word with distinct and stately decorum. "It certainly sounded like ghosts. It could have been ghosts. Ghosts have an affinity for the cemetery. They feel comfortable there. You could say they feel very much at home in the cemetery," she said a bit desperately.

"Dear," Lady Mary said, patting Clair's arm in sympathy. "You couldn't have known that it wasn't a ghost. It could have been. Quite easily indeed. Easily."

Ian stared at all three women, his amusement obvious. "I am agog with curiosity. If it wasn't ghosts haunting the cemetery, what could it have been? Let me see," he teased. "Was it a goblin? No. Goblins aren't real, I recall being told only recently."

Clair pursed her lips, her eyes twinkling.

"Could it have been that dreaded *v*-word? A vampire?" He gave Clair such a devilish smile that she almost melted on the spot, her embarrassment easing greatly.

But Ian's look had not gone unnoticed by either Lady Mary or Lady Delia. Carefully, Lady Delia composed her features and remarked sweetly, "No, it was pigs. Smelly pigs, rooting around the headstones at night."

Clair glanced down, hoping the ballroom floor would open up and swallow her, but knowing in her rational mind that it wouldn't. She had been the butt of these jokes too many times, and it still hurt.

In spite of himself, Ian caught himself chuckling. Lady Delia giggled. However, Aunt Mary, a veteran of Clair's debacles, kept her grin to herself. It wasn't every niece who could cast for pearly ghosts and end up with swine.

Yes, Lady Mary remembered the ghostbusting mission at Murray Manor had caused her niece quite a bit of old-fashioned embarrassment, not to mention that it had set her back several months in her observations of ghostly spectrals.

Loyally, Lady Mary patted her niece's arm. "It was a mistake anyone could make, dear. I'm sure ghosts sound just like pigs rooting about on their nightly haunts." It really had been naughty, she thought, for Delia to bring the subject up.

Clair wanted to roll her eyes. "Thank you, Aunt," she managed, a rueful smile on her face. Her aunt always meant well, but if Mary wasn't putting her foot in her mouth then she was somehow maneuvering to place Clair's there as well.

Lady Delia wiped a corner of her eye, her mirth still obvious. The shrew was always at her best when making sport of someone else, Clair thought sourly. It wasn't fair, she argued with herself. Delia looked all pink innocence but had the heart of a killer. She'd flesh out a person's weakness and then go full steam for the jugular.

"By the by, did you ever manage to find any evidence of ghosts at all?" Lady Delia asked.

"No. However, I am now working on something altogether different. Much more spectacular than spectrals. It's important. Really, really important research."

"It wouldn't take much to outdo pigs," Delia said.

Glaring, Clair wished just once that she hadn't been born a lady. What she wouldn't do to the black-haired witch. She took a step forward.

Ian, sensing that the battle of wits was moving into a physical reclaim, quickly placed a restraining hand on her arm. "My lady, it is the waltz you promised me." Bowing to both Lady Mary and Lady Delia he said, "If you will excuse us, please."

Lady Delia frowned and Lady Mary smiled. Chalk one up for the baron, Lady Mary thought. The handsome devil had extracted Clair with *haut-ton* finesse, diverting a scene, escaping Lady Delia's clutches, and bringing a smile to her niece's lips. Yes, he would do quite nicely for a husband. She watched Ian gracefully sweep Clair into the waltz.

On the dance floor, Ian had to keep reminding himself not to hold Clair too tightly. She felt so incredible in his arms, and light as an angel. Her gaze narrowed on him, making him feel he just might be the devil.

"You're scowling at me," he remarked calmly.

"Ladies don't scowl," she replied stiffly.

"Ladies don't get caught up in catfights in the middle of balls," he responded dryly.

He was right; he had her there. Still, his amusement at her pig disaster rankled. "How clever you are. Yet gentlemen don't make sport of ladies or insult their gowns," Clair said.

Her earlier hurt had turned into chagrin at Ian's utter lack of compliments on her attire. He should at the least have been stunned by her appearance. She knew she was in good looks. She had to be. She had spent three cursed hours getting ready for this cursed ball only to have the cursed baron insult her ballgown, when she could have been plodding ahead with her investigative work. She had another vampire suspect to study; perhaps she should be off studying him.

Ian eyed Clair's gown, his gaze lingering on her abundant charms. A spark of anger filled his eyes. "There is not enough of that gown to insult."

"Really, my lord, you go too far! Madame Le Fronge said it was the latest in Parisian fashion."

Ian knew that Madame Le Fronge was one of the foremost dressmakers in London. But obviously the woman was an idiot.

"Clair, don't get yourself in a tiff. The gown is lovely on you. What there is of it. I can't take my eyes off you—and neither can the other so-called gentlemen of the *ton*. And I use the word 'gentlemen' lightly."

"I would accuse you of having a screw loose, if my uncle Victor had created you." Clair glanced around. "No one is paying attention to me."

"In that case . . ." Ian trailed off as he danced her out the open balcony doors. The terrace was awash in soft moonlight that gilded Clair's face and hair.

Releasing his grip on her arm, he moved a step back, staring down at her. "You're wrong, Clair. Men do look at you, and often. If you would just get your head out of your books, you'd see that."

"Balderdash," she replied. He was embarrassing her.

"You need to quit reading so much about life and live it," he advised gently as he led her over to a corner on the terrace deep in shadow. "Take time out from your studies and endeavors and just live."

"I would expect that kind of rakish comment from a rogue."

"I'll show you rakish," he said. Giving a wolfish grin, he pulled her into his arms and held her tightly against his heated body. Ignoring her gasp of surprise, he kissed her.

Clair returned the kiss shyly at first and then with a vigor that was startling. The friction of his mouth working against hers was delicious. His tongue entering her mouth was incendiary. She could feel his body heat envelop her, and she could feel something pressing against her stomach.

His arms were strong against her back, his hands questing. She felt the pull of his gravity thoroughly. A long, drawn-out moan escaped her.

With that soft sound from Clair, Ian's kiss took on a will of its own. White hot heat flooded him as he explored the depths of her mouth. All Ian could think was how he wanted to devour the honeyed sweetness of Clair.

Their kisses quickly heated his blood to the boiling point. He pushed his tongue inside her mouth again. She was like an electrical storm flashing through his system, jolting him back to life. His member was hard and throbbing, heavy with need. She arched back, the movement pressing her ample breasts against his chest. He could feel the nipples pebbling.

Growling, he trailed kisses down her neck to her daring décolletage. His tongue flicked out, causing Clair to gasp and grab his hair. He nipped her nipple and she shivered. It was almost more than Ian could bear. His hunger for her was sharp-set. He wanted to throw her to the ground and bury himself so deep it would take a week to pull himself free. Somewhere deep inside Clair, she knew that she should stop Ian. Ladies did not do this. Ladies did not feel passion, they only read about it. Ladies did not go out on balconies and then go up in flames. *To hell with ladies!* She grabbed his hair and pulled him closer.

Unexpectedly, they heard the sound of footsteps in the garden directly below. Ian broke apart from Clair, his nostrils flaring. Looking down at her, he arrogantly noted Clair's dazed expression and red lips, bruised by passion.

"I-I . . ." she stammered. She tried again, her breathing almost back to normal. "I should apologize to you." My God, she fretted. It was worse than she'd thought. She had become a salivating strumpet. She was losing her dedication to duty along with her moral fibre. She hadn't thought about the vampire nest since Ian arrived in the ballroom. What would Uncle Victor think?

Ian shook his head. Once again Clair had shocked him. "I should be the one offering an apology," he said. His voice was husky with unfulfilled lust.

"No, I acted very unlike myself—more like I imagine a woman of the street would act in a similar circumstance." Ian tried to interrupt, but Clair waved him off. "I know a lady should not act the wanton, and I am after all a lady by birth and degree, but I am also a Frankenstein. And Frankensteins have a fierce passion for scientific inquiry."

Ian smiled. "Yes, I know."

"Then you do understand."

"Understand what?" Ian was at a complete loss.

"My response to your kiss was inevitable. You see, we seem to have some kind of electrical current, a spark, so to speak. This spark intrigues me. I feel it must be quite similar to Oersted's theory on magnetism, where two opposing poles attract one another. I had so wondered what caused poets to write such passionate sonnets as I have read. Now I know," she remarked. She turned and began walking away.

Suddenly she stopped and looked back over her creamy white shoulder. "After experiencing passion myself, this centripetal force, I wonder that there is not more poetry in the world. A veritable deluge of it."

Ian sighed, frustrated. He was giving her his best kiss and she was thinking of magnets? Still, he couldn't keep his eyes off her as she strolled away, her shimmering green gown a beacon of light. She had done it again: stunned him. Clair Frankenstein was like the unfettered ocean rushing off in ceaseless journey toward distant shores. And how could he resist her pull? She stopped once and looked back, smiling at him, a smile for him alone.

Grimacing, he studied her. So she thought him an experiment. He had been many things to many people in his life; however, an instrument of scientific inquiry was not one of them.

Then all at once he smiled wickedly. Just wait until the next time he kissed her. He would give her a charge that would knock her garters off!

And just what in the bloody hell was centripetal force?

Guess Who's Coming to Dinner?

The first thing Ian noticed as Brooks led him into the Frankensteins' Blue Salon was that there was not a speck of blue to be seen. The second thing he noted was that the walls appeared decorated in a fur-and-feathers motif. The theme continued through every space available, including the four floor-to-ceiling mahogany bookshelves, which were filled with stuffed animals and birds.

A colorful macaw was perched on a tall gold stand in one corner of the room. In another corner, a magnificent tiger of gold and brown lay in repose. An owl was suspended from the ceiling in midflight. Crouched on all fours atop a gilt end table was a fat tabby cat with two lime green lizards frozen at his feet. One wall was completely covered with every kind of head imaginable, from a twelve-point buck to a grinning ferret. It was a virtual den of taxidermy, and it gave new meaning to the phrase, *The night has a thousand eyes.*

Ian raised an eyebrow, centuries of aristocratic breeding explicit in the motion.

The much put-upon but very proper Brooks explained stoically, "Lady Mary is quite proud of her hobby. In fact, it is rather a sideline of hers."

Ian raised both eyebrows. "Taxidermy?"

"Many people, rather than bury their pets, prefer to have them stuffed. That way, they have their loved ones with them forever." With a straight face, Brooks turned to the group of people standing at the fireplace and announced loudly, "The Baron Huntsley."

The small group turned toward Ian. He took in their faces, though some of them were hidden by shadow. He felt a crackling, creative energy which seemed to roll through the room. It gave him a queer start.

Bustling forward in a gown of flowered blue silk, Lady Mary made him welcome. "How glad we are that you could make our dinner party. Come meet the others," she requested sweetly.

The first of the men to whom Ian was introduced was a Mr. Harre, who was visiting from the Isle of Man. His pale blue eyes were red-rimmed and he sniffled constantly. Lady Mary confided to Ian that Mr. Harre's pet turtle had recently died. He had come to her for the funeral, which was set for tomorrow. The tortoise was to have a full burial at sea. Feeling sorry for the grief-stricken Mr. Harre, Lady Mary had generously invited him to tonight's dinner.

The next man Ian met made a stark impression. The young man had dark, brooding eyes and a grave and stern decorum that made Mr. Edgar Allan Poe seem a decade older than he really was and steeped in perpetual sorrow. With reluctance, Mr. Poe turned from his study of a beguiling raven on a perch. Both men observed the formalities.

Next Ian was introduced to a Mrs. Annabel Garwood, a woman of Lady Mary's age who was dressed in a bright yellow brocade gown with purple trimmings and a yellow turban set atop her flaming red hair. The turban had a speckled band which secured it in place.

Her daughter, Miss Arlene Garwood, made known as Clair's closest friend, was dressed in a less garish fashion than her mother. Unfortunately, she had inherited the carroty red hair color. The rather plain young woman, however, did have eyes a remarkable shade of green. Intelligent jade eyes, Ian determined after careful study.

But it was the next introduction that most captured his attention.

"Professor Whutson is an old acquaintance of the family," Lady Mary remarked, smiling warmly at the jolly middle-aged man. He was round of face with long grayish brown sideburns. "He and Clair are great friends, for they are always poking their noses in dusty old tomes or conducting some scientific study here and hence."

"Honored," Ian said formally. He had met Professor Whutson before. At the time, however, he had been in disguise—a disguise so total that no one except his own mother would have recognized him.

"Professor Whutson is interested in solving all sorts of whodunits and such. He is quite brilliant," Lady Mary professed proudly.

"No, no, my dear Mary. It is Dr. Homes who is the brain behind the brawn. *His* conclusions are genius, and his methods of reductive reasoning are truly remarkable. My friend Homes takes the most daunting and difficult of criminal cases and solves them with amazing aplomb. I am only a novice compared to one such as he," Whutson protested modestly.

"You work with Durlock Homes?" Ian knew two and two was four, but he didn't like the answer and he didn't like coincidence. Ian knew that Durlock Homes had a sterling reputation. Homes was a mastermind at solving puzzles and problems of any kind. He had met the redoubtable tuba-playing crime-solver when Dr. Homes was on the case of the Sine of Five. Homes had pursued the solution relentlessly, wearing himself down until he fell ill. He hadn't stopped until he solved the riddle.

Ian wanted to howl with frustration, distrusting and disliking the connection between Clair and Homes. If Homes were helping Clair with her research, then heads would fly . . . literally. United, Clair and Homes would undoubtedly uncover some secrets of the supernatural world. Blood would be shed, and Ian was afraid most of it would be Clair's and Homes's.

"Yes. We consult together on cases—or rather I provide a sounding board for Homes's theories," Professor Whutson replied.

"Nonsense. Quit hiding your light under a bushel. You are of great importance. Dr. Homes told me so himself when I saw him in July," Lady Mary scolded. "You always did take too little credit for yourself," she added as she patted Professor Whutson on the arm. She continued, "Homes may be a genius, but you have common sense, and that is worth more than I can say about most men of scientific bent. They all too often don't possess a whit. Most scientists and scholars I know are like little boys playing with matches. They do so regret it dreadfully when they get burned but are hell-bent on making their fires," she confided.

"You do me too much credit." Whutson waved off Lady Mary's comments, a slight flush on his rotund face.

"Fiddlesticks. You know my brother Victor is as bright as any scientist inside his lab, but if events fall outside his laboratory and his experiments, he is like a half-blind bull blundering through a china shop. While the resultant events might be fascinating to watch, the effects can be shattering," Lady Mary finished.

Whutson and Ian both chuckled, and the professor acknowledged it was true. Brooks's announcement of a Mr. Dudley Raleigh interrupted the congenial exchange.

Mr. Raleigh had a washed-out look. His skin was like fine, wrinkled parchment, giving him the impression of a man used up and spent by a life of folly. Again Lady Mary made introductions, relaying that Mr. Raleigh was an old beau of Lady Abby's from before her marriage and widowhood.

Ian was left standing with Professor Whutson as his hostess scurried off to converse with Mr. Raleigh. It was a fortunate event for Ian, leaving him to pursue his inquiry into just how much the good doctor knew about Clair's supernatural research.

"I take it you have known the Frankensteins a long time?" he began casually.

"Since Clair was in diapers and Lady Mary was a young beauty," Professor Whutson replied. "I met Victor when we were both enrolled at the University of Vienna."

"Then you've had the pleasure of watching Miss Clair grow into adulthood."

Professor Whutson's smile was kind. "Yes, she has always been a great delight. Always scampering in and out of her uncle's laboratory, putting her dolls among the beakers and Bunsen burners. Clair was a fearless child, filled with mischief, playing hide-and-seek in the cemetery when her uncle Victor was on one of his grave-robbing expeditions."

Professor Whutson reminisced fondly as if such missions were an everyday occurrence and the career of choice. Ian blinked, having the strangest feeling of descending into a kaleidoscope of Frankenstein follies—a most odd fall indeed.

"She used to wear her uncle and me out with her unending questions. 'What makes butterflies die so soon after they metamorphose?' 'Why do the stars live so far away and where do they go when they go to sleep?' 'How many vampires does it take to close a coffin?'" He chuckled. "She was always a whirlwind, a true credit to the Frankenstein name."

The last made Ian stand straighter. So, he thought, it appeared Clair's interest in the preternatural was of childhood origin.

"Yes, Miss Frankenstein is quite an amazing student in the more mystic-type studies," Ian probed. His focus sharpened; yet outwardly he remained the perfect picture of a bored gentleman. If Professor Whutson was ignorant of Clair's recent work, Ian didn't want to alert him.

"Quite," Professor Whutson replied.

"Do you confer with her on her studies?"

"Clair confers with no one. She sticks that pretty little nose of hers to the ground like a good bloodhound and goes after the scent. I can tell you that she's caused a gray hair or two on her uncle Victor's head." The doctor chuckled affectionately.

Longing to breathe a sigh of relief, Ian merely smiled. Now he knew which enemies were at the gate, since Watson and Holmes were clueless about Clair's current quest. "How does Miss Frankenstein come up with her hypotheses? Does anyone help her?"

"No. She does that too by herself. Amazing brain that girl has. Probably the most forward of backward-problem-solving I have had the privilege to witness. She learned to walk before she could crawl, learned her alphabet from Z to A, and solves a mystery beginning with the end and working in reverse to the beginning. Truly amazing."

Which explains, Ian thought smugly to himself, the case of mistaken identity.

A new man entered the room, a tall mustachioed fellow, and Whutson gave a start. "There's that incorrigible Arthur again. He's always following Homes and me around, pestering us and asking the most personal details about our casework, then getting everything wrong. I'm going to give him a piece of my mind."

And with that the professor excused himself, leaving Ian to study the room and its odd assortment of guests. Ian noticed that Poe fellow standing alone by the fireplace, where dying embers wrought their ghosts upon the floor. He seemed lost, a man in a dream within a dream. Ian walked over to join him.

"Mr. Poe?"

Edgar glanced up at Ian, nodding, his face sphinxlike. "Baron Huntsley," he said quietly, his attention returning to the raven.

Ian cocked his head, studying Poe. It appeared as if he were receiving some psychic revelation. It was as if Mr. Poe was peering into the darkness of his soul, pondering things no mortal man had before thought.

"Nevermore," Mr. Poe whispered.

"Pardon?" Ian asked, perplexed by the comment and by the odd thin man standing before him.

"Nothing."

"You seem alone with your thoughts." Ian grimaced in disgust. He had smelled the cloying scent of opium before. If Edgar wasn't an addict yet, he was well on his way. Which was a shame, Ian thought. Opiates and liquor might first stir a creative fire, but in the end the addiction extinguished the flames, leaving talent in the ashes.

"No. Not alone." Poe motioned to the raven. "Do you know that I believe this bird is a prophet, a thing of evil? Bird or devil, I know not which."

"I rather thought the bird was dead and, though not buried, most certainly stuffed," Ian remarked.

"He speaks to me, quotes to me."

"Shakespeare?" Ian inquired, deciding to humor him.

"Milton. *Paradise Lost*," Poe answered solemnly.

"I see," Ian said and he did. It all made perfect sense. The bird was quoting a man who had lost paradise on earth to another who had lost his marbles in the Frankensteins' Blue Salon. Abruptly Ian took his leave. Poe remained locked in mortal combat with the stuffed raven.

Lady Mary intercepted him scant moments later, remarking upon her niece. "Clair should be down soon. She is helping Lady Abby dress. Lady Abby is Clair's great-aunt."

"I look forward to enjoying Miss Frankenstein's

company. Her recent studies have quite captured my attention."

"Yes, when one is part of the study, it tends to capture one's fancies." Lady Mary winked at him.

"So you knew of Miss Frankenstein's suspicions?"

"There's not much that gets past me. I've known what Clair was working upon for quite some time. Not to mention that I attended the tarot card reading. It was all most frightening, a truly remarkable event." Lady Mary tapped her fan thoughtfully against her chin. "Such a shame, in a sense. Clair was so sure you were one of those undead things. It would have made her day if you had been the leader the of the pack."

"It could have made her dead," Ian argued sternly. "As her aunt, don't you feel a need to stop this particular road of inquiry?"

Mary patted his arm. "Dear boy, trying to stop Clair is like trying to halt a particularly nasty electrical storm."

Ian frowned. He really wanted to dislike the round little woman, but he couldn't. Her warmth was infectious. Damn, just like her niece.

"You Frankensteins are obsessed with those storms. Using them in your experiments, likening yourselves to . . . But being electric and unpredictable doesn't keep Clair safe."

Lady Mary smiled slyly. Her Plan A, *To Catch a Baron*, was falling marvelously into place. She almost felt like a master thief at the ease with which she had so far maneuvered the handsome baron. It was like taking candy from a mere babe. "You're worried about my niece."

"Yes. Miss Frankenstein should be attending balls, not hunting vampires. She should be painting watercolors or embroidering like other young ladies of her class, not running around at all hours of the night peeping into coffins."

Lady Mary seemed to ponder for a moment. "Clair is a cerebral being, often living only in her mind. And you know what they say, you can't make a silk purse out of a sow's ear." She stopped, her brow wrinkling. "Although, if anyone could do it, Victor could." Seeing Ian's strange expression, Lady Mary patted his arm. "I digress. You are worried about my niece. I can say honestly that most of her studies into the otherworldly have been fairly harmless—like those pigs in the cemetery or the devil in the belfry."

"Devil!" His heart froze. Devils were such hotheaded little creatures with nasty tempers, always sticking their little pitchforks here and there. Ian had often thought their temperaments were probably a result of the ugly little horns on their head poking into their brains, along with spending much of their lives breathing sulfur and brimstone. That would tend to make anyone a trifle testy.

Lady Mary pooh-poohed him. "Stop looking like you're going to bite me, my lord. It was merely a case of mistaken identity. This devil was only an alias for the old vicar of Scratch Parish. He was a bit touched in the head, you know."

Ian wanted to ask if the old vicar was a family relation. "I see. Another case of mistaken identity," he said instead. "There seems to be a bit of that going around."

"Well, one could see it like that."

"Yes, one could. However, we were speaking of Clair and her new, very dangerous studies. I can say, with all due respect, that Clair is no match for a vampire."

Lady Mary only smiled more brightly. She would

wear her blue velvet ostrich-feathered hat with the pearl inlays to the wedding.

"You don't seem frightened for her in the least," Ian objected.

"Of course not, dear boy. I sleep much better at night knowing she now has you to watch over her while she is pursuing her field research into vampires and werewolves."

Before Ian could do anything more than wipe the astonished expression off his face, Lady Mary bounced off in her merry way. Bloody hell! The dratted woman thought he was a babysitter.

Crossing his arms on his chest, Ian glared, daring anyone to approach him. Enough was enough. Nothing else was going to disturb him tonight. But as often happened, his best-laid plans ended abruptly.

The grand door to the salon was flung open. A tall, stately, elegant, and yet pompous woman entered the room with Clair by her side. The aging dame was dressed in an Elizabethan-period gown of fading green brocade, complete with tall white ruffles around the neck. A gold jeweled crown was set atop her silver hair. She stopped before Ian, a regality in her manner. Eyebrows arched, she gave Clair a pointed look.

"My great-aunt, Lady Abby Frankenstein," Clair said anxiously, searching Ian's face for a reflection of his thoughts.

Clair had suffered many insults regarding her greataunt Abby's eccentric behavior, each one a tiny nail in the coffin of her reputation. She didn't believe Ian was a shallow man, but experience had taught her the virtue of being cautious where her family was concerned.

A loud cough to her right side brought Clair back from

her worries. Glancing at the stern expression on her great aunt's face, Clair quickly conceded, "Great-aunt Abby is also known as Queen Elizabeth of England."

Ian bowed formally over Clair's great aunt's hand, a courtier's smile on his face. He assumed an expression both polite and serious, an expression suitable for meeting one's monarch.

Clair felt the tension in her muscles ease greatly. She hadn't even realized she was holding her shoulders so tightly.

Another cough came, louder this time. Clair finished the introductions. "Elizabeth the First, Queen of England. The greatest queen of all time—even if someday there happens to be an Elizabeth the Second."

"I concur," Ian said, then smiled into the eyes of the older woman. Deep lines fanned outward from the edges, but did nothing to dim the audacious brightness in her gaze.

"I am charmed by the honor you do me," he said quietly to Lady Abby.

The woman bowed her head regally and moved on to greet the other guests, a study in queenly demeanor. Ian stared after her.

"I take it Lady Abby has a slight problem with reality?" he asked.

"Oh, no," Clair protested. "Aunt Abby is normal—except when she is having one of her episodes. This time she is Queen Elizabeth. I must admit Elizabeth is one of my favorites."

"She has other people she impersonates?" Ian asked, fascinated in spite of himself. Not withstanding what Clair said, Lady Abby's normalcy was a moot point. As far as he was concerned, the woman had more bats in the belfry than Westminster Abbey.

"Oh yes. She believes she is everyone from Caligula to Shakespeare." Clair searched his face for some sign of revulsion. Happily, she found none.

Ian kept his expression blank, a habit long ingrained. He had been right. Victor Frankenstein wasn't the only one a few cards short of a full deck in this family. No, it appeared Clair's nut didn't fall far from the old Frankenstein family tree, he mused sardonically.

Imps of the Perverse

Clair sat gloating like Cheshire, her friend Jane's well-fed cat, as she and the other women made polite chitchat and the men finished their brandy and cigars. As far as she was concerned, the dinner party had been a raging success—the one small exception being when Mr. Harre had gotten weepy at the sight of the turtle soup being served.

The talk had been lively, the meal superb, and Ian looked spectacular in his evening clothes. He was dressed wholly in black, with a white waistcoat embroidered with red thread that matched the red ruby pin in his fashionably tied cravat. The handsome devil quite took her breath away.

Ian had also acted with remarkable courtesy to both her aunts, not even lifting a brow when Great-aunt Abby had called out, "Off with their heads," when the senior footman forgot to pour her more wine.

Clair couldn't help but beam. Ian seemed to take in

the eccentricities of her family with a remarkable calm, like a lone oak standing tall against the woodcutter dancing gleefully around its trunk. She felt almost sure that he was interested in her, which made her heart quicken and her insides feel as if tiny butterflies were alighting in her stomach. It was a truly exceptional sensation for a woman who had learned to compartmentalize her feelings, placing them in tiny boxes to be safely stored away, while she devoted her life to her career.

Breathing deeply, she savored both her feelings and confusion like the men did a fine port after dinner. It was amazing what an attractive beau could do for a woman's outlook on life.

Noting her friend's agitation, Arlene sat down next to Clair on the green-striped settee. "Clair, you look provokingly thoughtful. I bet I can guess what you're contemplating so thoroughly." Arlene grinned. "One very handsome baron?"

Clair sighed. "He is handsome, isn't he? Probably the handsomest man in all of London . . . England . . . make that the whole British Empire!"

Arlene giggled. "I can't believe it, but it appears you, my scientific brainiac, are smitten. This is quite the red-letter day."

"Yes, I do believe I am. It's like being bitten by bed-bugs and not minding. I should be thinking about my vampire theories, but instead I'm thinking of how green Ian's eyes are," Clair confided conspiratorially.

Before she could say more, the salon was suddenly filled with the smells of cigar smoke and a faint trace of aged brandy as the men entered. Clair smiled affectionately as Professor Whutson approached. He was one of her favorites among her uncle's cronies.

"What a fine meal, Clair. I am so glad I could attend." Whutson patted his belly.

She hugged the older man. "So am I. We have missed you. But I know Dr. Homes has kept you quite busy," Clair said sincerely. "Tell me, what is he involved with now?"

"Tobacco."

"Tobacco?"

Whutson laughed at her expression. "Yes, Homes is busy testing different tobacco ash. The other day I opened the door and smelled thick smoke. I thought a fire had broken out, only to find Homes studying tobacco ash."

Clair's laughter pealed out like the tinkling of bells. Professor Whutson shared in her mirth, chuckling long and loudly.

"Homes has deduced that he can solve many mysteries if he can tell from where certain tobaccos originate."

Clair's smile faded as she grew intrigued, her mind instantly recognizing the possibilities. "Yes, of course! That is quite astute of him. I imagine tobacco is much like a fingerprint. If Homes can determine where villains buy their tobacco, I feel sure it would cut down on investigation times."

"Quite, my dear." Giving her a quick peck on the cheek, he motioned toward Lady Abby, who was setting up court. "I do so enjoy confounding Homes with these readings, for I always relate them carefully when I arrive home, and he is always astounded that your aunt is always correct."

Clair laughed brightly. "You are a wily old fox."

"If so, I am in good company," he said cheerily. "Come, let's enjoy another adventure of the tarot cards."

The two joined the group around Lady Abby, who prepared to begin her readings. "Come, my subjects, it is now time for the cards." So saying, she sat down in a tall Louis XVI chair and pulled out her tarot cards. "Who will be first?"

After no one answered, Lady Abby dramatically pointed a finger bedecked with rings at Mr. Poe, who had once again taken up his post by the stuffed raven, that ominous bird of yore. "You there, leave that bird alone and come here."

Mr. Poe hurried to obey the royal request, seating himself in front of Lady Abby. "My lady."

"Do I know you, sir? What tempest has tossed thee to my shore? Have we met before, perhaps at Windsor Castle? Did you make obeisance to me there?"

Poe shook his head, looking ill at ease.

Ian shook his head, amused that the man was embarrassed talking to a make-believe queen, but perfectly fine with being enamored of a dead, stuffed bird.

"Come now, sir. No need to be shy," Lady Abby advised haughtily. "My, you are a beguiling little fellow." Turning around to face Raleigh, she added ceremoniously, "Raleigh, we must give him an appointment at court."

Mr. Raleigh nodded from across the room. "Yes, Bess. Perhaps I can put him on as Dresser of the Wardrobe."

Lady Abby seemed satisfied. "A most worthy position. What say you, Sir Poe?"

Clair hid her grin. Mr. Poe looked like a fish out of water, but then Aunt Abby often had that effect on people. Her great-aunt was as delusional as they came during her episodes, a wonderful old lady full of spit and vinegar. Of course, she also had a heart as vast as the bluest of skies.

Mr. Edgar Allan Poe finally managed a weak nod as Abby adjusted her heavy gown and shuffled the cards.

The cards were drawn, yet remained facedown as the sounds of silence descended upon the room. The only exception was the ticking of the pendulum clock on the fireplace mantel, ticking away the hours of every human life.

Lady Abby glared ruthlessly at the offending clock. "To the tower . . . take it to the tower. Brooks! Brooks! Take it away, it offends us."

The long-suffering butler hurried forward, a rare mutinous look on his face. Ian repressed a grin. If this were the *Bounty*, Lady Abby—alias Queen Bess or whoever the hell she was this week—would be walking the plank.

Brooks quickly bundled up the hapless clock and took it away, muttering under his breath. "They don't pay me enough to endure this."

"Now, Mr. Poe, pay attention to the cards," Abby commanded as she turned three tarot cards over. "By the heavens that bend above us, you have drawn the Tower and the Chariot!" She shook her head. "But also the Moon, which is good." She looked arrogantly at Mr. Poe. "You will have fame. The power of your words will evoke strong emotions and images. Perhaps you will know great fame, but it will come with a cost. A very great cost. Perhaps the cost of your heart. The road will not be easy."

"My writings, they will sell?" Poe questioned eagerly.

Lady Abby studied him, seeing in his eyes the mark of a demon. Mr. Poe was a haunted man. "Yes. Hear the tolling of the bells. Iron bells." But Lady Abby knew the price Mr. Poe paid would be high: his sanity and his life.

The man laughed with delighted abandon. "I was so afraid, so afraid. But I will become a great writer after all."

"In time. All in God's good time. But not all of this fame will come in your *own* time."

"What do you mean?" Poe demanded. His laughter faded.

"Your greatest fame will be after your death," Abby prophesied.

"But, but," Poe stuttered, his expression confused and defeated. "My writings. My destiny is to be a great writer. An author of great renown."

"You already are, sir. You need no man to tell you that your macabre words have a life of their own, and that they will be remembered for decades to come." Lady Abby smiled regally, then indicated for him to rise. "Go now and head thy soul away from stealing shadows and birds."

Poe stood, hesitating, afraid to anger the old lady, but his curiosity was unsatisfied.

"Begone, I say," Lady Abby demanded boldly in a tone that would have done Elizabeth Tudor proud. Mr. Poe had no choice but to back away, a confused expression on his features.

"My lord." Turning slightly in her chair, Lady Abby addressed Ian. "Now it is your turn."

Ian felt apprehensive, but he sat down before the grand dame. He didn't want his fortune read, knowing his own future far too well. Still, in this gathering of giants he couldn't risk refusing and having questions asked.

"Now, Baron, draw three cards," Abby instructed.

She nodded as she handed him the deck to shuffle. "Many men are mere puppets who come and go, formless men who do the bidding of others. But you are not such a one."

Ian glanced up at the old lady, but he remained silent as he picked the three cards. He drew the Tower, the Hanged Man, and Death. Ian heard a few hushed murmurs of concern over the last card.

Lady Abby stared at Ian for a long while, her expression grave. "Your life has been magic, but also a tragic adventure. At times your journey in life has been obscure, other times lonely."

He nodded.

"There is great change in your life, continual change. The Tower indicates this. Always there is change, but at the cost of destruction," Lady Abby explained to everyone, studying Ian closely. "Strange how this change is such a constant thread throughout your life. You keep so many things hidden."

Ian shifted uncomfortably. Lady Abby was touching on secrets that needed to remain hidden. "My life has been what it should be."

Lady Abby shook her head. "No, my lord. Destiny causes you to chase the wind and the moon. You struggle to accept what is written upon the wind. Some spell shall bind you."

Behind him, Ian could sense Clair moving closer. Her curiosity seemed almost a living thing.

Lady Abby pointed to the next card. "The Hanged Man indicates that you are undecided about a situation. You do not know how to act, therefore you choose not to act at all. That will not do. You must act in order to preserve your destiny."

"And what am I undecided upon?"

Lady Abby only smiled a mysterious smile and shook her head. "Ride boldly down the valley of shadow. Ride boldly." She pointed to the last card. "The card of Death."

"That's something I don't fear."

Lady Abby looked deep into his eyes. "No, you are not afraid, but death is stalking you, you know. He rides a big black horse, and he is legion to immortals."

Clair gasped, moving to stand by Ian's side, her concern a palpable thing.

"He stalks us all," Ian said quietly.

"But methinks he chases you harder than most. You have outwitted him so far, but be wary, my lord. Death rides a dark horse and he rides it fast. And as the Norsemen used to say, he rides also the night wind." She inclined her head. The tarot reading was finished.

Ian took Lady Abby's hand, giving it a courtier's kiss, then stood as she motioned at Mrs. Garwood to take a seat.

Clair guided him to a corner in the room where they could stand without being overheard. "I am sorry about the reading, Ian, it was really quite grim."

Ian smiled down at her. "Clair, I don't believe in such things."

She put her hand on his arm, beseeching him with her eyes. "But you should. My great-aunt may be a bit of a character, but she is quite good at her cards. She warns you to be careful. Please do so."

Ian grinned. "Her cards told you that I was a vampire," he reminded her.

"Her cards told me that there was something other-worldly about you."

"You see how wrong she can be?"

Clair shrugged. "Everyone is entitled to a mistake or two."

Ian chuckled. "Well, that one was a doozy."

"Don't you ever make mistakes?"

"Not since I was in leading strings."

Her gray eyes twinkling like the evening sky, she teased, "I see I can add modesty to your list of admirable traits."

Ian could feel the strong pull of attraction. Luckily, it appeared to be mutual. Yes, he thought, he was well satisfied with the progress of his Plan A, *The Seduction of Clair Frankenstein*. The affair was proceeding as planned. Clair was becoming enamored of him. Soon he would have her concerned only with his kisses, have her walking about with her head in the clouds and not on the walking dead.

A loud, "Humph!" interrupted their exchange. Clair and Ian quickly glanced around to find Lady Abby standing and holding out her dress, upon which a large wine stain was spreading.

"Out, damned spot! Out I say!" Lady Abby quoted dramatically.

Ian whispered, "Isn't that Shakespeare?"

Clair nodded. "She gets her characters confused sometimes. Well, there's no help for it. I need to take her to the maid so she can get changed. I'll be back momentarily."

"I wait with bated breath."

Clair arched an eyebrow and left.

Instead of joining the others, Ian decided he needed a few moments of peace, letting the conversations swirl around him. He could hear Professor Whutson commenting to Mr. Raleigh on another of the Homes cases. Lady Mary was enthusiastically showing Mr. Poe her taxidermy specimens.

Brooks broke Ian's concentration as the butler entered the room carrying a note on a silver platter. The servant glanced around, then exited.

On gut instinct Ian followed, and Brooks led him to a back room near the kitchen where Clair was just leaving. The butler handed her the note while Ian hid in the shadows of the stairwell.

"Aha!" Clair exclaimed.

"Oh no, Miss Clair, not again." Brooks clutched a hand to his chest, a mournful expression on his homely face.

"Oh, Brooks, you are such a worrier."

"With more than good reason. Now what have you gotten yourself into?" the butler asked cautiously.

"Brooks," Clair sighed, giving the man's shoulder a fond pat. "The game is at hand."

"Miss Clair, you *really* worry me when you start imitating that Durlock fellow." His voice was filled with reproach.

"My dear fellow, if it were up to you, I would still be in the nursery."

"Yes, you would. Safe and sound, and not out gallivanting around the cemeteries and in people's crypts. It's not fitting for a genteel lady like yourself."

"Dear, dear Brooks, you know better than most that a Frankenstein can't quit once on the trail of a scientific breakthrough. The truth at all costs."

"Don't quote the family motto to me again. If I have heard it once, I have heard it a thousand times, and that's the plain truth! That little motto could get you dead and buried. Or even worse," he scolded like an old maid, "it could get you two big holes in your neck. How would you like that? How would your aunts like that? You know Lady Abby can't stand the cold and how my arthritis acts up in the damp night air."

"What has that got to do with anything?"

"If you become one of those undead fiends, where do you think we will have to go to visit you? The cemetery, that's where!"

"Now, Brooks, I will be fine." Affectionately, Clair again patted his shoulder. "I will be leaving a little after eleven."

Suddenly, she frowned. She could get in quite a predicament over this purloined letter, which would lead her to the secret assignation, if Ian got a devil in his head. Well, there was no hope for it; she would have to hurry Ian on his way home.

"Leaving where at that hour?" Brooks chided, his feathers ruffled like a feisty bantam rooster.

"To the Honorable Christopher Wilder's house." Clair said the last over her shoulder as she scurried away.

Ian shook his head, remaining in the shadows and listening to Brooks's muttering: "Let's just hope the Honorable Christopher Wilder is an honorable man."

Ian grimaced. The Honorable Christopher Wilder was anything but honorable where women—ladies or whores—were concerned. Ian knew him fairly well from the clubs of ill repute scattered across London. Wilder was a renowned rake, a connoisseur of all that was fleshy, female, and curvy, the bawdier the better. He loved the chase, the capture, and the capitulation. Only, after the fact, Wilder got bored and roamed to new unplowed pastures.

Running a hand through his dark hair, Ian reevaluated things. Perhaps his Plan A needed a few revisions. He smiled deviously. If Clair Frankenstein planned to pay a surprise visit to the Wilder residence, she was in for a big surprise herself.

The Vampire Buster

The road to hell was paved with scientific inventions, a vampire, lust for Ian Huntsley, and breaking and entering twice in one week, Clair decided. She was doing Uncle Victor proud, she mused as she glanced up at the night sky.

Slithering clouds of gray covered much of the half moon, which provided Clair with the darkness she needed to scale the ivy-covered walls of the Wilder property. She was in luck. It was a great night for burgling. And she was ready, dressed in tight-fitting doeskin breeches and a black velvet jacket.

Clair checked her mountain-climbing equipment once more, then swung her rope and grappling hook, which connected with the wrought-iron balcony. Quickly she began her silent ascent up the pale brick wall. As she climbed, she grinned, thinking that one could never underestimate the appeal of a hard-fought silence.

Scrambling over the balcony edge, she laid her rope discreetly to the side. Taking a quick glance back at the ground below, she noted nothing but shadow. No movement. Good, she applauded silently. No one was the wiser that she was here.

The open doors of the balcony lured her forward, revealing a bordello-like chamber of appalling taste. It seemed the Honorable Christopher Wilder was enamored of the color red, in particular the very bright hue known as crimson. His carpet was red, along with the walls, not to mention the bedhangings and spread, all done in vivid tint with interwoven tiny gold flecks. His room was enough to give a person a red scare, Clair decided.

In spite of her revulsion at the utter lack of good taste, she smiled. Uncle Victor had hit the nail on the head once more. Vampires *did* sleep in the red.

Espying the large wardrobe dead center in the room, Clair moved toward it. The perfect hiding place. She would be able to see the Honorable Christopher by leaving a small crack in the door, but he wouldn't be able to see her. She only hoped his feeding habits weren't too messy.

A voice behind her interrupted her thoughts, and she whirled around. She should have been terrified. Instead she was only horrified. Drat! Ian!

"Miss Frankenstein, we do seem to meet in the strangest places, and you always seem to be breaking and entering!"

"Good grief, Ian. What are you doing here?" she asked

nervously, chewing on her bottom lip, her heart still racing from the unexpected shock.

"I could ask you the same question," he snapped.

"I asked you first."

Ian counted to ten. It didn't work, so he counted to ten once more, studying Clair. Tonight she was dressed in another of her unique breaking-and-entering costumes. This one was complete with breeches.

In spite of his pique, he couldn't help noting with grand approval how Clair had longer legs for her five-foot-and-not-much-more frame than he would have thought. Very nice legs, in fact. Indeed, legs that looked like they would feel great wrapped around his waist as he plunged inside her.

Reluctantly, he snapped himself back to attention. "Clair, I am here to stop you from your rendezvous with Wilder."

She gasped. "What rendezvous?"

Irked by her mad dash to disaster and her penchant for sticking her nose into things that went bump in the night, Ian alleged, "You aren't here to make mad, passionate love with him?" Knowing full well she wasn't.

"Have you lost your mind? What would make you think a thing like that?"

"What would make me think that? Could it be because you are standing in the man's bedroom? Which reminds me, how in the bloody hell did you get in here?" Ian inquired coldly. He couldn't leave her alone for more than a moment without her courting trouble.

"I climbed."

Strolling to the window, he glanced out at the rope. "That explains the strange getup," he remarked, glancing down at her trousers. "I guess I should add mountain climbing to your considerable list of talents."

"Uncle Victor and I spent three summers in the Alps," she explained softly. "I even climbed the Matterhorn." Ian's forbidding expression worried her. Surely he couldn't believe she was interested in a man with such poor taste in home decoration?

"How did *you* get up here? I know you didn't come through the door."

He smiled. It was wicked. "I leaped."

"What a bounder," she said, giggling. "In a single bound?"

"Of course."

"My, you must be some sort of superman."

"I would be more than glad to show you some of my other abilities, and as we are in the bedchamber . . ." His dark green eyes twinkled. "Oh, but I forgot you are to meet Wilder."

Exasperated, she rolled her eyes. "No! No! And double no! I came to watch him slake his vampire thirst. My informants told me he is to be with Lady Montcrief tonight, and you above all people know what an appetite—"

Ian shook his head, interrupting. "Clair, Clair, what am I to do with you?" Suddenly he glanced toward the door. "Right now, I guess I'd better hide you."

"What do you hear?" she asked nervously. She couldn't be caught; that would alert Mr. Wilder to the fact she knew he was one of the undead.

"Footsteps on the stairs." Grabbing her, Ian shoved Clair toward the wardrobe. Opening the door, he speedily pushed her in. He followed quickly behind, closing the door with a snap.

"It's a tad crowded in here," she complained softly.

"It's about to be a tad crowded out there." He smiled in the darkness, breathing deeply. Clair's fresh scent surrounded him, whetting his appetite to taste her sweet, soft flesh.

"It's so dark. I can't see a thing," she complained. "Ian, watch what you're doing."

"Shhh," he whispered. "They're entering the chamber."

"Ian, move! Your hand is on my breast," she urgently whispered.

"I thought it was your foot." He savored the feeling of her plump breast, envisioning it naked. His hunger grew. He wanted her beneath him doing nature's primal dance. Unfortunately he was in a wardrobe, a most undistinguished place for a tryst, especially for a peer of the realm. Clair really was bad for his dignity.

In a pig's eye he'd thought it her foot; Clair thought crossly. The man was a randy goat through and through. And she was stuck in a wardrobe with him for God knew how long. Hmm, she changed her tune, what a lucky lady she was.

"Bounder," she whispered. His hand now held all of her breast, his thumb circling the nipple. She shifted uncomfortably, wanting something indescribable, for it was something unknown to her.

"Sneaking snoop," he whispered back.

"Lusty libertine."

"Nosy Nellie," he murmured, leaning close to kiss her. She held her hand up, stopping him. "This isn't the time. I need to see Wilder feed."

"This should be some trick. Has your uncle Victor

designed some sort of gadget that sees through wood?"
Ian mocked.

"Hush," she whispered. Quietly, she turned the handle on the door. "Bloody hell. It's stuck. Of all the luck," she grouched.

She had made it unseen inside Wilder's red bedroom, and now she couldn't see the sight she needed to see. She was beginning to wonder if Ian Huntsley wasn't rather the opposite of a good luck charm.

Ian gave it the old Oxford try. The result surprised him. "It does appear to be stuck. What an interesting situation. We could stay in here until we rot or I could bang on the door and plead with Wilder to let us out."

His anger was slowly building. Once again, Clair had run headfirst into disaster, this time dragging him with her. In all his days of spying, he had never ended up in the untenable position of being stuck in a wardrobe. What was worse, Clair didn't even realize what a disaster she truly was or the danger she was in!

Ian drew Clair nearer, his hot breath on her ear. "Of course, when Wilder asks me why you and I are in his wardrobe, I will have to tell him that we were spying on him. Then I imagine I will be meeting him with pistols drawn at dawn," he finished grumpily.

"Don't be stupid. He can't meet you at dawn. The sun would fry him to a crisp."

Though neither could see the other, each knew they were glaring furiously.

Reaching into the pocket of her breeches, Clair retrieved a slim pick. A moment later, Ian heard a slight click.

"What are you doing?" he whispered.

"What else? Picking the lock."

"My, my, is there no end to your nefarious talents?"

"Put a sock in it, my lord," she snapped.

As the latch gave, Ian hissed. "Don't push on the door." The words of warning came too late, and both Clair and Ian were dumped unceremoniously on the carpet.

The tableau was straight from a tawdry farce, Ian thought. Wilder was literally caught with his pants down, a shocked expression on his features. Dressed in nothing but black garters and nature's grace, Lady Montcrief was on her knees, worshiping Wilder with her mouth.

"My stars, Ian! I got it wrong again. Wilder's not biting her. She's biting him!" Clair gasped.

It was more than Ian could bear. It was classic Frankenstein. He fell to the floor, howling with laughter.

It was an hour later—filled with sermons, curses, and one or two dubious explanations, all of them coming from Ian—before Clair was returned home to her bedchamber.

Dispirited, she glanced around. The room was decorated in Wedgwood blue and creamy white, with chairs of similar hue, while the settee and window seats were all upholstered in a delicate floral pattern. Well-stocked bookshelves lined the walls and a fire flickered in the blue-marbled hearth.

The logs in the fireplace shifted, causing tiny sparks to shoot outward into the thin mesh screen. Clair stared gloomily at the flames, recalling with shame Ian's lengthy and virulent lecture on the way home.

Ian had been fierce in the closed coach, trying to impose his will upon her. But no matter how he lectured, threatened, or cajoled, she wouldn't give up her dreams of winning the prestigious Scientific Discovery of the Decade Award. She wouldn't give up her chance to be a published scientist of renown, no matter what Ian growled and no matter how many harsh lectures he subjected her to.

She could still hear his stern tone, telling her that she needed to live in the real world and give her scientific research a rest for a while. But he didn't realize that science was her life on every level.

She remembered the look Ian gave her, which had scorched to her very soul. She was terribly afraid that she was falling in love with the devious wretch. But she would stick to her guns. She didn't care how hotly Ian looked at her with his passion barely banked. Or how his dark green eyes blazed as fiercely as the flames in her hearth. Or how long he pleaded and threatened her to stop work. She wouldn't give up her quest. She was first and foremost a Frankenstein and a seeker of the truth.

Aunt Mary, sitting beside her in a white cotton nightgown, finished pouring some tea. "Now, dear heart, care to tell me about it?"

"It was an unmitigated disaster of the first degree," Clair replied mournfully. "And worse, I made a complete jackass of myself."

She winced, remembering her words about Lady Montcrief's bite. Ian had scornfully explained that Lady Montcrief might be a vamp, but she was no vampire. He went on to explain in a rather formal, clinical manner just exactly what Lady Montcrief was doing to the Honorable Christopher Wilder—an act Clair felt wasn't very honorable in the least.

Clair bit her lip, thinking that she would rather suck on a lemon than do that to Wilder's male member.

Lady Mary patted her niece's hand companionably. "Did I ever tell you about the time Victor was seventeen years old?"

Clair shook her head.

"Well, you see, Victor got a rather inflated opinion of himself, and decided he could challenge the Fates and win."

"What did he do?"

"He chained himself to the gables of the roof during a nasty electrical storm, threatening the lightning to strike him."

"What happened?" Clair asked. This was a story about her uncle that she had never heard before.

"What do you think? The fool boy got struck by lightning. It was rather amazing that he lived."

"Of course!" Clair squealed, her eyes alight with excitement. "I always wondered where he got the idea for using electrical currents to stimulate dead cells in the reanimation of dead flesh. I asked often enough, but he would never tell me."

"Of course not. Your uncle Victor is a proud man and he lives on your hero worship. He would never want you to see him in the guise of fool."

Tenderly Clair hugged her aunt, the woman who had been like a mother to her ever since her parents were killed in a boating accident when she was four. She understood the moral lesson her Aunt Mary was imparting: *Everyone makes foolish mistakes, but only the foolish give up their dreams.* "Thank you, Aunt."

"Good. Now, no more mopes. You merely had another case of mistaken identity. You will just have to buckle down and dig deeper. I have complete faith that you will find that nasty nest of vampires."

Picking up her teacup, Clair sipped thoughtfully. "Aunt, I thought you weren't too fond of my vampire study."

"Heaven knows I'm not, but it's important to you. You are too much like your Uncle. If you stopped what you were doing, it would kill off a part of that marvelous creative spark that is so integral to your makeup. I wouldn't want that. You wouldn't be Clair Frankenstein anymore."

"I know you have been afraid of the dangers I might face, but truly the only danger I have been in is making a fool of myself."

Lady Mary giggled. She knew Clair was beginning to feel better. It was due of course to her indomitable Frankenstein spirit, a force with which to be reckoned. "I must admit I have worried much less since Baron Huntsley entered the scene."

"Hmm. I am beginning to think he is unlucky for me."

"I see," Lady Mary murmured mysteriously. "He is not quite as handsome as some of the other young men of the *ton*. I believe his jaw is too square, his nose a trifle too long."

"Oh no, Aunt, you're wrong. He's truly gorgeous in a wild and handsome way."

"He is rather arrogant at times," Lady Mary proposed. She carefully regarded her niece's reaction.

"Not at all. Well, only to toad eaters," Clair defended devoutly.

"I heard that he is a seducer of innocents." Lady Mary suggested, her tone bland. Now she was getting to the heart of the matter.

Clair blushed. "He has been a perfect gentleman to me," she began, then stopped, remembering his hot, strong hand on her breast.

Watching her like a hawk, Lady Mary pounced. "Clair, is there something you'd like to tell me?" She didn't quite approve of the old ruse of getting a man to the altar through a compromising situation, but if the compromising did occur, then the compromiser was most definitely going to marry the compromisee.

Warily Clair eyed her aunt. She knew that tone. Mary Frankenstein was plotting something, probably something to do with wedding dresses and wedding cakes and a certain crafty baron. But while Clair desired Ian to be in love with her, she would not force him into an unwanted leg-shackle.

She leaned over and kissed her aunt's cheek. "No. Ian and I have done nothing to be ashamed of. I wish I could say the same for the not-so-Honorable Christopher Wilder. I would like to tell Arlene and Jane about what I saw. But it wouldn't be proper. Besides, they probably wouldn't believe me."

Her aunt diverted, Clair went on to describe the scene which had occurred upon her emergence from the wardrobe. Much to Clair's chagrin, her always-dignified aunt ended up in much the same position as Ian: rolling on the floor, shaking with laughter.

"If Great-aunt Abby were here right now, she could appoint me her court jester," Clair remarked rather stiffly. That only sent her Aunt Mary into another fit of laughter.

Reconnaissance in the Garden of Good and Evil

The formal garden was filled with lush, rich vegetation. The strains of a waltz filtered through the large stained-glass balcony doors, and from the ballroom soft golden light spread out across the deep green foliage.

Ian lifted his head and sniffed the air. It was filled with a myriad of smells, but one scent in particular: *Clair*. Surveying the darkly shadowed areas, he spotted a very shapely bottom stuck into the air. He would know that derriere anywhere.

He knew it, had dreaded it, had been prepared for it, but still her unrelenting audacity made him grit his teeth. She was like a feisty terrier with a particularly juicy bone.

Ha! he thought. When Clair Frankenstein got the bone between her teeth, she was off and running, leaving everyone else behind. But he had no choice except to follow.

He stepped lightly, approaching his unsuspecting victim as silently as death. Clair never heard him coming. Leaning over, he seductively breathed on her neck. "Boo!"

"Ouch!" Startled, she banged her head on the shrubbery under which she was halfway hidden, tangling her hair in its limbs. Frustrated and a trifle wary, she complained gently, "You scared the life out of me."

"Better me than some other villain lurking in the shadows," he remarked sternly. He began untangling her hair from the boughs of the bush.

As he did so, Clair motioned Ian to squat down by her side. "Be quiet."

Ian gritted his teeth. "Who, or should I say what, are we spying on now?"

"I resent that."

"No. You resemble that."

"I am not spying, I am merely on a scouting mission," she hedged.

"Who is your victim this time?" Friday-faced, he tried for a modicum of civility. It was not an easy feat, as he was fast being driven around the bend by Clair's scampish antics. And she was driving at a fast clip.

She narrowed her gaze at him. "Really Ian, you would think I was committing a murder or something."

He bared his teeth. It was not a smile. "No, but I might be. Clair, how many times do I have to warn you?"

"Four thousand, five hundred, and two," she said impishly.

At odds with his annoyance, he felt a desire to kiss

her. "Very amusing." The twitching of his lips turned into a lopsided grin.

"It made you smile."

The wily rogue was just too tempting for his own good. Or hers. Clair had no time for romantic nonsense right now. She was on another investigative quest into the unknown. Who knew what earth-shaking discovery she might make tonight? She was due. Who knew what hideous fiend lay hidden in the guise of nobility? Who knew what salivating beast she would reveal, what scandal so spectacular that the world would take note. Not to mention what scientific theory she could prove to awe the judges of the prestigious *Journal*'s award. The world was at her fingertips—or rather half a garden away, lurking in the guise of humanity.

Dragging herself out of her thoughts, she grinned up at Ian. "Yes. I most certainly made you smile," she noted.

"Better than crying, I guess." Ian sighed wearily. "You know, Clair, I might be a fool, but I am not a stupid fool."

She cocked her head, studying him like some lab specimen. "Pray explain."

"Look around you, Clair." Ian gestured to the night.

Excitedly, Clair asked, "Is it a vampire bat?"

Ian sighed louder. Taking her chin in hand, he lifted her head, positioning it. The moon was hard to miss, way up in the sky.

He said, "The moon in all its silvery splendor, its glistening remnants of moonglow. Some say that on a night when the moon is blue, all those couples who gaze upon it are struck . . . moonstruck."

"Is that like a disease?" Clair asked.

Ian shook his head in resignation. "No, Clair. They are struck by *love*." Putting a hand to his ear, he continued with his lesson in romance—as much romance as one could try for when one squatted behind some yarrow bushes. "Listen to the music of the night. It has a cadence, a rhythm all its own. A romance all its own. And here I am, and here you are, male and female all by ourselves, alone in a garden. I am with a most beautiful woman and I am watching for . . . vampires. You do see the irony in the situation, don't you?"

Slowly, he leaned over and kissed her. She tasted wet, spicy, and yet sweet. Her lips were the softest velvet, her sigh a song of beauty. She had a scent all her own, like just before a rain in the Welsh mountains. It was a smell he distinguished from a thousand other females. Clair stirred his appetites and made him ache with want.

Clair breathed Ian's smell, too, a smell like dusky autumn leaves and tart apples. He tasted feral and fierce and made her blood hum. She sighed into his mouth, again feeling that unfamiliar throbbing between her legs. She released another breath, this time from vexation. Ian was turning her into a terrible trollop, a hopeless hussy. However, it was a heady feeling.

With regret, Ian broke off the kiss, knowing this wasn't the time or place for seduction. Frustrated in both body and spirit, he stared at Clair's wet, pink mouth, carnal cravings eating at him. "Be glad I have overcome my regrettable tendency towards cannibalism," he said.

She smiled, a bemused expression on her heart-shaped face. Yes, she and Ian clearly had an intense gravitational pull towards each other, like the sun and the moon. The attraction was definitely changing her into a helpless harlot.

"You are vampire-hunting again, I take it," Ian said.

"In a manner of speaking," Clair replied sheepishly.

"You know, Clair, someone should have told you a long time ago that you shouldn't count your vampires before they hatch."

"How silly of me," she teased. "And all this time I thought it was chickens."

"If only it were," Ian remarked regretfully.

"Shush," she warned, staring through the shrubbery at the opposite end of the garden, where a small rose arbor covered in red and white rambling roses stood reposed in half shadows. Tiny lanterns filled with candles flickered overhead, and a tall brown-haired man was escorting the charmingly lovely and charmingly lewd widow Lady Montcrief into its depths.

"My, she does get around," Clair observed dryly.

Ian's eyes widened at the sight before him. He glanced in horror at Clair. "Oh, no! Not Asher. You couldn't possibly be idiotic enough to be spying on the Earl of Wolverton."

"Hush. I told you I wasn't spying," Clair whispered.

"Bloody hell! The deuce you're not. Just lurking in the shadows like a spider waiting to pounce?"

She punched him in the arm, all semblance of decorum fled before the winds of her ire. Ian was making her furious with his unreasonable attitude. He knew she was a scholar of the supernatural—unpublished as of yet, but a scholar nonetheless. This was her mission of scientific discovery, and Ian had no right to make her feel like a Peeping Tom just because of a few hair-raising kisses. He had no right to dictate to her.

"If you're so concerned about being seen, you can leave."

Ian scowled furiously. "If I left, I am sure it would improve my humor. But unfortunately I can't. By God, Clair! You are in way over your head. This is no small thing. The earl is a thoroughly ruthless, cunning adversary. You don't want to make an enemy of the man."

He trembled with anger. Clair was rushing in where only fools would tread—which, come to think of it, described her perfectly. She was a bluestocking kook. And yet, to his grave misgivings, he was crazy about her. Now his queer bird was going to try and dissect Neil Asher, the Earl of Wolverton. The man would chew her up and spit her out without a twinge of conscience. Asher had no soul and hadn't for a very long time. He was infamous for both lechery and just retribution, a man both revered and reviled. And for bloody damn good reason.

"I am not making an *enemy* out of him, only a supernatural predator!" she explained.

"I'm sure he'll be delighted with that distinction," Ian said. "I can hardly wait for the end of this farce!"

"You pig!" Clair snapped. "I'm not wrong this time. I am absolutely, positively sure. Beyond a reasonable doubt, any doubt. The earl is a bone-crunching, marrow-munching fiend of a werewolf. And I shall prove it!"

"Damn, Clair. Keep your voice down. Do you want him to hear?" Ian warned. He lifted her chin to meet his burning gaze. "How in bloody hell did you come upon this remarkable lack of deductive reasoning? What dubious fodder did you glean from the rumor mills?" He was enraged. She was treading in deep water and he, Ian Huntsley, was forced to drown her or save her pretty neck. "Clair, I'm waiting for my answer."

Glancing up at Ian with a rueful smile on her face, she explained. "It was staring me in the face all along. Indeed, I feel rather foolish about it. It was rather elementary. He is the Earl of Wolverton. I just assumed that was too easy."

His patience at an end, Ian snapped. His eyes a furious shade of green, he grunted, "What does the Earl of Wolverton being the Earl of Wolverton have to do with werewolves?"

Clair looked at him as though he were a loaf short of a baker's dozen. "Pay attention, Ian. Wolverton. Wolf. Werewolf. Good grief! His coat of arms has a wolf on it. I must have been blind. Wolverton is the werewolf of the vampire nest." Her eyes gleamed with smug satisfaction. "I reasoned it out last night."

"The Earl of Dover has a dragon crest. You don't see him out and about breathing fire and eating innocent maidens," Ian snarled. Then, recalling some of the old earl's proclivities, he wanted to kick himself. Bad example. The Earl of Dover did eat maidens—the fairer, the better. "I take it you have more than his coat of arms and family name to condemn the man to his furry fate?"

Nodding, Clair began to tick off the points on her fingertips. "Number one, he's never seen on the night of the full moon, which makes perfect sense since were wolves can only transform into their animal form on full moons, regardless of provocation or predilection. You know they absolutely have no choice in the matter but to go from man or woman to wolf form."

Yes, Ian knew, but he hadn't realized Clair was aware. "Go on," he urged gravely, concerned. Asher would not take this lying down, and neither would several other groups he knew.

"Secondly, I was informed by several jewelers that the earl can't wear silver—he has a terrible allergy to it. Thirdly, Wolverton is very fit and handsome. Shapeshifters generally are fit. I deduce it's from all that running about on nights with full moons and the energy it takes to metamorphose," Clair explained, a speculative look in her eye. She continued to study the figure of the alluring earl.

Ian's scowl darkened further as she talked. "Go on," he forced out, gritting his teeth. This woman was dangerous, deranged . . . and driving him wild with her soft, pink lips.

"Number four, several waiters have revealed that the earl only eats his steak rare."

"The man should be hanged!" Ian gasped.

"That's not all," she hissed. Better people than Ian had mocked her. For a man as bright as he, Ian could be such a dimwit. He just wasn't getting the whole wolf-man picture.

"I am all agog. Do tell," he said.

"Fifthly, the Earl of Wolverton has animal magnetism. I calculate it must be a werewolf thing—pheromones and all, you know. His lovemaking is reputed to be even superior to your own." There, that should shut him up, she speculated. From her limited experience and what limited gossip she and Arlene had heard, men were worrywarts about their bedroom skills.

"The man should be worshiped as a god," Ian growled sarcastically, jealousy flooding him. He would show her magnetism. He could be an animal anytime she wanted.

"Don't be flippant," she snapped. Drat! Ian was still being an addlepated twit. For someone so strong and intelligent, he reminded her of a ten-year-old. And he wasn't paying attention. He couldn't see the werewolf in the forest for the trees.

"Sixthly, Wolverton owns wolfhounds."

Exasperated, Ian ran his hands through his thick hair. "So do I! So does my cousin Galen and so do a hundred other men. What has this got to do with the price of tea in China?"

The bloody woman was an enigma with windmills in her head, stirring up all kind of ill breezes that would undoubtedly blow his careful world away.

Vexed, Clair complained, "Ian, keep up with me here."

"I'm trying, Clair. I'm trying." Trying not to strangle you, he thought waspishly. Clair Frankenstein made him madder than any other person alive, dead, or undead.

"I have done a study."

Ian glowered. How he was beginning to hate those five little words. They were words which spelled Ian's descent into the madhouse—or, he reasoned sardonically, he could just move in with the Frankensteins.

"The wolfhounds' footprints hide the werewolf prints. Anyone tracking a werewolf would see that there are wolfhounds in the vicinity and, seeing the werewolf prints, would believe that they are those of the wolfhound," she explained happily.

Ha! Ian thought. The bloody fool woman acted as if she had found the Rosetta Stone. He arched a brow, begging her to explain, wishing she would become a mute in sudden retribution for irritating him and delving into matters otherworldly. He wished to no avail. Plan A, *The Seduction of Clair Frankenstein*, was no longer proceeding as planned. He couldn't even distract her from her quest with a romantic tryst in a garden with the smell of roses and gardenias filling the air and the mystique of the glowing moon. His attempts were a dismal failure.

"However, I do know how to find the truth," she continued.

"I expected no less," Ian muttered.

Excitedly, she explained the solution to the problem of wolfish prints. "You see, you follow the wolf's footprints or wolfhound prints until they turn into those of a man—or vice versa."

She was so proud of her new hypothesis that her plump white breasts were quivering. The view of the valley of his dreams caught Ian mentally unaware, and a pulse of desire surged in the vicinity of his nether regions. "Neil Asher is not a werewolf in any form or fashion," he groaned.

Now Clair's breasts quivered with anger. Ian stared, transfixed at the delectable morsels. In the back of his mind, he wondered why he was overcome by stupidity every single time her chest came onto display.

He shook his head ruefully. It would take a better man than himself to ignore these sudden near-violent urgings enveloping him. Yet he was a fool with a capital *F* to be thinking of rutting with Clair when the Earl of Wolverton was less than a garden away.

Peering through the hedges, Ian was suddenly afraid that he was not the only one with ravishment on his mind. Ian noted the play of moonlight across Lady Montcrief's bare breasts. Asher was feasting on them with insatiable delight.

Quickly, he grabbed Clair's arm. But she was spellbound and tried to pull away, entranced with the scene.

Ian stifled a groan. He knew exactly what Asher

would do if the earl learned he had been center stage in a lewd display. It would not be a pretty sight. "Come on, Clair. Now!"

"Just a minute. He's at her neck again, ignoring those rather impressive breasts. He's apparently a neck man. If I didn't know he was a werewolf, I could be persuaded to believe he was a vampire."

"Bloody hell, Clair! I thought you were interested in science, not voyeurism." Ian jerked her towards him, debating whether to toss her over his shoulder and haul her off like a bag of sailor's laundry.

"Ian. Please wait a minute. I want to see the animal magnetism part."

"Asher is not a shapeshifter! I promise you," Ian snarled. "Or a vampire," he added for good measure.

"Gammon you say! I know he is and I want to see," Clair argued. She tugged on her arm, which Ian was holding in a viselike grip.

That's it! Ian thought, maddened. He had run tame long enough. Without finesse or gentleness he dragged Clair out of the garden, paying no heed to her protests and less than ladylike curses. But as he dragged the little spitfire along, he worried that Asher knew they had been in his garden spying.

Once they set foot on the terrace, Clair hit him in the groin, causing him to double over in agony. The woman might be short, but she packed a punch.

"Cad!" she complained coldly as she turned away from his pained expression. Then she entered the ballroom alone, muttering to herself, "The truth at all costs!"

Ian narrowed his gaze and slowly straightened, aching. He said with a sigh, "It appears the cost is all mine!"

The Good, The Bad and The Big, Bad Wolf

Miffed with Ian, Clair left him standing alone by a large faux-marble column. Her thoughts were in chaos. She was surprised her punch had affected Ian as it had. Perhaps he wasn't as strong as she thought. Of course, she had meant to punch him in the stomach, but he was so much taller than she was.

She was slightly sorry that she had punched him. But the man did make her lose her temper like no one else. He also made her feel beautiful, and her blood hummed whenever he was near. The attractive baron made her want to sing with joy, if only she could sing without everyone wincing.

In one way it was flattering to have Ian worry about her well-being. It showed that he cared enough about her to be concerned. Nevertheless, she was incensed that he didn't grasp the importance of her objectives or her work. She was no weak-kneed, faint-at-the-drop-of-a-garlic-clove female. How could Ian not recognize this? It was as if he, despite being a male member of the human race, could not be reasoned with. Or maybe because of it. He was too emotional about the whole situation.

"How dare he take me off my werewolf watch!" Clair grumbled.

With womanly wisdom, she decided to let him stew in his own remorse and guilt for treating her as less than the dedicated scientist she was. To teach him a lesson, she flirted shamelessly with those gentlemen of society who did not walk swiftly away when they saw her coming.

"Miss Frankenstein," a familiar voice said cordially behind her.

Turning, Clair found herself facing her friend Jane's brother. Brandon was not quite six feet tall, with light brown hair and greenish gray eyes. He had freckles and a long thin nose. He was not a handsome man, but he was not unattractive either.

Brandon Van Helsing was one of *the* Van Helsings, the world's foremost hunters of vampires. The family had been hunting the fiends since before Charles the Second was crowned. Normally Clair would have known nothing about the real occupation of the Van Helsings, since knowledge of their secret vampire-slaying society was on a need-to-know basis and shrouded in great secrecy. However, Uncle Victor had been admitted more or less reluctantly into the secret society upon the development of Frederick. Fortunately her uncle had confided in her, swearing her to secrecy about the scourge of bloodsucker society, which left Clair and Jane free to discuss various theories and questions regarding the otherworldly.

"Brandon, it's a delight to see you! Is Jane here in London with you by any chance?" Clair asked, peering about for a glimpse of her short, plump friend.

Brandon shook his head regretfully. "No. Father still insists Jane stay out of London, ever since the regrettable incident."

Clair frowned, recalling Jane's regrettable incident. It was when Jane fumbled a vampire staking for the second time, an unheard-of thing in Van Helsing history. But really it was not so remarkable when one considered that the sight of blood made her nauseous and dirt made her sneeze. Mausoleums and caskets were just filled with all kinds of smelly dirt, Clair thought morosely. Major Van Helsing, Jane's father, was a dictatorial tyrant. Jane deserved better than being entombed in the country for the past two and a half years for the slight mistake of fleeing the scene of a failed fiend-slaying.

"When will Major Van Helsing let sleeping dogs lie?" Or even sleeping vampires? Clair asked herself silently.

Brandon shrugged, his eyes dark with repressed indignation at his father's treatment of his sister. "However, Jane isn't at the country estate. Our aunt in Holland took a serious fall. Jane has gone over to keep her company and help nurse her back to health."

"When will she return?"

"Two to three months," Brandon answered.

Clair nodded thoughtfully. "Perhaps a change of scenery will do her good."

Brandon nodded. "My thoughts exactly."

"And you, Brandon? What are you about these days?"

"This and that," he replied mysteriously.

Clair shook her head. "You Van Helsings are always so secretive. All that cloak-and-stake stuff."

Brandon swiftly surveyed the nearby members of the *ton*, but they all seemed totally consumed in their own conversations, paying no attention to him or Clair. "Watch yourself, Miss Frankenstein. The walls have ears."

"True," she agreed, thinking of the Blue Salon.

"So, what are *you* up to now? No more ghosts in the cemetery?" he teased.

"Watch it, yourself," Clair warned. "You know how I feel about porcine humor."

Brandon snorted.

"Besides, I am involved in a new undertaking of quite significant value."

"Something to do with the Scientific Discovery of the Decade Award," Brandon stated.

"Yes," Clair replied, surprised.

"I saw Jane in the country not long after you wrote to her. She told me that you were trying for the award. But she didn't mention the subject material."

And she wouldn't, Clair thought smugly. Jane had been sworn to secrecy.

Seeing her sly expression, Brandon snorted again. "Keeping secrets, are we?"

She nodded. "We Frankensteins can be just as secretive as you Van Helsings."

Brandon laughed out loud. "Right. A seven-foot monster is certainly not fodder for gossip."

"Humph!" Clair responded, and she walked away. Sometimes Brandon Van Helsing was too big for his breeches. Really, Clair thought, at times men were such . . . men. They were infuriating, aggravating, unworthy, and irritating.

"Now where are you, Ian?" she muttered, trying not to care if he had noticed her in conversation with Brandon, who was an eligible bachelor if you didn't mind him out running around cemeteries poking the undead with sticks in the dead of night.

She spotted him a second later, leaning back against a wall and watching her. Smiling to herself, she went about her business of driving Ian crazy. Perhaps her friend Arlene could give her some helpful hints about making him pay for his crimes.

Ian watched Clair stoically, his arms crossed over his chest as he leaned back against the wall. He had noticed Clair conversing with the younger Van Helsing. He had watched Clair and her friend Arlene dance and flirt with various town fops. He would have been livid with jealousy if he hadn't known her heart really wasn't in this pettish display. He hid a grin. His Clair was an independent woman, rebelling against his masculine authority and the fact that he had spoiled her less than scientific fact-finding mission.

He wanted to ask Clair to dance, but he knew with an instinct born of years of experience with feminine pique that she would rather chew nails than comply. She was an entity unto herself, an odd angel whose fluttering wings breathed fresh air into a world which had long grown stale for Ian. Her sweet smiles gave balm to his wounded, weary spirit, just as her kisses sent him soaring heavenward. It was fascination, he knew, that old black magic she did so well, which made her unforgettable.

Ian recognized their relationship had little future,

most especially if one or both of them ended up vampire food. The rational part of his brain sternly advised that he wasn't ready for a leg-shackle anyway—anytime, anyhow, and in any form. Marriage was a trap which, once well-sprung, could catch and capture his heart and tear it out if he ever lost Clair. Knowing Clair's penchant for trouble, the scenario was entirely too possible. Besides, he was too wily a hunter to see himself caught.

But then, he contemplated, when was he ever wily around Clair Frankenstein? When was he even rational with her? She could ask for the moon and, if he happened to be in one of his stupid modes, which was generally when he was staring at her breasts, kissing her lips, or even listening to her metaphysical prattle, he might just try to move heaven and earth to get the damn thing.

Yet he was being rational now. While he was drooling over Clair, Ian was also keeping a wary eye out for Asher, pondering what he could do about his conundrum. He hoped fervently that Clair hadn't already captured the crafty earl's nefarious attention.

As the night sky changed from the ebony darkness of midnight to the more somber hues of early morning, Ian received an urgent message. He had no choice but to leave, since the note called for his immediate and personal attention. Reluctantly he left, placing a well-advised word of warning in Lady Mary's ear to keep a close eye on her niece. The message thrilled Lady Mary's little matchmaking heart. Another was thrilled as well, but for different reasons. A figure standing in the shadows of the upstairs gallery's balustrade shrewdly watched Ian's departure. The tall man smiled fiercely, his sharp teeth glistening in the semishadow.

"Hold on to your hats. This could be a very bumpy night," Neil Asher gloated as he made his way down the staircase, his prey ever-present in his sight.

Oblivious to the earl's interest, Clair stood by the punch bowl watching Arlene dance, thinking that she had been remiss in writing to her friend Jane. It had been too long since the last update.

Unexpectedly, she felt a tingling foreboding. Glancing about, Clair felt her chest constrict. The Earl of Wolverton was beating a direct path toward her. He moved with a fluid grace, his hair the color of roast chestnuts, gleaming like copper in the soft glow of the chandeliers. His broad cheekbones and firm, square jaw hinted at his Germanic heritage, while his coloring was claimed by his English ancestry. Yes his exalted lineage was evident in his proud manner. And anyone who dared approach him was halted by the earl's disdainful sneer.

In an abstract way, Clair noted he was a good two inches taller than Ian, and Ian was a tall man. "Must be all that raw meat he eats," she murmured, the scientific part of her brain registering his flawless characteristics while the womanly part registered his magnificent sex appeal.

Asher smiled again, this time with unqualified carnality. His prey was near. He pounced.

"Allow me to introduce myself. I'm Neil Asher, tenth Earl of Wolverton."

Like quicksilver, Clair comprehended that the earl wore his exalted ancestry like invisible armor, girding himself against annoyance by the lesser beings of the world. "My lord, you must excuse me, but we haven't been formally introduced," she said stiffly, turning to leave. His words stopped her abrupt departure.

"Miss Frankenstein, I didn't think such formalities need exist between the two of us. In fact, I feel as if we are already on intimate terms. At least, you certainly know some intimate details about me."

Clair's curiosity got the better of her. "And those details are?" She noted that the color of his eyes was like chipped ice, with a darker blue around the edges. She also noted that he was watching her as if she would make a tasty treat. In a strange way, that was excellent. It was more fodder for her werewolf theory.

"Come now, don't play coy with me," Asher remarked patronizingly as he looked his fill. Clair Frankenstein was a rare beauty, exotic in spirit and unmatched in eccentric ancestry. Alone she would have interested him, but with Huntsley recently sniffing at her skirts, her value increased tenfold. He couldn't and wouldn't resist tweaking the baron's nose by stealing this lady out from under it.

"I assure you, I'm not," Clair rebuffed, looking into his eyes. Suddenly, she felt as if she were rappeling down the face of a glacier into the deep unknown. She blinked.

"Hmm," he said. "We'll see about that. It would seem that you know personal things: when I get up, go to bed, what I like to dine on . . ." He hesitated, building the suspense. "My illustrious techniques in the bedchamber. Indeed, tonight it seems you got a personal view of my seduction skills, with the Lady Montcrief playing a rather key role."

Clair gasped at his indiscretion. "You, my lord, are no gentleman."

137

Asher laughed, the sound chilling her to the very core.

"And you my dear, are no lady, in spite of the impeccable packaging." Pulling out his quizzing glass, he looked her up and down. Then he smiled lasciviously.

Clair's eyes flashed. Ha! The old wolf wasn't nearly as smart as he thought. She would soon see him howling at the moon. Haughtily she remarked, "And you, my lord, are a wolf in sheep's clothing. One with too fine of an opinion of yourself. In fact, you're so top-lofty, it's a wonder you don't tip over."

A flash of surprise crossed his features. Asher narrowed his chilly blue eyes. "Pardon?"

In spite of his irritation, Asher found that she fascinated him. He was used to being adored and feted, or having others fear him. This Miss Frankenstein was a different flavor altogether.

Clair wanted to pinch herself for stupidity. She needed to befriend the earl, not vex him. "Please excuse my ill manners," she apologized.

The earl continued to study her, his gaze leering. "I could excuse a pretty little morsel like you many things."

Good intentions forgotten, she snapped. "How nice. But I'm afraid I can't excuse you any."

"Ouch," he said, though he looked unmoved. "What sharp little claws you have. Perhaps you would like to try them out on me sometime—preferably soon," he suggested.

Clair ground her teeth, wanting to slap the fur from out beneath his skin. Years of her aunt's training, however, came to her rescue. "I must politely decline," was all she said.

Slyly, she dropped her silver charm bracelet on the

floor by the earl's shiny boots. "How clumsy of me. Would you mind picking that up for me?"

Asher chuckled. "It appears closer to you than me. I must politely decline."

Just as she had surmised, he wouldn't touch the silver. Another piece of wolfish evidence. "Aha!" Clair retrieved the bracelet herself, hiding her smug smile. "If your august personage won't mind, I really will be taking my leave."

Asher grabbed her arm in a lightning-quick move. "My, my, you are a surprise. You have me all aquake with desire to see what you'll do next."

Clair looked pointedly at her arm. Slowly the earl released it, haughtily tilted his chin, and held his hands up in the air in a placating gesture, silently commanding her to stay. It didn't work.

"I think, my lord, you indulge your desires overmuch. It reminds me of a pig feeding at a trough," she retorted.

He laughed in spite of the insult. "You do me injury. But I must reply that desire is what separates us from lower beings."

Clair's early desire to flee fled. The earl had presented too good an opening to let her temper get the better of her. He was talking about being a werewolf, she felt certain. "Please, do go on."

"I am a something of a scientist myself. I believe in survival of the fittest. Those who lead in the world are born to do so. Those who are less superior and can't keep up are useless and disposable. After all, they are of no account in the grand scheme. This is a brutal world, where the elite are masters as they should be."

Of course! Clair reasoned that a werewolf would consider itself at the top of any food chain. That the earl was so open with his malevolent remarks surprised her. She wondered if he'd had too much to drink. Then she pondered if werewolves could get drunk. She contemplated: if a werewolf ate a human who was drunk, could that werewolf end up foxed?

"And you, being a noble, are part of this elite membership?"

Asher flicked a piece of lint from the cuff of his midnight blue jacket. "But of course, my child. I'm an earl. Centuries of good breeding—superlative breeding—are in my blood."

His tone was matter-of-fact, which was so much more than Clair Frankenstein had dreamed. In this man's heart lay a great darkness, where killing was no more immoral than eating an apple. Civilization and the centuries had reduced him to only feeding until his thirst was lessened, but it was never quenched. It didn't seem fair for a creature such as himself, a creature of unbridled passions and hunger, a species so savage few would knowingly dare cross him, and none of those would live to tell the tale. But this new century was very modern, and he was obviously too much the gentleman to kill for sport or for dinner. Otherwise she would know something of his crimes.

"How fortunate to be so far above us all," Clair remarked coolly.

After giving her a thoroughly dressing down with his eyes, Asher glanced around at the other members of society. He chuckled. "Without qualification."

Motioning to all the members of the *ton*, he added, "Look around you. These are cattle, existing merely for the sake of their own existence. They eat, drink, and seek their guilty pleasures, living and dying fast and furious.

At the moment of their deaths they cry out for forgiveness, though the only regret most have is when they are caught raiding the cookie jar. I'll make no bloody bones about it. They're freaks in the circus of the damned."

"And you, my lord, are different? Don't you seek these same guilty pleasures for yourself?"

"Definitely," he professed, sending a heated glance at her breasts. "Would you care to help me obtain them?"

She cocked her chin and gave him an icy stare. His forwardness was not to be believed. "Again, I must decline. You are out of my league," she demurred frostily, feeling very much the fly to his spider.

"But Huntsley isn't," he said, an odd look in his eye.

"I fear you are too perceptive." She turned away, wondering what web he was spinning and how intricate the design.

"My pretty, don't play the blushing miss with me! You and Huntsley have become grist for the gossip mill."

She raised a dramatic hand to her breast and looked back. "I can't believe you would condescend to listen. You with your earldom and superior mind."

"Tsk, tsk. Such a sharp tongue. I wonder if your baron will be able to dull it. Well, he is an enterprising man, especially when he is on the hunt."

Clair smiled coolly. "You make me sound like a fox to be run to ground."

"And torn apart, depending on who catches you. Take my advice, my dear: Huntsley is a law unto himself. He's devoured more elusive prey than you before, and will most undoubtedly do so again." Asher wanted to toy with her, subtly coax her, wanted to poison her good thoughts of the baron.

"He has been all that is gentlemanly," she retorted,

her eyes flashing. This puffed-up earl had no right to decry her Ian!

"Huntsley will do or say whatever to whomever in order to gain whatever his heart desires," Asher went on.

"And you know this how? He's never named you friend in my hearing."

"Nor would he. We are mere acquaintances who met by chance—competitors, if you will, at cards or in conquests of a more, shall I say, carnal nature?"

"Then you know him little."

Asher chuckled, shaking his head. "I know the type. Too well, I know what Huntsley is capable of to gain his ends. Right now he's playing a waiting game, cat to your mouse. In fact, he is playing the oldest game in the book."

"And what, pray tell, is that?" Her scorn was obvious. Clair didn't like what the earl was saying about Ian. She didn't like the earl's snobbish philosophy. Mainly, she didn't like the earl.

Although, in all fairness, before she met him, she had been prepared to give the earl the benefit of the doubt, since he was a werewolf. In her logical manner, Clair had diagnosed that it must be a difficult life as a wolf-man: never eating apricot tarts; always having to watch out for steel traps: always having to keep wolfhounds rather than her personal favorite, the spaniel. And then there was being genetically disposed to such big teeth, which would cause a person to bite their tongue a great deal whenever they shape-shifted. Or having to bear the indignity of ending up naked as the day they were born after shifting, and having to constantly hide clothes all over God-knew-where to prevent any tricky nude situations from occurring.

However, now that she had met the toplofty earl, she decided he was a dog of a different color.

"The oldest game besides 'hunt or be hunted' is much the same—the game between man and woman. Woman and man. The same game I'm playing now. I want you," Asher stated boldly, his chilly blue eyes appraising Clair hungrily.

"Then you're a muttonhead, even if you are an earl and one of your supercilious few. I know you're quite accustomed to getting everything your heart desires, but this time you're off the mark."

Asher shook his head, a lazy grin on his face. "Nothing is beyond my grasp, nothing in this whole bloody world." Amusement was clear on his cold but magnificent visage. He knew he had scored a hit or two with his poisoned-dart comments on Hunstley. He had also enraged Clair Frankenstein enough to make sure the fiery lady would remember and think of him.

"*I* am," she remarked adamantly. Then she strode off regally, leaving him to his own company.

Clair Frankenstein was much more complex than he had first thought, Asher realized. She was also a stunningly beautiful woman with a voluptuous body and a spirit to match. A female who was indifferent to his regard, which set Asher's predatory instincts into overload. And to make matters even more interesting, Huntsley owed him a lover, for stealing that opera singer out from underneath his nose. Yes, Huntsley owed him that dark debt.

Asher cursed under his breath. He would have Clair Frankenstein come hell or high water. And Huntsley be damned, if he wasn't already.

The Scientist
Who Knew Too Much

Clair was in a brown study. Despite her great expectations of her tale of two vampires in the city, she had ended up with an expected twist. It was a dickens of a dilemma. It seemed, she mused, that for a scientist who knew so much, as of late she often knew too little. She needed to reassess and reevaluate her work in order to learn how to proceed, although she knew she was right about the Earl of Wolverton being a werewolf.

Brooks's announcement of Baron Huntsley interrupted her thoughts. Clair hid her smile as she saw him walk into the room. He made her heart do a funny little pitter-patter. He looked as if he had gotten little to no sleep last night. Good, he could join the club.

Clair was still angry with him for abruptly dragging her out of the garden the night before, and for his quick departure from the ball without a word to her. He needed to get into the spirit of things—which spirits were vampires and werewolves. She wouldn't bend an inch. She would show Ian a thing or two—mainly that Frankensteins couldn't be intimidated or dragged willy-nilly from gardens.

As Ian entered the room, he noted Clair's posture and expression. Yes, she was still most definitely angry at him. The thought was irritating. She had no right to be peeved because he cared enough to try and stop her from getting Asher's back up. But she was a female, and their reasoning wasn't always reasonable, no matter how a man tried to interact with one.

Ian had come prepared to do penance. Seeing Clair sitting in the library, framed in bright sunlight from the huge bay window behind her, he caught his step, standing and staring at her. She was so very lovely and so very much alive, obviously enjoying life in all its complexity.

He smiled. Clair was a vision of everything that was spring, in a morning gown of mint green silk. She sat in a gilt-wood chair in front of her massive teak desk, across which books and yellowed papers were haphazardly piled. Ian hid a grin at the total chaos of her workspace, presuming there was somehow a method to her madness.

After several minutes of heavy persuasion, he finally got her to admit to having an encounter with the earl. His ugly suspicions of the night before were now unfortunately confirmed.

Ian sought damage control. "Don't invite him into your house or your life."

Clair stared in disbelief. Ian had done everything but draw her a picture on how the Earl of Wolverton could not be a werewolf or a vampire. If she hadn't known better, she would have thought Ian had been trying to pull the proverbial wool over her eyes. "You stated last night—and most emphatically, I might add—that the earl wasn't a werewolf or a vampire!"

Ian could almost see the steam coming from her ears. Defending himself, he cajoled, "I am almost positive that he's not either. However, just to be on the safe side please do as I ask. Don't let Asher enter here, and stay far away from him on the full moon. Even better, stay home all the time."

Clair fumed. She had been up most of the night worrying about the earl's mysterious comments warning her away from Ian. She knew Ian had the reputation as a rake of renown, yet since he had been wooing her, she was seeing a different side of his roguish tendencies, a side quite special. She had noted it recently, whenever Ian looked at her. Dare she call it love?

After hiding a yawn, Clair couldn't help but return Ian's smile. But what was she doing smiling? Her night had been filled with confusion. She had worried about how the earl found out about her interest in him as a werewolf. And how much exception would he take to the fact? If the earl was dangerous, just how much of a deep ditch had she dug for Ian and herself? At this rate of worry, she was going to have gray hair before she was thirty.

She began to worry that Ian was going to be killed because of her, and then she worried that if Ian was, would he ever forgive her? Then she worried if she could ever forgive him for dying. "It would appear that I have opened a Pandora's box," she said aloud to herself.

Ian crossed his arms, commenting gravely, "Clair, my love, you have no idea."

Clair stood, traversing the room to where Ian stood,

placing her hands in his. Imploring him with her smoky gray eyes, she begged, "Please, Ian, tell me truthfully. Is the Earl of Wolverton the Wolfman of London?"

"No." He answered without a twinge of remorse. Lives hung in the balance. Bending, he bestowed a tender kiss upon Clair's brow, then slowly moved away to the shelter of the bookshelves—away from her fresh, clean scent and luscious body, away from temptation.

Clair scrutinized him thoroughly, her analytic brain observing every nuance. "I would hate to call you a liar. However, going back to our earlier conversation, you did warn me not to invite him in. Why is that?"

Ian shrugged, schooling his expression. "I'm jealous."

"In a pig's eye," she retorted.

"You told me you thought he was a handsome," Ian reminded her, closing the distance back to her side, unable to help himself. He loved being near her, her smell, her laughter, the way the shadows of the room highlighted her heart-shaped cheeks.

"Handsome is as handsome does. Asher scares me a little, reminds me of a lofty king spider casting out his web and spinning it in little melodramas."

Ian nodded gravely. "An apt description," he remarked, knowing he would have to go to Plan B, since Plan A had been sent down in flames. Plan B was of a crafty sort, a Machiavellian plan. Brilliant, even if he did say so himself. It was a plan designed to keep Clair tilting at windmills. It was sure to guarantee that she would be kept safely away from the supposed Big Bad Wolf, the earl. He would call it the *McGuffin*, in honor of his friend Sir Albert Hitchcock, who had devised it for the war ministry. It was a plan where the real object of interest was replaced by another object in order to distract and confuse.

Ian tenderly squeezed Clair's hands. "Clair, I have been thinking long and hard over your research. I know how important you think this project of yours is to your Frankensteinian destiny. . . ."

Releasing his hands, she went to stand by the window, staring out at the vibrant landscape. "It isn't just my destiny or my dreams, it's every man's or every woman's. It seems to me that a man's work will live beyond him, while his dreams, without substance, are only dust in the wind. Does that make sense to you?"

Ian nodded solemnly. "Yes. And that's one of the reasons I stopped by today."

"Yes?"

"Well, the other day I was remembering what you told me about the warlock or warlocks in a vampire nest. So I decided to do a little research on my own. I think I know who your warlock is."

Her eyes shining brightly, Clair almost skipped back to where he stood. In spite of all of Ian's dubious feelings on her work, he had decided to help her! He was interested enough in her to be interested enough in what she cared about. He had actually spent time and effort in searching out the warlock of the London nest, a feat she had tried at and failed.

She grinned, her eyes sparkling with happiness. Ian was her unsung hero. Although, she wasn't dim enough not to know the reason behind Ian's picking out a warlock to research instead of encouraging her hunt of the werewolf. Where werewolves were long and sharp of tooth, warlocks weren't. One was danger with fangs, the other's danger lay only in ancient spells. It was as simple and as complex as he thought her in less peril from magic. Yes, Ian cared more for her than he admitted. "Who?"

"The Duke of Ghent."

"The Duke?" Clair repeated, surprised. "Are you sure? He seems like such a jolly old man. Aunt Mary knows him. And he's a *duke*."

"You believe Wolverton is a werewolf and he's an earl," Ian accused.

"True. I guess supernaturalism is an equal-opportunity employment."

Ian studied her, a reluctant grin on his face. He knew she was going away again into that dizzy maze of her mind. Patiently he waited, wanting to kiss her silly.

"Okay, why this particular duke?" she asked.

His grin grew. The trap was sprung. He would now lead Clair off in a different direction. And though he regretted his false directions, at least this path wouldn't plunge her to her death if she took a right turn.

"The duke is always mixing up spells and chanting while he cooks. He has a pentagram painted on his bedroom wall. He owns three black cats. Oh yes, and a black dog too," he ad-libbed, making most of it up as he went.

Ian knew he should feel guiltier. He knew he should probably be more concerned, but he really didn't see how Clair could break into the Duke of Ghent's home. The duke was known for his paranoia due to years in the war. All he owned, most especially himself, was heavily guarded. "The duke also dresses in those long warlock robes," he added, inspired.

"Warlock robes?" Clair hid her smile. Ian was so adorable trying to help her scientific quest. Of course, he didn't have a clue at all about the work an actual hypothesis actually required. He had gotten lucky on his first try and she was proud of him, like a mother hen watching her chick leave the nest. How she wanted to hug the handsome dolt! At this moment in time, she discerned, she had never felt closer to another human being. It was almost frightening, her desire to be held by him and to hold him, to comfort and caress him for all the days of her life. If only Ian were the marrying kind, she would set her cap for him in a London minute.

In a pig's eye, she thought in horror. Where had that last traitorous thought come from? She had decided long ago that she wasn't the marrying kind, either. She had her science to pursue. She had the prestigious Scientific Discovery of the Decade award to pursue. She had *Ian* to pursue. Drat! She needed her attention focused on things that howled at the moon, not this magnificent man in front of her. Still, if anyone could make her dream of wedded bliss, it was Ian, mere mortal though he was.

"You know, those garments that devil worshipers wear," he was saying.

"The cowls?" she asked, trying to suppress a grin but failing.

He scowled.

"I know. You're not a fashion expert on the occult."

"Clair, Clair. What am I going to do with you?" Ian took her into his arms.

"Kiss me?" she suggested.

Ian did as the lady requested, and their passion once again ignited. Unfortunately, before Ian could sample a taste of her forbidden virgin fruit, Lady Mary entered the library looking for her embroidery. Fortunately for his status of single white baron, the kiss had only just begun. He broke away in haste, a silly grin plastered on his lips. He fled to his carriage still wearing the expression, causing his footman Tiger, who had been holding the horses, to give him an odd look. Inside, a flustered Clair and a flushed but smiling Lady Mary watched his leavetaking. The library hummed with anticipation. Lady Mary was delighted. Her Plan A, *To Catch A Baron*, was going so smoothly that she wanted to pat herself on the back. She could just see Clair in her wedding finery. She would be a true sight to behold.

Glancing at her niece from the corner of her eyes, Mary observed the pink flush upon Clair's cheeks. Clair was in love with Ian; she just didn't know it yet. Yes, it would be a splendid match. The match of the century, and Mary would have been an integral part of the wedding of the two great families. She did so love a good wedding.

"The baron is really a most intriguing man, quite the catch of this season or any season," she remarked casually, carefully hiding her marital plot. She would see the baron all the way to the altar, or her name wasn't Mary Frankenstein.

Clair reseated herself at her desk, interpreting the speculative gleam in her aunt's eye. So that is the way the wind is blowing, she thought. She couldn't really blame her aunt, since some of those same thoughts of church bells and wedding cakes had been intruding upon her own dreams.

Studying her niece out of the corner of her eye, Lady Mary picked up her embroidery, chuckling. Raising her head from her notes, Clair glanced at her. "Something amusing?"

Her aunt smiled a secretive smile. "Nothing really. Oh! I did receive a letter from Victor today."

"Have they found Frederick?" Clair asked somberly, concerned for her adopted cousin, who was a like a big, big, *big* brother to her, even though his left arm and both ears were younger in origin.

Her aunt waved her hand in the air. "Yes. Nothing to be concerned about. Frederick came home, no worse the wear."

"Does Uncle Victor know what caused him to run away?"

"It appears that a group of young men were running around impersonating poor Frederick. They are all wearing those sixteen-foot-long clodhopper boots he wears and sporting bolts in their necks," Lady Mary explained patiently. "Frederick was quite upset about the whole impersonation thing at first. He thought they were making fun of him. Then Frederick learned they were imitating him because they admired him. You know, rather like all those young bucks in town imitate that Beau Brummell person."

"I'm glad Frederick is in fashion now. He's had a hard time of being different. How is Uncle?"

"My brother has calmed down somewhat since Frederick came into his own," Lady Mary explained. She smiled affectionately. "I was always fond of the giant tyke, myself."

"Yes. Frederick has always been like a big brother to me. Remember the time he held me up in the window so I could scout out the vicarage? And he saved my life a time or two," Clair reminisced. "Remember when the crazy old vicar tried to spear me with that pitchfork?"

Her aunt's face took on a greenish cast. "How could I forget? If Frederick hadn't routed the old devil, you'd have been seriously injured or burned."

"Dear Frederick, owner of my heart."

"No, sweet. That was Mr. Applebee's heart Victor used."

Both women laughed. Looking down at the notes she had jotted, Clair changed the subject. "By the way, Aunt Mary, what do you know of the Duke of Ghent?"

Her aunt's expression became distant. "Julian was very fresh in his salad days. He was quite the rogue. He lives much quieter now. I know he has a fondness for cats, black in particular, and is always going to see that play Abby drags me to—*McDougal?*"

"*McBeth*," Clair corrected. She went on to partially explain the conversation between Ian and herself, although she left out the part accusing the Duke of Ghent, not wishing to worry her aunt with fear for her safety.

Clair then relayed the warning about never inviting the Earl of Wolverton inside their home, albeit suspiciously. Ian knew more than he was saying about the mysterious Asher. In fact, Ian was being as mysterious as the earl. Which was not surprising. But now, instead of one mystery to solve with the wolfish earl, Clair also had to puzzle out the baron's excuse for hiding what he knew. It appeared everyone was hiding something. Aunt Mary, Ian, the Earl and the Duke of Ghent—only Frederick was an open book.

Clair sighed. When had life gotten so complex? She had to find the weres, but where were they? Did Ian know where the weres were and who was a werewhat? If so, then why was Ian remaining silent on the subject? She signed again, wishing she could ask, "Will the real vampires and werewolves please stand up?"

"But dear," Lady Mary said, "if the Earl of Wolverton comes to call, we must invite him in."

"Ian advised us against it," Clair warned.

"But that would be badly done," her aunt chided.

"Better than well done and eaten," Clair remarked, closing the book she had been referencing. "Now, what is for dinner?"

"We are starting with stuffed grape leaves and a Caesar salad, followed by roast mutton with olive tapanade, and wine, of course," Lady Mary replied, setting her embroidery down.

"Ah, yes. I had forgotten. Aunt Abby is Julius Caesar this week."

"Which is fine by me. I am too old to curtsy all the time. I find it quite tedious on the knees," Lady Mary remarked tartly. "Abby is upstairs right now telling the maids the die is cast and making plans to invade Egypt."

Clair shook her head. "I know. Yesterday she told me that if I was serious about Ian, she would bribe him with the city of Alexandria as a wedding present."

"Well, what young lady could ask for more as a dowry? Not to mention the prestige of having Julius Caesar as a wedding guest. Just think how jealous Cleopatra would be!"

"Et tu, Brute?" Clair asked laughingly. But all in all, it seemed just another typical day in the house of Frankenstein.

After dinner, she wrote another letter to her friend, remedying the recent lack of updates:

Dear Jane,
I spoke to Brandon last night and he informed me you
left for Holland a few days ago. I am sending this to the
Van Helsing country estate with orders that it be for-
warded to you at your aunt's house in Holland. You

must tell me all about your adventures there, and are the wooden shoes comfortable?

Ian, that handsome clever man who is not a vampire, is helping me advance my goals regarding the supernatural world. Well, he's not actually helping, but rather is following me around. I believe he may be smitten. I, in return, find him quite remarkable—for a mere human. I must admit he has consumed a bit too much of my thoughts and time, time which would be better spent with my research.

Since last I wrote, I found out that the Honorable Christopher Wilder is not so honorable. I caught him in a compromising position with a noble lady of less than noble reputation. He is also not a vampire. It was quite distressing: the undressing and the fact that neither the lady nor Wilder were sucking each other's blood—other things perhaps, but not blood. Oops! Sorry. I know how you feel about the b-word. Anyway, Wilder is not a vampire. Which is most discouraging, but I know my duty to the Frankenstein family name and motto. I will prevail.

Fortunately, I have two new leads. My latest theory is that I have uncovered the werewolf of the vampire nest. I believe it is the Earl of Wolverton. How silly not to have recognized it before. Ian insists I am wrong. Did I mention how strong he is? Ian, not the earl. Of course, as a werewolf, he would also be strong. The earl, not Ian.

Ian believes that the Duke of Ghent is the warlock of the nest. Did I mention that Ian is helping me with my research and he is extremely intelligent for a mere mortal who is not a scientist? Ian, not the Duke of Ghent.

As for other news, we received word that Frederick has come home again. We were all greatly relieved, though confused. There had been several Frederick spottings across the countryside, which turned out to be Frederick impersonators and not my dear adopted cousin. But he is home now, safe and sound, all six foot eight inches of him.

With fondest regards,
Clair

P.S. Great-aunt Abby came into my room whilst I was sealing this letter. She sends her regards and says to tell you not to miss the English sailing against the Spanish Armada this week. (She has been Queen Elizabeth quite a bit in the past two weeks.)

A Neil in the Coffin

Ian wanted to be anywhere—perhaps fighting dragons, or cavorting naked with mermaids or even old Nessie herself in Loch Ness—rather than here waiting on his nemesis.

But boot perched against the crypt, Ian stood patiently. The sun disappeared from the sky and night encroached. He could hear the scraping of the skeleton-like branches of the trees on the top of the mausoleum. And as the last rays of the setting sun vanished, the coffin lid popped up with a loud creak.

Ian surveyed the inhabitant with disdain. "I see you've changed your sleeping habits. No longer sleeping at home?"

However sleepy the man's hooded eyes, the anger burning in them would have made a lesser man weep with fear. "It seemed circumspect, considering the situation," Asher grunted, his gaze glacial. He stretched, his long body unwinding. "Come to put a nail in my coffin?"

"No, Neil—although the thought is tempting." Ian was wishing himself in a thousand different places, but instead he was stuck with this grumpy vampire. Somehow he had known Asher wouldn't be much of a morning person. Or was that evening person?

"More than tempting, I'd wager," Asher scoffed, carefully exiting his coffin. He watched his foe with bright, burning eyes. Ian Huntsley would pay for this desecration of his bedroom. And Huntsley would pay in a way that was close to his heart: Clair.

"I'll tell you why I'm here. . . ." Ian trailed off, his body tense, his senses on full alert.

"Let me take a guess. The fair Clair," Asher said. "Do you think a Frankenstein by any other name would still be a Frankenstein? That's part of her trouble, you know."

"I have better things to do with my time than stand here listing to you butcher Shakespeare," Ian growled, moving forward threateningly. "Leave Clair alone. You'll live a much longer undeath if you take my warning to your black heart."

"What a brave man you are. Foolish, but brave nonetheless," Asher stated, the sharpness of his voice just shy of a razor's edge. His look could have frozen lava. "I have lived centuries, yet you dare to threaten me?"

Ian pulled a vial of holy water out of his pocket. An enraged vampire was not a thing of beauty, and was deadly as an asp. He didn't want to tangle with Asher, but he couldn't back down either.

"I see you have come prepared," Asher snarled, his

sharp white fangs glistening in the glow of the candles Ian had lit nearby.

Ian knew he was walking a tightrope between foolish threats and useful ones, and he prayed he didn't slip. "Leave Clair alone. I know the whores of London would hate to see that pretty face of yours scarred by holy water."

Asher's cold laughter filled the tomb. The sound slid down Ian's back, making him flinch. "Our dear Miss Frankenstein has been a busy little bee, flitting here and there. She knows about Wilder."

Knowing how fast Asher could move, Ian watched carefully. His senses were on alert, but Asher simply grabbed for trousers, quickly slipping them on to cover his pale, strong legs.

"She thought Wilder was a vampire. Now she thinks he's just an ordinary lecher."

Buttoning the cuffs of his shirtsleeves, Asher shook his head. He wanted to smile but didn't. Instead he became as still as marble, his face an expressionless mask—a vampire trick he had learned as a fledgling. He loved baiting Huntsley. "She's too close. She's ready to point the finger at me."

"It's not what you think. Clair suspects you're a *werewolf*." He waited, focused on Asher's reaction. To his great surprise, the vampire threw back his head and laughed.

When he was done, Asher wiped blood-red tears of mirth from his eyes. "What a queer start. What a queer duck Miss Frankenstein is. It's all in the stock, the breeding—the blood, you know. That bloody damn Frankenstein pedigree."

With remarkable aplomb considering his current fears, Ian replied, "I thought you would be a bit more upset by my revelation. It's not everyday one is accused of being a werewolf."

Asher chuckled and wiped a speck of dirt off his gleaming black Hessians. He had been called worse.

Ian scowled, seeing Asher's amusement. "Ah, yes. You have been called a wolf a time or two, but only by females you've bedded." He began to pace, carefully keeping his distance from the *Nosferatu*. "Now, what do you plan on doing about this?"

"Shall I play Lancelot to your Arthur?" Asher grinned, thinking of what he would give a lot of lance: Clair's fragrant, sweet flesh. And when Clair was totally his, Huntsley would lie down and die like a wounded dog. For Asher knew something Ian hadn't realized yet: Ian Huntsley was in love with Clair—the kind of love that happens only once and lasts even after death did you part.

Ian's pacing stopped abruptly, and he glowered at Asher. "You won't touch one drop of her blood. She's an innocent in all of this."

"Ha! She started this whole ludicrous mess by poking her nose into things which are none of her affair! In this cat's case, her curiosity has very well killed her."

Ian shook his head. "We're in a gray area here. There's no need for violence. She thinks you're a wolf, not a vampire."

Asher shrugged. He wasn't planning to kill Clair; he was going to kiss her senseless and drink her blood. But what Huntsley didn't know did hurt him, which was just what Asher wanted. "Semantics. Dead women tell no tales. I'll err on the side of caution." He struggled into one of his black Hessian boots. They were made to fit tightly, showing off his well-made calves. "Clair is human, and mortals have a major tendency to gossip."

Ian wanted to smash the complacent look off Asher's face but knew he couldn't. He wasn't strong enough to defeat the vampire in a battle. He also knew that if he had staked Asher while Asher was still in the coffin, Asher's nest of vampires would seek retribution not only against him but also Clair. He grimaced. He was going to have to do some fast-talking. Pointing at the vampire's boots, Ian remarked with a sangfroid air, "You missed a spot. I guess everything runs smoother with your valet. Your *human* valet."

"Your point," Asher snapped, his patience gone. Huntsley had invaded his territory. Huntsley had been waiting inside this crypt with holy water in hand when he opened his coffin. Huntsley could have easily killed him. Someone would pay!

"Your valet, Renfield, is human. And as far as I know, Renfield has never told another living soul about you and your nest."

Asher shook his head. "Correction: My valet is my human *servant*. A pointed difference." He snickered as he finished putting on his second boot.

Ian snarled in disgust. "Come on, Asher, we need to reach some kind of compromise."

The vampire raised a tawny brow. "Now it gets interesting. Are you suggesting I make Clair my servant?"

"Over my dead body," Ian growled, his rage a living beast.

"With pleasure." Tying his cravat with a flourish, Asher faced Ian, fangs extended, his ice blue eyes glittering with golden flames.

Ian backed off a few more steps, watching Asher's complete transformation from man to vampire. Fortunately he had encountered the metamorphosis before. Still he observed, and his fascination was apparent, his angst palpable.

The blue of Asher's eyes was now almost overshadowed by the golden flames. His gums had receded, highlighting his inch-long fangs, and his fingernails lengthened to needle-fine points. Concern for Clair was the only thing that kept Ian from leaving the crypt. He unstoppered the vial of holy water and held it high for Asher to see. In his other hand, he pulled out a sharpened stake—Van Helsing model number four.

"I'll take you with me, or at least hurt you. You know that if holy water touches your skin, your flesh melts. It's no idle boast, Asher. I won't let you hurt Clair."

"Perhaps. Perhaps not." Asher shrugged philosophically. "Who can say? But I'll wager a monkey that I will come out the victor."

"As always, Asher, your vanity overcomes your common sense."

Asher snarled, his fangs glistening. Ian tensed, waiting for the attack, his life flashing before his eyes in a series of colorful images of love, laughter, and ultimately grief and unfulfilled responsibility.

Then Asher grabbed his cape, his eyes returning to their usual glacial blue. "I don't have time for this, Huntsley. Come. The night is calling me. It vanishes quickly and too soon will slip into dawn." Asher donned the heavy dark cloak. "Clair Frankenstein is a danger to me and my kind! Think what wholesale slaughter could happen to my people if humans became aware of our existence. Think what a bloodbath would occur if mortals knew of us. They would attack us, we would decimate them. How would your Clair feel if she were the one responsible?"

Ian shook his head. "She won't tell, even if she figures it all out—which is doubtful."

"The deuce you say. You're moonstruck, my chap. She's a Frankenstein. Of course she'll tell. She'll write about my species in some obscure scientific text. Of course, in this case, the more obscure the better." Asher opened the mausoleum door.

Ian held up his hand, motioning for Asher to stop. "I think you should be aware that her family is close friends with Durlock Homes."

Asher halted. "Bloody damn! That man's a bloodhound once he's on the scent. He never tires and he never stops!"

"Homes would take it amiss if anything happened to her," Ian went on as they exited the mausoleum. Asher was in the lead; no way would he have the vampire at his back.

Night surrounded them, its scent so strong that Ian could taste it. The silence was ominous as he awaited Asher's decision.

The vampire stood with head thrown back, bathing in the glow of the moon. Then, recalling himself, he finished their business. "I must admit I don't want Dr. Homes on my trail. He's almost as good at the hunt as one of my kind."

"Don't forget Clair's uncle and his monster," Ian added.

"Victor? The man's a bedlamite. Still, it seems Miss Frankenstein has a veritable dragoon of dragonhearts saving her neck. Literally."

"One more thing. Call it blood for thought. As of tonight, I've put Clair off your scent."

Asher appeared intrigued. "How?"

"By giving her other quarry to pursue. You might call it a false trail. A very false trail."

"You underestimate your *petite chère*. She's made of sharper stuff. I doubt you've solved my problem."

Ian clenched his fists. "Asher . . . stay away from her."

The vampire raised an elegant hand. "No need to get your hackles up. You've given me a great deal to reflect upon," he countered as they came to the edge of the cemetery. "By the way, how did you discover my new sleeping quarters?"

By the tensing of Asher's shoulders, Ian knew the question wasn't casual. He answered truthfully, "I tracked you."

"Well, don't ever do it again!" Asher commanded, his expression deadly. "Though I should have known. You Huntsleys were always masters of the hunt, yourselves. Too bad we hunt different prey. It would have been a challenge to see whose skill was superior." And so saying, Asher vanished into the mist.

Bell, Cookbook, and Candle

Once again, Clair's mountain-climbing ability served her well. She scaled the Duke of Ghent's walls like a mountain goat, just as crafty as a fox, she had avoided the guardians of the gate and those surrounding the duke's palatial mansion. It was, in fact, the great expanse of the place that increased Clair's chances of not being seen.

As usual, Clair had been her pragmatic, resourceful self, memorizing the layout of the duke's home. Methodically, she started her search in the lower rooms, investigating the library, the morning room, and the duke's study. Finding nothing of interest, with the exception of one black cat curled up in a ball, she continued toward the kitchen.

She made her way silently, needing to be wariest of all now, for the kitchens of the wealthy were usually filled with busy workers, working diligently with flour on their aprons. Clair tilted her head to listen to the sounds of chanting coming from the closed kitchen door.

"Eureka!" She thought in triumph. Finally she would catch a culprit red-handed, or at least holding a book of spells.

Quietly, she pushed the kitchen door open, praying it wouldn't squeak. Once again, luck was with her; she noiselessly made her way through. Inching her way forward, she crouched behind a large green cupboard. Peeping around it, she saw that the kitchen had been modernized with all the newest in cookware, including a yellow brick Dutch oven set majestically in the center of the back wall. The heat from it warmed the room, making for a cozy nest.

To Clair's surprise, there was only one person in the kitchen. He was standing with his back to her, near a stove. Two fat black cats lounged lazily nearby, one at the man's feet and the other beside the oven. Clair instantly recognized him as the duke. The man's hair was silver, his clothing was elegant, and he wore well an air of command. He was dressed in soot-colored satin breeches with a smoking jacket of a deep ruby hue. A pair of dark ruby house slippers completed the ensemble.

Clair was disappointed in his dress. He wasn't wearing what Ian had called "warlock robes." She pondered a moment and then decided that the duke probably couldn't run around in his occult costume without rousing the suspicions of his servants.

The duke, stirring something in a large black kettle on the stove, remained unaware of her. Unfortunately he had stopped chanting.

Gathering her courage, Clair crept forward until she was leaning around the duke. The spellbook she'd been so determined to view was in reality a cookbook. "Where's the eye of newt?" she muttered to herself.

"Drat!" she added. A troubled frown crossed her features. "Out of the frying pan and into the fire."

Startled, the duke dropped the ladle he'd been holding. "Who in the blue blazes are you?" he asked.

Trying for a composed look, Clair politely answered, "I am Clair Frankenstein."

The name raised one of the duke's imperious eyebrows. Taking a quizzing glass out of his jacket pocket, he looked Clair up and down. Then, pointing to a small round table in the corner of the kitchen, he motioned her to sit. "Aren't you the Frankenstein who used that new-fangled recording device to capture pigs rooting around a cemetery?"

Bloody hell, Clair thought, borrowing one of Ian's favorite curses. It seemed her fifteen minutes of infamy were lasting a bit longer than fifteen minutes. "I was going to record *ghosts*, Your Grace."

"Intentions, intentions. It looks as if you ended up with a pig in a poke."

Clair raised her eyes to the ceiling. How she hated such humor at her expense. She would never live down those little oinkers. The initial flashbacks from the porcine incident had people pointing and giggling at her—or worse, oinking at her. One clever gent had even sent her a roast pig with a dozen violets. That had been the breaking point. Clair had quit eating pork—a feat not easily done, since the Frankenstein cook made the most delicious bacon and eggs.

The duke took in the bright flush on her face. He smiled. "What are you doing haunting my kitchen?"

"Would you believe I was hungry?"

Shaking his head, the man picked up his soup ladle and began dishing stewlike substance into two bowls. He placed one in front of Clair.

Suspiciously, she sniffed. It smelled delicious. "Is it poison or bat wings?"

"Heavens no, child. Chicken wings in red wine stew." He placed the second bowl to the right of Clair. "Would you care for a glass of chianti to go with it?"

Clair nodded warily, waiting for an explosion or a demand for further explanation as to why she had sneaked into his house. It wasn't long in coming.

"Now, tell me what all this balderdash is about." His voice was stern with centuries of breeding as he poured a rather generous amount of wine into a very tall glass. "And don't try to bamboozle me, my dear."

She knew a command when she heard it. Sensing honesty was the best policy, she replied with the truth. "I thought you were a practitioner of the black arts."

"Good grief, no!" he said, flabbergasted. "I am a practitioner of the culinary arts. To be honest, I haven't blackened anything in the kitchen since I was a wee lad."

Drat! Drat and double drat! She had done it again, made a fool of herself, always rushing in where even angels feared to tread and falling flat on her face. How could she have made such a mistake again? Wait a minute! This fiasco was courtesy of one sneaky, odious toad of a baron. The realization narrowed her eyes. It was her caring, helpful Ian who had started her on this primrose path, leaving her to face the folly. She was a lone rat on a fast-sinking ship. She would kill him with her bare hands, she envisioned. Or boil him in oil, then tie him to the mast and burn him for treachery.

"Won't you try my stew, my dear?" The duke asked. "It's one of my new recipes," he added as he motioned to the cookbook on the counter.

Politely, Clair took a bite. It was as good as it smelled. She was a bona fide idiot and this duke was a bona fide chef. "It's delicious. Amazing, Your Grace."

He took several sips of his wine, obviously pleased. "Some wine?" he asked again.

"Yes, thank you." Maybe she could get bosky and forget this whole misguided adventure. Or, Clair mused, maybe she would lop off Ian's nose with a carving knife. That would be a funny sight.

Mulling over her options, she recognized that if she had only had a brain and Ian only had a heart, she wouldn't have stumbled into this kitchen. Indignantly she brushed back a lock of her golden hair and tucked it behind her ear. "Your Grace, I am a bit confused."

"I can see that. I take it this is another of your pigs in a poke."

"Your Grace, I do beg pardon, but I am really getting tired of everyone bringing up that misadventure."

He chuckled. "I can well believe it. Now, let me introduce myself properly. I am Julian Maurice Oswalt. But my friends call me Ozzie," he remarked as he leaned over and patted the fatter of his two black cats. "You, I think, may call me Ozzie." The cat purred loudly, eliciting another chuckle from the duke, who pointed a finger at the contented puss.

"This is Aurora, mother to that one over there," he informed Clair, inclining his head toward the smaller of the two cats, who lay snoozing peacefully at the foot of the stove. "That is Samantha. Both are bewitching felines."

"They are pretty," Clair agreed. "And, in a way, they are partly responsible for why I'm here tonight."

Ozzie raised an eyebrow. "You're a cat burglar?" he asked. Then he winked.

She laughed. "Of course not. I'm here because I thought you were a warlock."

Ozzie chortled. "I see. I know people think it odd that I only keep black cats, but as a boy my dearly departed mother gave me one. These are her great granddaughters. The cat's, of course. Not my mother."

"I didn't know dukes could be so sentimental," Clair said.

"We do take our sentimental journeys—all in the dark, of course. Yes, sentiments and passions are frowned upon for a duke, as is cooking. What would the *ton* say if they knew I was my own chef?" he asked sadly.

"They'd want to stew you in your own sauce, I would imagine."

"Correct, Miss Frankenstein."

"Call me Clair," she offered. She quite liked this eccentric duke. "I must say you are a bit of a surprise. In all fairness, you should have called for your guards to cart me off to the fleet for this cursed business. But you didn't. Why is that?"

"You are a Frankenstein, and having a long acquaintance with your family, I have learned to expect the unexpected from you. You know, you look a great deal like your aunt Mary did when she was your age. She was quite the coquette in her day, and the loveliest woman I ever beheld." Ozzie smiled nostalgically. "Now, tell me the whole story of this new project. I have a desire to be entertained."

So Clair did just that, starting at the beginning and

leaving nothing out. The duke sat quietly, sipping his wine. He was indeed an inspired listener, filling her wineglass and bowl whenever needed but rarely commenting. After she finished, he gave some suggestions on how to go about finding the werewolves and vampires. But he cautioned her to be careful, reminding her how upset Aunt Mary would be if she got herself in danger. He agreed that Ian should be boiled in oil. He also agreed that men, with himself being the exception, were black-hearted knaves. Finally, he sent his warmest regards to Clair's aunts, most especially Mary; then Ozzie, the wonderful cooking wizard, sent Clair on her merry way, reminding her that there was no place like home.

Less than hour later Clair was seated on the pale gold and blue floral settee, her bare feet nestled in the thick plush Turkish carpet of her aunt's bedchamber. Shadows flickered on the walls from the rise and fall of the flickering flames of the fire in the large blue-marbled hearth, and seethingly Clair explained the night's comedy of errors. After her explanations, she was even more incensed.

"Odious toad! Philistine! Cowardly cad! I can't believe his nerve! His absolute gall! What does he think me? Stupid, I'll wager. Ian is the veriest pillock!" Clair roared.

"Now, now, dear, the baron doesn't think you a nodcock. He's just underestimated your bulldog tenacity," Lady Mary soothed, patting her niece's arm.

"Flattery," Clair muttered.

"But true. All Frankensteins have bulldog determination. It's an inherited quality, you know."

"Now I'm a bulldog?"

"Better than an ass, my dear," Lady Mary said. She poured some jasmine tea into a delicate porcelain cup.

Clair shook her head. "Ian is the ass. An unmitigated jackass of a man!"

"It's in men's natures," Lady Mary confirmed sincerely. "Even more unfortunately, they often bray and kick."

"Ian's a beast!" Clair continued bitterly.

"Most men are. Have a cup of tea, dear. It will calm your nerves," her aunt advised as she handed over the cup and nudged a plate of teacakes across the small mahogany foot table.

"He's a monster," Clair ranted, scrambling for other names to call her betrayer.

"Don't be silly, dear," Mary admonished, taking a sip of tea. "He's nothing like Frederick."

Clair rolled her eyes. "Ian Huntsley is going to be sorry. I'll make him eat his words. He betrayed me. You just wait and see."

On her way home from Ozzie's, she had conducted an absolutely brilliant plan. She called it Plan B, *The Sting*. Ian was going to get pricked by jealousy, drown in his own perfidious nectar. Clair would pollinate the Earl of Wolverton with honeyed words, buzz around him, and cloud the issue of her research. Being the queen bee, she would not get stung and she'd be able to scout out London's nest of supernatural predators. Yes, her Plan B was a masterpiece of Machiavellian planning. The idiot drone—that would be Ian—didn't stand a chance.

"I don't believe I like that look in your eyes," Mary said. "It generally bodes trouble."

"Mainly for Ian. He is such a . . . such a . . . *man!*" Clair had run out of insults.

"And thank heavens for that," her aunt said, patting

Clair's arm again. "Where would we be without the silly creatures?"

"In paradise."

"And very, very lost there, I'm afraid. Now eat your scone and drink your tea. You'll feel much better."

Clair sighed. Her aunt's recipe for curing tragedy was stuffing one's face until one felt much like one of her taxidermy subjects. But Clair wasn't ready to eat her way out of her pique. "I would have been utterly mortified at mistaking His Grace for a warlock, except he was such a great sport. And an amazing cook," she added as an afterthought.

"Yes, Julian was always a kind heart," her aunt reminisced, expression melancholy.

Taking in her aunt's demeanor, Clair speculated there must have once been something between them. "He told me to call him Ozzie, and he asked much about you," she said.

"Ozzie, indeed. Such an undignified name for such a fine figure of a man."

"He's rather old. I'd say at least in his early fifties," Clair said, probing for a reaction. She got one.

"The face may age, but the heart does not. In here," Lady Mary replied, pointing to her chest, "in here, we're all still beautiful young debutantes in our first season."

Hmm, Clair mused. Live some, learn some. There was more here than met the eye, she decided. "I take it you knew His Grace well at one time?"

"My dear, you are prying."

Clair laughed heartily. "That too must run in the family. I do believe I inherited that particular trait from *you*, Auntie."

Her aunt blushed.

Clair continued her questioning. "Do tell. Was Ozzie one of your gentleman callers?"

Lady Mary smoothed her creamy lace nightgown, her expression one of woe. "I knew him when I was a debutante."

"How well?"

"Little scamp! We courted for a while. Alas, it didn't work out. He was quite the catch of the town, top-of-the-trees in his heyday."

"What happened?" Clair was beginning to be concerned by the wistful look in her aunt's eye.

"He was caught in a compromising situation with another young girl who was making her come-out that season. They were married a week later."

Clair was shocked. "Ozzie has too much honor to compromise an innocent, I would think," she said.

"Yes, he does and he did. The young girl and her mother engineered the compromise. Julian was trapped."

Clair was upset to discover this secret anguish of her aunt. All these years, and she'd never known Mary had once been deeply in love. And apparently she still was. "Is that why you never married?"

"I never found anyone to compare. No matter the passing of the days or years, the memory of Julian still clove to me of wondrous days of long ago." Lady Mary stared off into the distance for a moment; then, recalling herself, she said to her niece, "It's another characteristic of our ancestry. It seems most of us Frankensteins only love once and always too well."

Tears sparkling in her eyes, Clair hugged her dear aunt tightly, wishing she could ease this heart long broken. "I am so sorry. I never knew."

"It's spilt milk now, Clair, and has been for some time."

"I don't know. He asked specifically about you tonight, and more than once. Besides, hasn't his wife been dead for over a year now?"

Mary nodded. "That may be, but Julian would never approach me. His honor would hold him back. He knew how badly he hurt me."

Regarding her aunt's downcast features, Clair smiled. "I hope you don't mind, then, because I invited Ozzie to dinner in a few days." She hadn't, but that point could easily be remedied with a quick note on the morrow. Clair grinned. It appeared she had inherited another Frankenstein characteristic: the matchmaker gene.

Friday the Thirteenth

Of course it was the Friday the thirteenth, Ian groused. His luck had gone from bad to worse as the day progressed, beginning when he awoke to find his valet had fallen down the stairs dead drunk. This left Ian with no recourse but to polish his own riding boots. To make matters more difficult, there was not a drop of champagne in the house to put a spiffy sheen on the Hessians, since Ian's valet had finished off the last four bottles in the wee hours of the morning.

Next Ian had discovered the upstairs maid was pregnant, and that the footman responsible was suspiciously on leave visiting his deceased grandmother.

Following that, Ian sat down to breakfast to discover that the cook had burned his kippers. A few inquiries confirmed his suspicions. His valet had had a partner in crime in finishing off the champagne.

With domestic matters so grim, Ian had wisely decided it would be prudent to take a ride in the park. Unfortunately, on the way his roan horse had thrown a shoe, clipping a little old lady's shin. The early morning hours had ended with Ian being beaten over the shoulder with a reticule.

As luck would have it, his cousin Galen had been riding by and witnessed the whole affair. Ian knew well that there would be chortles throughout the Highlands when Galen went back and told the sordid tale to his brothers. All in all, Ian conceded dismally, it had not been one of his finer mornings.

But then came the icing on the cake to this unluckiest of days. Clair threw his dozen roses—he'd been trying to apologize for telling that smidgen of a white lie about the Duke of Ghent in order to protect her—smack dab in his face. Ian now sported a half dozen scratches on his cheeks from the thorns. His day's luck was staying true to form.

Lady Mary witnessed the bristling Clair and her amazing throwing arm. She then watched as Clair stormed off in a cloud of ill humor. The gentle lady tried to explain to Ian that her niece had a smidgen of temper, but then was interrupted by Lady Abby, who entered the room in one of her bizarre costumes, complete with Roman toga and grape leaves for a crown.

Before Ian could say "Jack Frost" he was sitting in the Blue Salon listening to Abby's plans to march on Rome. He was also having a tarot card reading, for all the good it did him. The three times Ian drew cards, he drew blanks, white cards in the tarot deck. Enough was enough. Tucking his tail between his legs, Ian beat a strategic retreat home to lick his wounds and doctor his scratches.

Which led him to now, when he was standing alone at the rout hosted by the Rogers family, wondering dismally how his Plan B had failed so miserably and hoping desperately to see Clair. He knew she was angry with him for his deceit, and he'd expected that, but he really hadn't expected her to be so furious she wouldn't let him explain. And to be honest, he really hadn't expected her to be able to break into the duke's domicile. He had been spectacularly wrong on both accounts.

Gloomily, he leaned against the wall. He spotted Clair flirting with a pink of the ton. As always, she was ravishing. Her hair was pulled high on her head in a Grecian knot, with floating tendrils around her shoulders, and it shone brightly in the light of a dozen candles.

She was wearing a gown of silver-blue satin interspersed with creamy lace. The lace circled the dress's hemline and puffed sleeves, and edged the deeply scooped neckline, which more than showcased Clair's splendid bosom. Ian wanted to worship at the shrine of those magnificent breasts. Bloody hell, he cursed to himself. The way his luck was running, he would be more likely to suckle a pig's tits than Clair's.

Scowling, he noted how the young buck with Clair was trying to stare down her dress. He was going to kill the stripling, and definitely planned a word with Lady Mary on her niece's risqué choice of gowns.

Feeling Ian's gaze upon her, Clair looked up. She donned a mask of cool disdain and pointedly ignored him. But with lashes lowered, she observed him discreetly.

She hid a gleeful smile, silently congratulating herself on her luck. How delightful that Ian was staring at her, and from the expression on his face, he was no happy gentleman.

Yes, this was her lucky day. She had finally found the exact color of green ribbon to match her poke bonnet, which she had been searching for the past two months, and she had won ten quid while playing whist with Great-aunt Abby. She never won playing cards against her great-aunt; Clair reasoned it was because the woman spent so much time with tarot cards.

Risking another peek at Ian, who was staring at her grimly, Clair raised her chin in the air a notch higher. Yes, she mused, this was her lucky day. Ian was miserable—which he should be, the conniving, callous cad. He was a cad who had betrayed her, made her look a fool. He wasn't fit to kiss the toe of her shoe. He wasn't fit for human company. How dare he tromp on her precious dreams? How dare he make a mockery of her research? How dare he judge her aspirations to be less worthy than a man's, and then play her false? The bounder! He probably didn't share a single hope in her chest.

Brandon Van Helsing interrupted her silent ranklings. "Clair, how pretty you look tonight! Like a budding rose, picked fresh," he flattered.

Clair smiled. "My thanks, Brandon. And you look quite the man about town yourself," she praised, noting that his dark gold jacket went well with his dark brown hair. "I have written to Jane recently and am awaiting her reply."

Brandon nodded. "I hope all is well with my younger sister."

"Yes. I hope she quite enjoys her visit to Holland, although nursing the injured can be less than exciting. Still, I'm sure Jane will come back with some marvelous sketches of birds." Clair noticed a slight tightening of Brandon's jaw, knowing birdwatching was proscribed among the career-oriented Van Helsings, with their black capes, black bags, and cemetery fetishes. How dear Jane with her love of birds and artistic temperament had ever come from that deranged clan was a question Clair had asked herself more than once. Jane was truly a bird of a different feather.

"True. She has quite the talent for taking an object and making it appear to come alive on paper," Brandon remarked, thinking how his sister's bird-watching tendencies greatly disturbed their father, who would much rather Jane turn her bird-watching into vampire bat–hunting. "I will be visiting with Jane in a few days, for I am leaving for the Continent on the morrow," he stated.

Clair cocked her head, studying him. The man was on the hunt. What vampires was he tracking? "Business, or making the grand tour?"

"The tour," Brandon said, with only a slight hesitation.

Clair knew it for a lie. Rather than making the grand tour, as many of the sons of the aristocracy did— visiting museums, music halls, brothels and gaming halls—Clair would bet a quid that Brandon's tour would include cemeteries and mausoleums. "I see you take after a certain baron here tonight."

"Pardon?" Brandon asked, perplexed.

"Oh it's nothing," Clair remarked sweetly. Men could look a lady in the eye and tell such big fat lies. She wondered if it was inborn to the male nature or if they attended some class on telling fibs.

Before Brandon could respond, Claire's bosom friend Arlene Garwood joined the group. Pleasant hellos were exchanged; then Brandon took his leave. Clair gave express instructions for him to tell his sister that she was missed.

As soon as Van Helsing left, Arlene commented on Ian's and Clair's locations—far apart. "So you two haven't reconciled yet?" she asked. She kept glancing back and forth from Clair to Ian; she had heard the whole sordid tale of Ian's treachery when Clair arrived on her doorstep at the unheard-of hour of nine in the morning. "After all, he did try to explain. And he gave you those lovely roses."

"Hmmpf." Clair snorted, unmindful of decorum. "No. And I won't reconcile with him. Not yet. There's more here than meets the eye. I'll wager a monkey that Ian is keeping secrets from me. And if he thinks that his gift of roses was enough, old Baron Charming has another think coming. I'm going to show him no mercy."

"Oh no, Clair. You have that gleam in your eye. That same gleam that almost got us drowned when searching for mermaids when we were young. That same gleam that got us locked in the attic for half a day when you decided the rats there were really ghosts. What are you up to this time?"

"Nothing yet," she remarked as she dragged Arlene behind a group of large potted ferns. "Now Ian can't see us."

"Clair," Arlene warned, shaking her head. "Not another one of your plans. Don't do anything you'll regret. You hold strong affection for the baron and he, I sense, for you."

Clair pursed her lips, steering the conversation away from her plotting. It was a brilliant plan, as plans went, but knowing Arlene as well as she did, she knew her good friend would try and talk her out of it. She wrinkled her forehead in frustration. Arlene never appeared to notice how truly inspired Clair's plans were. Still, Arlene was a good, loyal friend, even if she was a tad slow at some things.

"You know, I believe Great-aunt Abby is right about men. She said that they always bring indigestion and insomnia into a lady's life while they are courting, while she waits for the gentleman to call. Then, after, they bring on crying jags and plate-throwing. I would be better off without Ian Huntsley darkening my doorstep." But even as Clair said the words of pique, her inner voice was crying out, "No!"

"Great-aunt Abby has a point. But think how bloody boring life would be without them," Arlene half-teased.

Clair sighed. Arlene was right. Her life had been really quite fine before Ian entered the picture with his debonair good looks, but Clair was still afraid that if he left, everything would be a shadow of its former self. Somehow the wretch had wriggled and squirmed his way into her heart. The worm! He really was a bad apple and deserved her Plan B, *The Sting*, even if Plan B included Asher, the proverbial fruit of the poisoned tree.

But beggars couldn't be choosers. She knew she had little choice but to pretend to have a tendresse for the Earl of Wolverton. She hoped it would drive Ian crazy with jealousy, and pay him back for his villainous lie. Her brilliant plan also would give her time alone with the earl to gather information. It was an inspired campaign, *Plan B*. And Clair was highly anxious to put it into play.

"You haven't seen the Earl of Wolverton here tonight have you?" she asked her friend slyly. "I've been searching for him, but nothing so far."

Arlene paled. "So that's your intention?" she gasped. "Gads, Clair. It will get you maimed or dead or even worse. You'll end up all furry once a month." She shuddered. "If that happens, I have to admit it will put a crimp in our friendship. Mother will never allow me around wolves, even if one of them happens to be my best friend."

Clair rolled her eyes. "Do calm yourself, Arlene. I am only going to flirt with the earl a little and make Ian jealous," she explained as she pushed Arlene forward and away from the ferns. "Come on, let's see if I can find out if the earl has arrived."

Out in the main room, Ian impatiently shifted his feet, his eyes never leaving the area where Clair had disappeared. He scowled. Besides ignoring him, the little imp was hiding. Yes, today was a very unlucky day, he ruminated darkly. Very unlucky indeed. It was in this sour mood that his cousin found him.

"You look deuced down in the mouth, laddie," Galen professed. He joined Ian in holding up the wall. "I take it you're not still moping about the old lady beating you. Although, for a noted Corinthian such as yourself, I guess it would be a trifle humiliating." He grinned at Ian's expression and added, "You could always have popped her cork."

"Go away," Ian snapped.

"No can do. Misery loves company."

"I am fine by myself," Ian retorted stiffly.

"Aye, I can see that," his cousin said sarcastically. He glanced around the room. "You stand here in a black funk, your expression so forbidding that no one but me will dare come near you."

He gestured at several ladies standing nearby with hopeful expressions. "They are just waiting for a smile to come and lift that woebegone expression off your ugly mug."

Ian snorted derisively. "Just what I want—more women. I have enough trouble with the one."

"Ah. The light dawns. You are having a Clair problem, I take it. What has the lass done now—besides hiding in wardrobe closets, chasing vampires, stalking supposed werewolves, and driving you clear around the bend?"

"What else? The woman wishes me to the Devil."

Galen studied him then dryly commented, "A feat you have accomplished at least a dozen times if I recall." Pulling on his cravat, he added, "Damn, if you don't always find your way back."

"Very amusing." Ian ignored his cousin. His attention focused on Clair, for he saw her emerge from behind some ferns and flutter her eyelashes at some young fop. His jaw tightened. He knew Clair never fluttered her eyelashes. At least not at him. "Why on earth do we need women anyway?" he asked.

Galen glanced over at Clair. "To bed them, silly. Not to mention the continuation of the species."

"She won't let me within ten feet of her," Ian complained sourly.

"They also smell quite nice. I believe Clair smells of something fresh. Pinecones in winter, maybe," Galen suggested.

Ian glowered at him. "What are you doing sniffing about her?"

184

"Really, coz, take hold of yourself. Clair is a fine figure of a lass, but she is too much Frankenstein for me. If I ever do decide to take a leg-shackle, it would be someone more biddable, someone who would cater to my every need, who would sit quietly at home and raise my bairns. Not a Clair-type at all. I want someone a little less of a romp and, most importantly, devoid of a lineage peppered with lunatics."

"I've said nothing of marriage. You know how I feel about that estate. Watching one's mother nearly grieve herself to death over one's father tends to make one extremely cautious. Besides, how would Clair ever fit in with our family?"

Galen tested the waters. "She's a Frankenstein. She has that indomitable spirit." He was pretty sure his cousin was in so deep as to be drowning. He could see that Ian was in love with Clair Frankenstein. In some ways that was a good thing, in other ways it seemed very, very bad.

Ian suddenly stiffened. Asher had entered the ballroom. Noticing his cousin's distraction, Galen turned towards the door.

"I see Asher is doing the rounds. But why is he here? He despises routs."

"Clair," Ian explained in a growl. "Bloody hell!" He watched Asher approach Clair, a dazzling false smile on the man's face. "I should have killed him when I had the chance!" he snarled.

"My, coz, you do love to live dangerously." Galen thoughtfully watched the situation unfold while his cousin cursed.

With his usual savoir faire, the Earl of Wolverton strolled toward Clair, a pretentious and predatory air about him. Upon reaching her and her friend Arlene, Asher bowed, seduction clearly on his devious mind.

"Bloody hell!" was Ian's only comment. He watched with glittering eyes and a fierce expression.

Yes, Galen decided. The fat was in the fire. Ian was clearly in love, and Asher, the seducer of many a fair maid, was interested in the same bit of woman.

The Best-laid Plans
of Monsters and Men

"How you look, Miss Frankenstein. 'She walks in beauty, like the night of cloudless climes and starry skies,'" Asher quoted, an appreciative gleam in his eyes. "You are absolutely ravishing." Then, doing the pretty, he turned to compliment her friend. "And you, Miss Garwood, are delightful."

Arlene blushed, enchanted despite her fear of the earl. He was such a libertine, with such a wicked reputation. That was enough to put a blush on any innocent maid, especially when said earl was also reputedly the Wolfman of London. Clair raised a delicate brow.

Noting her poised coolness, Asher added, "Miss Frankenstein, I feel I owe you an apology for my less than gentlemanly remarks the other night."

Mischievously Clair quipped, "The Earl of Wolverton is apologizing? I feel the earth on its axis spinning to a halt. I fear the Elgin marbles will crumble to dust. Ah, St. Peter must surely be turning over in his grave." Smiling, she patted his arm with her fan and gave him a come-hither look.

Asher smiled wickedly, showing off his pearly white teeth. "Perchance are you flirting with me, Miss Frankenstein?"

"I believe I am too wise to do such a bold and dangerous thing."

Asher glanced around the ballroom. "Where is your champion?" he asked. Spying Ian, he added scornfully, "I see Huntsley is over there. He rather reminds me of a supporting column. Why, and he looks rather blue-deviled."

"I would say he probably is. Traitors never fare well, you know," Clair remarked coolly.

Asher chuckled, his expression smug. "Trouble in paradise so soon?"

Clair hit him with her fan. "You, my lord, are too pert for your own good."

"Let me show you how pert," he replied arrogantly. He took her arm, excusing them from Arlene, and said, "Come, my pretty." He led Clair to a window embrasure at the far end of the room. Pulling the curtains aside, he ushered her within.

She went without protest, amazed her plan was going so smoothly. She had baited the trap, and the wolf was biting.

Dropping the drapes back in place, Asher admired Clair's composure and beauty. "Alone at last," he said.

She laughed. "With only two hundred guests, give or take a few, all a simple shriek away."

"You are a charming minx," Asher teased, touched by how uniquely beautiful Clair Frankenstein was. She was relentlessly intelligent, with a burning desire to discover the unknown. She had a sharp wit that he admired, and her bloodline, though not quite as top-of-the-trees as he would have liked, was still acceptable. He barely even minded that she was a Frankenstein. Actually, having that monster in her family was a point in Clair's favor. If one already had a monster at home, why quibble at two?

"How astute of you to notice, my lord."

"Call me Neil," he enticed.

"It wouldn't be proper."

"Asher, then."

"All right," she agreed hesitantly. "In private."

"Ah, then you anticipate more private moments," he remarked. A devilish gleam filled his eyes. "Speaking of private . . ." He trailed off, moving closer.

Clair laughed, holding up her hands to ward him off. "You are all talk."

Asher grinned, hand over his heart. "You wound me. I have a rakish reputation to uphold."

"Uphold it with some other lady and behave yourself, Asher," she retorted.

"I will cease if you will grant me a boon."

"A boon?" Clair asked apprehensively. She understood that it was all well and good to make Ian jealous, but right now it seemed she had a tiger by the tail—or rather a werewolf.

Asher laughed at her fears. "Let me call you Clair."

Clair breathed a sigh of relief and nodded.

Before more could be said by either party, the drapes were shoved aside and Clair was suddenly standing face-to-face with a very angry Ian. "Have you no care for your reputation?" he cried. "Asher is a renowned womanizer, and here you are alone with him." His fists clenched, his green eyes burning with rage.

With undisguised interest, Asher examined the byplay between the two. "The cavalry arrives," he remarked.

Ian glared. "Stay out of this, Asher!" Returning his attention to Clair, he bitterly scolded her, "You don't know what you're doing. Believe me, Asher's bite is much worse than his bark."

Asher arched an elegant shoulder. "That's rather the pot calling the kettle black," he said.

Ian ignored him, searching Clair's eyes for some tiny spark of forgiveness. "Asher's not to be trusted," he went on.

"And you are?" Clair inquired coldly. As she took in Ian's fierce countenance, she could feel waves of jealousy rolling off him. Plan B was a smashing success. Somehow she managed to hide her triumph.

Her words struck Ian forcibly. With a pained expression, he beseeched her, "Clair, forgive me. Please? I am sorry, truly sorry. I never meant to hurt you."

Asher jumped in with both feet. "But you did hurt her, didn't you?" the top-lofty earl accused. Taking Clair's hand in his, he craftily added, "I told you Ian would wound you. It's in his nature."

Ian snatched Clair's hand away from Asher, a feral look coming into his eyes. "Back off, Asher. She's mine."

Clair snatched her hand away from Ian. "In a pig's eye!" And with those words Clair departed pertly, leaving a forlorn and frustrated Ian and a very amused Asher.

"She's an intriguing woman. You don't have to worry any longer that I will kill her," the Earl of Wolverton remarked.

Ian turned, his fists clenched. "She's mine, Asher, and what's mine I hold," he growled. He would never let Clair end with Asher. The earl wasn't fit to touch the ground Clair walked on. "Take my words to heart, Asher. Back away or blood will be spilled. Yours!"

"Oh, I do hope for blood," Asher taunted. "I could use a good drink."

Ian advanced, his eyes glowing a dark green. "This is no game. And Clair is not prey."

Asher only shrugged. "Threats won't work. Besides, you should be overjoyed that I no longer see Clair's research as a problem. In point of fact, I have resolved the problem with Miss Frankenstein's belief that I am a werewolf—or it will resolve itself." He shuddered in amused revulsion at the word "werewolf." His was noble blood, the blood of both earls and vampires, and certainly not that of some four-footed creature at the beck and call of the moon.

"And how, pray tell, have you done that?" Ian asked.

"I will invite Clair and her aunt to be guests at a small country house party I am having that starts on Tuesday."

Despite his anger, Ian caught on quickly. "Wednesday is the full moon. And when you don't change into a wolf, Clair will be there to witness your nontransformation."

"Quite." Asher's expression was bland, not revealing his devious Plan A, which he had named *From Here to Eternity* and had Clair in the starring role. The unshakable Earl wanted Clair with an intensity that shocked him.

"How will you manage the days?" Ian asked. "Clair is a suspicious creature by nature."

"Again, that is calling the kettle black," Asher laughed. Ian scowled.

"The guests will arrive late Tuesday afternoon. I will be called away on an emergency through Wednesday day, and Thursday the guests will be leaving in the morning."

Ian nodded, his expression grim. "Not bad. But Clair is going nowhere near you without me. I take it I am invited?" It was really not a question.

"I had really rather hoped to avoid it," Asher replied. He turned his back and departed.

"I will see you on Tuesday," Ian called out. His cousin Galen approached with a wry expression on his face.

"Gripping performance, coz. Dare I ask if there will be an encore?" he inquired.

Ian grunted and started to leave.

"Where are you going?" Galen asked.

"To find Clair."

"She left right after she spoke with you."

"Bloody hell! I wonder which rout she went to next?"

Galen shrugged and Ian stalked away, muttering under his breath, "Just wait till I find the little hellion."

"Isn't love grand?" Galen remarked to no one in particular.

Several routs later, Clair would have agreed with Galen's assessment in spite of her ill humor. She stood impatiently tapping her slippers as she waited for Ian to show up at the Bennington manor and glare at her. So far he had tracked her to the Faltisek fete and the Love rout. She was fairly sure that he would put in an appearance at the Benningtons', the last event of the evening.

Her anger was dwindling as Ian chased her around the town. At the beginning of the evening, she had wanted to give him a piece of her mind. Now she realized he had a huge piece of her heart, the swine.

Love was scary, exciting, and, utterly remarkable, Clair determined. And the reality of it was so much better than all her lonely midnight fantasies. Ian had touched an invisible part of her, hidden even from herself. He had made her whole. He both completed her and complemented her. Together they shared an inseparable nature like atoms with covalent bonds—a theory her uncle Victor was considering. If only Ian hadn't lied to her.

Clair felt a sudden brush against her sleeve and a cool wind on her neck. Startled, she turned to find Asher watching her with a proprietary look, his teeth white and gleaming.

"I should have known," she said. *Drat!* Ian still wasn't here.

Asher leered at her. "It must be my lucky night."

"Are you following me?" Clair asked, somewhat amused. Since Ian wasn't here, she might as well pursue her werewolf research.

"To the ends of the earth, Clair, the ends of the earth."

She laughed, the sound light and tinkling, causing Asher to smile. He could listen to her laugh forever. And he would, if he had his wicked way.

"Do you know, you are the first person to laugh at me in a very long while." It was not a question.

"How long? Ten years, twenty years? Hmm . . . a hundred?" she asked, crossing her fingers behind her back. It was a pretty weak ploy, but still she had to try.

In the pursuit of science, it was far better to try and fail than never to try at all.

The earl chuckled. "Come now, surely you don't think I am as old as that? However will my ego take this new insult?"

"With your consequence, I imagine you'll survive infamously well."

"Clair, you are a delight. Come away with me. We'll go to Paris and drink champagne in bed."

"Champagne gives me hiccups," she countered, keeping an eye out for Ian. Surely he would track her here, and soon?

Eyeing Asher, Clair got the feeling she might have bitten off more than she could chew. Especially when he said, "All right then, come away with me to the country."

When she gave him a frosty look, he added mischievously, "I am having a house party at Wolverton Manor from this coming Tuesday through Thursday, with a small ball being given on Wednesday. Would you and your aunt Mary do me the honor of attending?"

Clair wanted to jump for joy. The wolf was inviting her to his den! She could almost feel the plaque given for the Scientific Discovery of the Decade.

Yes, she would gain her proof, Clair thought, her mind spinning. But she had to admit to some surprise, in spite of her inner victory dance. Wednesday night was the full moon. All shapeshifters would shift into animal form during the full moon. How on earth did Asher plan to host a ball all furry and fanged?

The crafty earl must be plotting something. There was no way Asher could host a party Wednesday night, unless he planned to scare his guests to death with a demonstration of metamorphism. However, knowing the wily earl, Clair felt sure that Asher would come up with some emergency to leave his guests by themselves that night. But that would not stop Clair from getting her information.

"I would love to attend. However, I have a small problem. I have invited the Duke of Ghent for dinner on Tuesday and would hate to rescind?" Clair made it a question, hoping Asher would respond appropriately. He did.

"I would be delighted to extend the invitation to His Grace also," he replied gallantly.

"Then my answer is yes. Thank you." Clair beamed. Finally! This time, she was invited to a house and didn't have to break and enter to gather information. As an added bonus, Aunt Mary and Ozzie would have a chance to rekindle their old flame. And to top things off, Ian would be livid.

As casually as she could, she asked Asher if Ian would be attending.

"Over my dead body," the earl teased. Or was he teasing? "Speak of the devil, here he is. And yes, an invitation has been regretfully extended. One can always hope he will break a leg or neck before then."

Clair gave Asher a disapproving look, then peered around his shoulder. She spotted Ian making determined course toward them, his face the perfect picture of displeasure.

Asher studied Ian's face, registering the cold fury there. Bowing to Clair, he commented dryly, "I believe it would be in both our best interests for me to decamp." He gave her hand a courtly kiss. "But never fear, sweet Clair. I leave the field of battle tonight to return in victory tomorrow." Her fresh scent lingered in his nostrils as he walked off into the crowd.

Clair barely noticed Asher's departure as she watched Ian approach. Ian's face could be the pattern for a mask of wrath. His jaws were clenched, his lips pinched in a tight, fine line, and his eyes blazed like green coals. Heat rolled off him in fierce waves. Perhaps, she judged silently, she had pushed him a bit too far—just a tad. Perhaps Plan B was not quite as brilliant as she had thought.

Before Clair could even greet him, Ian grabbed her arm—none too gently—and hurriedly escorted her around the perimeter of the dance floor. He moved like a man on a mission, never giving his love a chance to speak.

Reaching the balcony doors, he pushed Clair outside and dragged her over to a dark corner on the far side of the massive stone terrace. Large ferns and other potted plants completely hid the place from prying eyes. There Ian glowered at Clair, barely keeping his already too heated feelings from boiling over and scalding her.

"I'm surprised I didn't catch you waltzing with the earl, arm in arm, cheek to cheek," he snapped.

Sniffing, Clair replied politely, "I wasn't in the mood to dance with wolves."

Ian shook his head. "Bloody hell! Enough is enough, Clair! I said I was sorry, damn it!"

Before she could utter a word in anger or defense, he grabbed her roughly by her shoulders and pulled her tight against him. She struggled, but to no good gain as his lips crushed against hers. Ian forced his tongue inside her mouth, breaching those sweet depths as he initiated a wild, plundering rhythm and held her in a bruising embrace.

His kiss burned Clair all the way down to her soul, setting her aflame. Cursing herself, she let the kiss continue, knowing that the lies had not been resolved, but she was helpless beneath the onslaught of his passion and her own. She could do no less than respond, since she stupidly loved this man—the betraying reprobate.

As experienced as he was, Ian recognized the exact moment Clair capitulated. In some dim part of his brain he knew he should stop kissing and start explaining while she was in a complacent mood, but he didn't. Asher's poaching had set forth a primal urge to make Clair his own. Ian ravished her mouth, taking her ample breasts in his hands.

By God! he thought lustily. Her bosoms felt as magnificent as they looked. Clair arched helplessly into his hands, powerless under his flaming kiss. She moaned softly, feeding his need to be deep inside her. Ian had never wanted anything as desperately as to make Clair his in both word and deed. Her fiery response had his body swelling near to bursting.

Grabbing the skirt of her gown, he pulled it to her knees and settled her on the terrace edge. Her skin was smooth as silk, he mused, as his fingers worshiped her thighs. Inching closer, he edged his way into the slit of her undergarments, groaning. She was wet and hot. Bloody hell, he needed to bury himself in her hot sweet place.

The touch of Ian's fingers on her cleft made Clair shiver. The feelings washing over her were like a tidal wave. Colors flashed in her mind's eye—colors of deep purple, amethyst, and lilac. She wanted to scream with pleasure. She wanted to shout with joy. She wanted to lie down and make love right this moment on the Benningtons' terrace. They could charge admission.

That single wanton thought brought Clair to her senses. Good grief! She was fornicating with Ian on the Benningtons' terrace with Aunt Mary and over a hundred guests in the ballroom less than five yards away!

Drat, drat, and double drat! Her lusty, wanton, red-blooded nature was going to get her sent to hell on a fast-moving train. She wrenched her head away from Ian, her breath coming in short jerky spurts.

"Ian, stop it," she warned, pushing against him. "Get your bloody hand out of my drawers."

Clair's words brought him to his senses. Breathing hard, Ian stepped back, straightening her gown. "Damn, Clair. I'm sorry. I didn't mean to. . . ."

"To what? Make love to me on the Benningtons' terrace?" she asked archly, her heart racing and her stomach churning, her body quivering with unfilled desire. She pointed a finger. "The Benningtons' terrace!" she repeated.

Frustrated at the reaction of his body, at Clair, and at himself, Ian ran a hand through his hair. "I didn't mean to get carried away. . . ." He trailed off, his chest heaving.

"On the Benningtons' terrace," she said again.

"Damn it! Can't we get past the Benningtons' terrace?" he asked. "I said I was sorry."

She slid down and onto her feet. "Sorry for trying to make love to me on the Benningtons' terrace?" she repeated a fourth time, wanting to smile at the irritated look Ian shot her. "Or sorry for sending me on a wild goose chase to the duke's? You lied to me, Ian. You looked me straight in the eye and lied."

Ian tightly clasped both her hands. "Tonight I got carried away. I would do nothing to harm your reputation or you. I told you what I did about the Duke of Ghent to keep you away from Asher. He is a dangerous man. I didn't want to see you get hurt, and yet I ended up hurting you. If I could take the lies back, I would."

Clair searched his face, seeking the truth. "You betrayed me. Would you do it again?"

He kissed her gently on the forehead. He knew her belief would either set him free or apart from Clair forever. "I will never betray you again, Clair. In any form or fashion."

Clair gasped. Coming from one of the *ton's* greatest rakes, here was an oath tantamount to a vow of fidelity. She hated to admit it to herself, but she had been worried about Ian and his reputation as a rake. If she ever gave her heart away, it would be forever. Fidelity was something crucial to Clair. Staring up into Ian's beloved face, she asked cautiously, "Including other women?"

He nodded solemnly. Clair hugged him tightly.

"I will also try to tell you the truth at all times if I can." Ian knew deep in his soul that there was no other woman for him. He had found the perfect mate in an imperfect setting.

The second avowal she wasn't too thrilled with. She dropped her arms. "*Try* to tell me the truth?"

Ian touched her nose with his finger. "Try, you minx. Sometimes truth is a relative thing. It's the best I can offer." He turned to go. "Sleep on it?"

Chewing her lip, she nodded as Ian walked away. It had been an exhausting night. But her investigation had taken a mighty leap forward. And all in all, Plan B had been one of her most inspired plans of all time, a plan that actually worked brilliantly.

Strange how the bee of jealousy had stung Ian. Rubbing her lips, Clair felt as though she had been stung herself. She grinned, remembering the old saying about the birds and the bees.

The Mirror Has Two Faces

" 'Does the imagination dwell the most upon a woman won or woman lost?' " Asher asked Renfield as he stood in his bedchamber and waited for the valet to finish tying his cravat.

"Tennyson, my lord?" Renfield asked politely. He had been the earl's human servant for over sixty years. With a flourish he finished tying the Oriental, a clever new twist in a long list of cravat styles, at all of which the valet knew he was the master.

"Yeats."

"I take it Baron Huntsley is the reason for your question?"

"As always, you are correct. How does this look?" Asher asked as he glanced into the oval gilt-framed mirror, studying his reflection.

"Outstanding, my lord," Reinfield replied somberly, brushing a speck of lint from a black superfine evening jacket. "I take it you are still annoyed about the opera singer and that unfortunate wager several years ago."

Asher scowled, soothing back a tangle of chestnut hair from his forehead. "She should have been mine. Bloody embarrassing losing the chit to Huntsley, especially after half of White's knew of the wager. Who knew the silly creature would prefer to give her favors to Huntsley rather than me? I had no idea the hussy had such deplorable taste."

"I can't understand it, Master," Renfield replied dryly. He put down the coat and held up two jeweled stickpins. "Diamond or ruby?"

"Ruby, I think, tonight."

"You know, sir, you could have cheated on the wager and mesmerized the singer."

"That, Renfield, would not be sporting. A wager is a wager." Placing the ruby pin in his cravat, Asher turned to face his valet. "How does this look?"

"Perfection, my lord."

Turning back to the mirror, Asher waited for Renfield to slide his evening jacket over his shoulders. "This time, Huntsley will be the one with egg on his face. The baron will be devastated to lose Clair Frankenstein to my sweet seduction. It is the perfect plan. What makes it even sweeter is that Clair is special. She has a quality I've not seen or tasted before." After he uttered the words, Asher felt again just how true they were. Clair was unique, and she would be his. And somewhere deep inside his glacial heart, a tiny sliver of ice melted, warming him. He knew instinctively that Clair would never bore him. She had a passion for life that would remain long after her death and quite likely would spice up their mating rituals.

Renfield made a final yank on Asher's jacket, smoothing its line. "Ah yes, the Frankenstein female. Isn't she the one that chases pigs? Are you sure you want her, my lord? Eternity is a very long time."

Though the valet spoke in a flat tone, Asher could sense the man's disapproval. "Quite." He gave Renfield a thoughtful look. "I am only giving Clair her first mark tonight." He knew his valet was not sure about the upcoming addition to their household. A new mistress would change the routine and rhythm of the house. Renfield would not take that lightly, being the old stick in the mud that he was.

"Hmm . . . The first mark. That will enable you to read any intense feeling she might have."

"Yes. It will enable me to tell just how passionately she feels for the baron."

"And the other six marks which will enable you to make her your consort? When will those be given?" Renfield asked stiffly.

"Do not fear yet, Renfield. I will give her marks two and three at the house party, but the rest will have to wait a month at least. You know it is dangerous to bring a human over too quickly," Asher said, thinking of the methods of marking a mortal for eternity. Mark two would enable him to read her dreams. Mark three would make her susceptible to his will. Marks four and five would make her stronger, sensitive to sunlight, and entirely under his control. The last two marks would make mind communication between the two of them possible and complete her transformation to the living dead.

"This will be our little secret." The warning was a command, one that Asher's valet could not willingly break.

"I hope the baron doesn't get wind of this. Won't he see the bite on her neck at the houseparty?" Renfield asked worriedly. "And Miss Frankenstein strikes me as a rather independent sort of lady. I don't think she will go gently into that good night. I take it, my lord, that you will be using your mesmerism talents?"

"You are a master of strategy, Renfield," Asher quipped as he placed his wolfhead ruby ring on his finger. "I won't be biting her neck this time, although that is my favorite place. I will choose a less obvious spot, since Huntsley and Clair have not copulated yet. Perhaps those delicious breasts."

Facing the mirror, he scrutinized his reflection, a look of cold pleasure on his face. "What do you think, Renfield? How do I look? Shall I make the fair maiden swoon?"

"You are a god. Miss Frankenstein will be overcome by her good fortune," the valet remarked stoically.

"I don't pay you enough, Renfield. Remind me to raise your salary in the morning."

"Beg pardon, sir, but you will be asleep in your coffin in the morning."

Asher ignored him. Studying his reflection in the mirror, he suddenly considered vampire myths. In reality, the *Nosferatu* could see their reflections. They were physically strong, but only twice as strong as mortal men. Their hearing was average, along with their eyesight, although their night vision was exceptional.

"I am glad some of the myths of the vampire have been greatly exaggerated," he said. He gestured at the mirror, indicating his reflection. "To think all this would be wasted if I could not view my own person."

"A disaster of epic proportions," Renfield agreed, keeping his face straight.

Asher grinned. His fangs glinted in the candlelight. "Do you know Clair called me top-lofty?" he said.

"Hard to imagine."

Asher sighed. "I wish that some of the old myths held true. I would like to turn Clair tonight, in one go. Still, if all my drained dinners turned, think where that would lead." He shuddered. "The entire unwashed population would be undead. What a perfectly ghastly thought. All those plebeians in caskets trying to turn into bats or wolves."

Renfield wore a look of distaste. "Impossible. Vampires can't shape-shift."

Asher gave his valet a piercing look. "Yes, Renfield, I know that. And you know that. But they don't know that. Their knowledge of the *Nosferatu* is still in the Dark Ages," he sneered. "By the deuce, they think we fly off at night on those little bat wings, eating bugs. Bugs! Or they think we shift into furry dogs. As if I would ever lower myself to become a wolf, running about on four legs in all that mud. The whole thought is revolting!"

Renfield nodded. "Yes. To be a werewolf would be a curse. There isn't much dignity in becoming hairy every full moon," he went on, tidying up the bedchamber now that the earl was dressed. "I certainly would find no pride in being the human servant of a flea-bitten master."

"Well, let us be grateful our dignity is intact," Asher said. "And be grateful that the only shape vampires metamorphose into is mist. One of my favorite inherited characteristics."

A movement in the corner of his eye caught his attention, and Asher whirled around, glaring as Wilder strolled into his private sanctuary.

"What is your favorite vampire trick?" the man asked, his interest obviously piqued.

"Dematerializing into mist or fog," Asher replied, his gaze narrowed on Wilder's sudden frown. "I forgot. You're still a hundred years too young to turn into mist," he mocked. "Now, why have you invaded my sanctuary? I have an appointment shortly." He made his voice like ice. He didn't like anyone in his lair unless he had personally invited them, even members of his own vicious nest.

"I came to discuss the Frankenstein problem. She is a danger to our race." Wilder's expression was cruel.

"I told you it has been taken care of," Asher warned, his eyes glittering with fierce impatience. "When she sees me waltzing the night away under the full moon and remaining both upright and devoid of fur, Clair will know I am not a wolfman."

Wilder paced the room anxiously. "What if she then decides you're a vampire, like she did me?"

"She won't. Her mind is on wolves. Now leave it be," Asher hissed, not wanting to reveal his plan to make Clair his vampire queen. It was too dangerous to let anyone know until he had the high council's approval. A master vampire was only allowed to turn two mortals every century. He had filled his quota over eighty years earlier. One result had been disastrous, the other not as bad.

The council would give their consent, Asher believed, due to the unusual circumstances, but he wasn't a hundred percent sure. He was also shrewd enough to realize that Wilder would be jealous. As master of the nest,

Asher had turned down Wilder's request to turn a human female only a few scant years ago in 1795.

It was a decision Asher didn't regret. Wilder was too selfish to nurture a fledgling vampire. He was also extremely moody and extremely cruel, sometimes exhibiting a ferocity that bordered on insanity.

Wilder shook his head. "She's a Frankenstein, for deuced sakes. They don't quit once they've got the bit between their teeth."

Asher growled, his blue eyes beginning to burn with golden flames, his fangs elongating. "Are you challenging me?"

Nervously, Wilder backed up a step. "I am many things, Asher, but a fool is not one them." He retreated to the door, his features frozen in a mask of rage, his fingernails needlelike points. "I'll leave you to your appointment. I just hope Clair Frankenstein isn't the end of us all!" And with those parting words, Wilder was gone.

Asher shook his head, the flickering fires in his eyes damped. "Ah, Renfield, the foibles of youth."

His valet only nodded, still staring at the door where Wilder had disappeared. "You must take great care, my lord," he said. "That one will rip out your throat. And I noted last night that Lady Montcrief was not well pleased with your interest in Miss Frankenstein."

"Were you spying on my boudoir playmates, Renfield? Shame on you."

Renfield sniffed. "Of course not, my lord. I was merely passing to refill the brandy decanter."

Asher smiled as he picked up his many-layered cape. "Now let us hope my bewitching Clair will soon be arriving at the cemetery."

"She is a most unusual female," Renfield agreed. "Most ladies," he said, stressing the word "ladies," with a doubtful look in his eyes, "would do anything to avoid meeting a man alone. A man they believe to be a wolf, and in a cemetery . . . ?"

"Most ladies are not Clair Frankenstein," Asher replied.

"The world must rejoice," Renfield snipped, thoroughly vexed at his master. "And please, my lord, do try not to spill your dinner all over your cravat again. Bloodstains are terribly hard to soak out of white linen."

The earl arched an aristocratic eyebrow. "Renfield! You try my patience at times."

He descended the stairs, a tiny doubt in the back of his mind. Clair was a lady, and meeting him alone at night as his note requested would put her in a compromising position. Would she come? His eyes flamed. She was a Frankenstein through and through. She would be there with her pulse racing. And if her heart wasn't racing when he arrived, it would be after just one kiss.

Sex and the Cemetery

Clair shivered as a cold blast of wind whipped her cape around her and rustled the skeletal branches of the trees above. It was pitch black at the Eternal Sleeps Cemetery, with the exception of her lantern, which cast a small halo of light to hold back the inky shadows.

Clair was cold, a little frightened, and very curious about Asher's mysterious note. She stood frowning, tapping her fingertips on the tombstone where her lantern rested. Ian would kill her if he knew what she was about. If she were fortunate, he wouldn't find out. She had used all of her persuasive powers to convince Aunt Mary of the need for secrecy, just as the note warned. Asher had stated he wouldn't tell her what he knew if Huntsley were involved.

Clair wished she could have told Ian, but he would either go off half-cocked or else have forbidden her to come. For a brief time she had thought Ian was coming to value her research, but his lie about the Duke of Ghent had proved that theory false.

She sighed, supposing she should be scared of meeting a werewolf in a dark, silent cemetery at night. Luckily for Clair, her many grave-robbing trips with Uncle Victor had prepared her for a scene such as this.

Asher appeared out of the grayish fog as if he had simply materialized in front of her. "You look frightened," he said.

She started at his approach, then raised her chin firmly in the air. She would show no fear. "Frankensteins are never scared. It's not in our blood."

Asher chuckled. "What is, then? Ghoulies, vampires and late-night walks in the cemetery?"

"Apparently so." She smiled slightly.

"I am glad you're here. I wasn't quite sure if you would come to our little tryst."

"How could I not? You knew your note would lure me. Now, what unusual activities have been going on here?"

"My, my, you do cut to the chase," Asher remarked, his eyes drinking in the beauty of both her face and her soul. Noting her impatient sigh, he spoke. "I have heard of some strange activity here at night. Unearthly noises and graves without bodies."

"It could be simple grave robbers," Clair replied cautiously, wondering what exactly Asher knew about her research.

"Or something more nefarious."

"And what would that be?"

"Those blood sucking fiends of the night—vampires. What else?" He waited for her reaction, noticing her fingers twisting in the folds of her cape.

"I see," she said, but she didn't. What was Asher's game? He was talking about vampires. She knew he must believe in them; after all, he was a werewolf. And she knew in a roundabout way they all belonged to the same preternatural club.

Cocking her head, Clair examined the Earl thoroughly. Maybe he was a werewolf trying to pretend to be a vampire trying to pretend to be human. It was a complex riddle, one worthy of the Sphinx. Or was Asher trying to gammon her like Ian had, leading her down a false trail with a false scent? "Vampires. Here at the Eternal Sleeps Cemetery?" she said.

Asher shrugged. "I thought it was a subject close to your heart. Your research into matters of the paranormal, I mean."

"It is."

"It is a very dangerous subject," Asher warned, stepping closer, Clair's spirit drawing him like a moth to flame. He felt his incisors begin to lengthen.

"It's not just my work, it's my calling, my destiny," Clair tried to explain, her voice filled with grim determination. Everyone was always trying to warn her away from what she knew to be right, what she knew to be essential to her mental well-being, what she knew she had to continue to do in order to be who she was and what she wanted to be in the future. She had to win the prestigious Scientific Discovery of the Decade Award.

Asher glided closer. "No, there is no escaping destiny." *And you are to be mine, mine, mine,* Asher repeated in a silent litany.

Cocking her head, Clair studied him, a slight smile forming as she decided what to say and what not. "Perhaps you do understand. 'The moving finger writes;

and, having writ, moves on; nor all thy piety nor wit shall lure it back to cancel half a line, nor all thy tears wash out a word of it.'"

Asher was moved by the glimpse of sorrow, bliss, and joy she revealed. It was a gift he would always cherish. "Omar Khayyam," he said.

She nodded, raising her face to his. "I have been and will always be Clair Frankenstein, be that a blessing or a curse. I would not change it for all the serenity or lady-like manners in the world."

Moved, Asher turned partially away. Placing his boot upon a tombstone, his eyes searched the night and he changed the subject. "There are shadows dark and low here. The secrets of the graves are echoes of the dying . . . dying . . . dead," he remarked softly. "So many dead. So many lovers lost to each other's embrace. So many mothers with hearts turned to dust. Laughing friends whose laughter has been silenced."

Clair focused on the sorrow evident in his eyes. She understood from her research that werewolves were not immortal, but they lived for over a century. It was an intriguing thought, but a melancholy one as well: they knew more than a hundred years of joy and grief, of birthing babies and bidding friends farewell on the journey to the unknown.

Asher turned to Clair, carefully studying her reaction to his next words. "Do you think that creatures of the night could be lonely?"

"I would say we are all prisoners of ourselves, loneliness being one of our worst jailors. If humans can shed tears, why not the supernatural? Yes, I imagine they know a great loneliness, perhaps more than any other."

Asher lifted her chin with his pale hand. He stared

into her eyes and gently bent down to kiss her lips. He kissed her tenderly, hiding the raging hunger filling his veins. The kiss stirred his dark soul, reaching into recesses he had long since thought shriveled up and dead from lack of warmth.

Her breath was the sweetest of scents, her taste a tantalizing hint of incredible delight. In the blink of the eye, Asher fell completely in love. Consequent with that love came knowledge. He would not make Clair immortal and risk the warm, generous essence of her human soul. She was too special to make into the chill undead. Although he doubted he could let her go completely. Perhaps if the Fates were kind they could be lovers. And Asher knew, with a smile, he would help Fate along in whatever manner he could.

Stepping back, Clair lifted her hand to her mouth in startlement. That kiss had been riveting. It was lucky she loved Ian, or else she might find herself involved with this attractive arrogant Wolfman of London.

Gently taking her hand from her mouth, Asher pressed a quick kiss to Clair's heated palm, wanting to do much more, when he heard the sound of rapidly approaching footsteps. Jerking his head upright, he scanned the darkness. "Expect any minute to have a mad dog at your door," he predicted in annoyance.

Clair glanced in the direction Asher indicated, seeing nothing really, just a slight movement of shadow. She turned back to Asher only to find him gone, vanished into the night like woodsmoke.

Before Clair had a chance to catch her breath, Ian appeared. He loped toward her, a fierce expression on his face.

"Bloody hell, Clair," he roared. "Have you lost your

mind! You could have been ravished! You could have been . . ." He trailed off, unwilling to say what Asher could have done to her alone in the dark.

"Where the hell is the pompous bastard?" He scoured the area with an eagle eye. Espying no movement, Ian grabbed Clair's arms and began to shake her. His heart had stopped in his chest when Lady Mary told him where Clair had gone tonight and with whom. It was at that moment he'd realized how he loved Clair: with an intensity so bright it might burn his soul to ashes.

"Asher's gone. The earl left right before you got here. He heard you coming." She was confused by Ian, by Asher, and by Asher's kiss. She loved Ian, this man whom she'd once thought was a vampire. She was attracted to Asher, a werewolf, pretending to be a man. It all had to be a huge cosmic joke. Whoever said love was easy was not seeing her life.

"Did my aunt tell on me?" she finally managed to spit out. "Ian, stop shaking me. You're hurting me," she chided sternly.

"Bloody hell! I'll do more than shake." With ruthless intensity Ian crushed Clair to him, taking her mouth with a raw hunger that left her breathless. It was a greedy kiss that both aroused and ravished, and he tasted her deeply.

Briefly, he let her up for air. She inhaled sharply. Now *that* was a kiss to raise the dead. Quickly, she glanced around. No one was climbing out of his or her grave. Her mini-inspection done, she turned her attention back to the very angry man in front of her.

Ian was staring at her with raw male hunger. Her heart danced in her chest as she felt hot wetness between her legs. Before she could say a word, he began nipping at her neck, sending little flickers of fire up and down her spine. She sighed, a sound that apparently drove him wild. He bore her to the damp earth, which smelled of damp leaves and rich soil.

The passion flared hotter between the two lovers as they kissed, almost bursting them into flame. Clair felt as if she were being consumed. Her love for Ian fed the fires of this great desire. She wanted Ian in the way a woman wanted a man. She wanted to give Ian the greatest gift she could give him, besides her love. She wanted to gift him with her virginity.

Grabbing his shoulders, she arched her back as he bit and kissed her neck. She had never known her flesh was so sensitive to the touch of warm lips. Liquid fire was streaking down her veins, making her feel alive and loved. Moaning, she whispered his name, "Ian. Oh, Ian."

The sound of his name from her kiss-swollen lips sent Ian over the edge. Desire flared through him. Jerking her gown, he pulled it to her waist and tore off her fine lace drawers. He was beyond thinking. This was war. This was hunger. This was primitive, basic lust. He had to have her now, to place his mark on her for all time. She would belong to no one but him from today onward.

Her naked splendor unveiled to him, Ian growled at the sight of the golden triangle of curls between her shapely thighs, his carnal hunger burning away his sensibilities. Hands shaking, he touched her sweet, hot cleft, groaning at the wet dew there. Without the leisurely petting he had oft dreamed for this night, without the words of love he had once imagined he would speak, he unbuttoned his pants, shoved them halfway down and pushed her legs apart. He was wild with desire, his flesh so hard he literally ached with the force of his erection.

He rolled over on top of her, resting on his elbows as he moved into position. He wanted to be able to see her face at the moment of possession. Holding her head between his hands, he stared into her smoky eyes, eyes that were heavy-lidded with lust. How he loved this woman!

Clair moaned, arching beneath her true love, struggling to get closer, needing to be one with him. Her insides ached with want for this wild beautiful man who lay atop her, looking down at her with such need and tenderness in his eyes.

"Please, Ian . . ." Clair hesitated, unsure of what she needed to stop the fierce ache between her legs.

But Ian knew. With one push, he embedded himself within her, breaking through her maidenhead and seating himself to the hilt. It was the most primal feeling he had ever experienced. She was *his*! Let no man put them asunder. Let no man try. Let no vampire try. He would kill any or all that would attempt to steal this wondrous woman. She was now his. His future. His destiny.

Caught in such overwhelming feelings of pride, possession, and lust, he sensed tears in his eyes. Then he felt Clair quiver, a whimper escaping her. Feeling the beast, he lowered his head to hers.

"Forgive me, Clair. I meant to go slower. I know it hurts, my love. But give it a minute," he gasped. She was the white to his black, the sun to his moon, and the youth to his aging responsibilities.

"God, Clair, how I love you," he said. He felt her lush

breasts against his chest, the nipples hard little circles. He felt the heat and tightness of her sheath, and he smelled the fresh scent of her woman's arousal and virgin's blood. He wanted to lick her there, taste her, and make her scream with ecstasy.

Dazed, Clair freed her hands from beneath his chest and, placing one on each cheek, she raised his head and gazed deeply into Ian's eyes. They were burning with a rawness she had never seen before, the green sparking like emerald fire. His jaw was tense, his neck corded. Tenderly, she kissed him on the lips.

"I love you too, Ian Huntsley," she murmured. She arched against him, tears staining her cheeks, a bemused expression on her face. This was what she had dreamed of in the long-ago dreams of a foolish young girl: love, pure and simple and true.

With the damp, cool earth beneath her and the midnight velvet of the night above, the stars were her guide. Clair arched up against Ian. She had to feel him move within her secret core now that the pain had faded. Her body was throbbing—hot, aching with an intense desire she didn't understand but instinctively knew only Ian could satisfy. Her movement triggered something inside him as Ian began to plunge his hips wildly back and forth. His movements became more forceful as Clair lifted her hips to meet his in a dance of love as old and fierce as nature and time.

Suddenly, Clair felt a building of some momentous force within her. Deep purple filled her mind with flashes of white lightning. The feeling built . . . built . . . built until it burst forth with a brilliance that left her frozen and in awe. She screamed a cry against the night.

The sound fired Ian's own primitive response. He

shouted as he thrust hard twice more and released his seed, claiming Clair as she held him in the cradle of her arms, clasping his head. With a lightened heart, he whispered words of love to her, some English, some in Welsh. His long days' journeys into lonely nights were now over. He had come home.

"Oh Clair, you are truly a miracle in my life. Are you all right?" he questioned anxiously. "I didn't mean to be so rough. I meant to wine and dine you, to kiss every delicious inch of your body. It was your first time and I should have been more circumspect, more a gentleman."

Clair laughed, the musical sound filling his heart. "I am living up to my family name. My first time making love and it's in a cemetery. You do know how to spoil a girl," she teased, kissing him lightly on the lips. "I think I rather like you wild and untamed," she decided after a moment. She brushed a dark, damp curl off his forehead. "No wonder no one tells us young ladies about this . . . this incredible, mind-altering, marvelous, earthshaking experience. If they did, we would all become wanton hussies with swollen bellies nine months out of every year," she finished enthusiastically.

Ian threw back his head and laughed a laugh of pure joy. He was free at last from the tribulations of his youth. He felt young for the first time since being a cub of fourteen, before his father's death and his mother's overshadowing grief, before the winds of time had blown his hopes into the dark abyss. "Marry me," he said.

Clair's head shot off his chest. "What?"

"You heard me. I want you to marry me. I would get down on my knees and ask, but it appears I'm already there," he remarked drolly as he twitched his legs, which were entwined with Clair's.

She shook her head, her palm against his cheek. "Ian, you don't have to do the honorable thing. I am almost twenty-five years old. I am not some young innocent."

"You were a virgin, Clair." He frowned. This was not going at all as he'd planned. She was supposed to be excited. She was supposed to be kissing his face in happiness, squealing with delight. She was supposed to be discussing her wedding dress.

"I know this sounds silly, but I am still not as innocent as some innocents truly are. I am a—"

Before she could finish, Ian interrupted her, impatience clear in his tone. He knew what he wanted. He wanted *her*.

"I know, I know. A Frankenstein. But I want to make you a Huntsley. Besides, together we are the perfect example of a covalent bond."

"Oh, Ian. You've been boning up on your science." Clair sighed admiringly.

He chuckled. He'd been boning up on something, all right. "Be my baroness. The Baroness Huntsley."

"But that is the point, Ian. I am a Frankenstein. I will be published. I will continue my research. I will win the prestigious Scientific Discovery of the Decade Award. And after that I will still be involved with my scientific research. How will you feel about me running all over God's green earth, chasing vampires and werewolves?" She asked as she must, her heart breaking. Ian would want her to give up her adventures; she just knew it.

"I wouldn't care for it too much. I would rather you run around God's green earth after our children. That will keep you busy and fulfilled," he added pompously.

She raised an eyebrow. "Yes. I want your children. Yes, being a mother and wife will keep me fulfilled. But I won't give up my scientific ambitions. I just won't, Ian. Not for all the tea in China."

"Or for being a baroness, either, I guess," he replied, stung. "I love you, Clair. We can work something out. Besides, you could already be pregnant." He put a hand possessively on her stomach. How he hoped she was. The thought of Clair carrying his child, suckling his child, stirred him deeply. He would teach his child the mysteries of living and giving. At such a dream, his heart swelled with love and a deep sense of abiding fulfillment. His John Thomas, who'd always had a head of its own, was once again ready and rearing to go.

Ian deliberately moved his hand to Clair's chest and began taking off her gown, which was crumpled around her waist. He hadn't gotten to important parts in his first round of lovemaking, such as the big one—nudity. Slipping the gown off her, he stared down in rapt fascination at the luscious bounty beneath him. Here was a feast fit for a king.

"If I am pregnant and that is a big *if*, then we'll cross that particular bridge when we come to it," Clair stated firmly, her eyes narrowing on Ian's playful fingers. They were now plucking at the nipples of her breasts. He was hoping to distract her, the bounder. She hoped he wouldn't stop.

"Marry me, Clair," Ian coaxed again as he began to nibble and suck on her breasts. He was getting distracted, and that wasn't good. Clair had to marry him, in spite of her indomitable spirit, which was apparently bred into the Frankenstein genes, and the sooner the better as far as he was concerned. There was no help for it. He would have to develop another bloody plan! For a military genius, his strategies were less than a stellar success around Clair. He was already on the third letter in the alphabet.

"Let's discuss it later, when we have all our clothes on," she said. Her body was heating up too fast. She squirmed.

"No. Now!" he commanded, reveling in the lush softness of plump, white breasts.

She moaned. He laughed.

Two can play at this game, Clair mused, taking his hot, hard arousal in her hand. He felt like smooth silk, his tip wet and glistening. She could barely close her fingers around it.

"Are all men this large? I know Frederick is enormous, but then Uncle Victor created him. Are their bollocks all this heavy?" Her curiosity was once again running amok.

Ian shifted slightly, beating his head against the ground in amused mortification. "Clair, my Clair, what am I to do with you?"

She grinned mischievously. "You could do that thrusting thing again with your hips. It drives me wild."

The look he gave her burned Clair to cinders. "It will be my pleasure," he replied. Then he was as good as his word. They both almost expired from it.

The Girl Who Cried Wolf

"Now that's what I'd call the house of a werewolf," Clair stated with conviction, her head bobbing outside the carriage window. She was scrutinizing Wolverton Manor, an imposing and sinister-looking structure of granite four stories in the air, the accumulation of several centuries' worth of architecture, gothic being predominate. Clair knew with one look that she had found the vampires' and werewolves' nefarious nest.

Ian sighed, glancing out the window at the massive structure high upon a grassy hill. He estimated they were still a good two miles away. He had tried to talk Clair out of the earl's house party, but to no avail. Since she refused to stay home, he'd refused to stay home. He couldn't just leave her to the wolves—or to the vampires, as the case might be. And no way was he letting his beloved travel to the earl's countryseat alone. Not with Asher on the prowl.

"Really, dear?" Lady Mary asked. She shifted on the soft leather seat and poked her head out the window. "How can you tell? It looks like a dozen other estates I have seen."

"I just can," Clair answered stubbornly. "This is the residence of the werewolf and his cohorts. This is the nest where he and his vampire cronies meet for plotting, blood-sharing, and orgies."

Ian rolled his eyes.

"My hypothesis won't be wrong this time," she snapped. Her pride and prejudice against the earl aside, all indicated Neil Asher was not what he seemed. Her sense and sensibilities all screamed that the earl was a supernatural creature. "It's even named Wolverton Hall. How much more blatant can one be?"

"Yes, dear," Lady Mary affirmed, her tone indicating her doubt. "But I do wonder . . ." she said, then stopped. Nothing riled her niece more than to have her theories debated.

"Yes?" Clair asked.

"Well, the Earl of Porkerston is not a pig."

Clair moaned. "Not pigs again." She would never, if she lived to a thousand, live that incident down.

"Calm down, Clair," Lady Mary cajoled, patting her niece's hand. "I just don't want you counting your werewolves before they're hatched, or whatever it is they do."

Ian gave a quiet snicker, and Clair shot him a cool glance then looked again at him in spite of herself. She couldn't help noticing his long shapely legs stretched out before him. The material of his docskin breeches fit to perfection. Drat! She felt a delicious ache low in her belly.

Noticing Clair noticing him, Ian gave an almost imperceptible smile. It barely curved his mouth but caused tiny creases at the corners.

Turning her attention back to her aunt, Clair replied, "You and everyone else, it seems."

The carriage hit a large pothole, its sudden lurch throwing Clair practically into Ian's lap, while Lady Mary hung on to the carriage straps, barely keeping herself upright. Noting how Clair's back blocked her aunt's view, Ian playfully pinched Clair's breast, just to see her reaction.

She didn't disappoint him. She puckered up like a prune and gave him a heated glance that almost caused him blisters.

"Rake," she hissed.

Ian smiled smugly, leaning back against the carriage seat. She was adorable when she was in a huff. She was adorable when she was in her brown study. She was adorable naked. He crossed his legs, wondering if his arousal was conspicuous under his breeches. He hoped Lady Mary didn't notice the sudden bulge.

Clair was exasperated. Everywhere there were doubters. She wondered if Newton had faced this heavy problem when he kept telling everyone about apples and gravity. They had probably just told him to go bake a pie. Had Trevithic almost run out of steam before anyone accepted his locomotive run on the power of heated water? "I'm not wrong this time," she said again.

"Hmm," Lady Mary offered. "If you are right, then this party is probably a very dangerous idea." She shivered briefly, then smiled at Ian. "I am so glad you are here, Ian, to help protect us from the big bad wolf."

Hiding his amusement, Ian replied stoically, "My

pleasure." Then he turned and grinned at Clair, hoping she was remembering their pleasures of the other night. She was. She blushed a becoming pink.

Bloody hell, he cursed silently. He was randy as a goat. Two tastes of the luscious Clair had not been enough—would never be enough. He had wanted to make love to her again, but commitments had kept him busy for the past two days.

"When is Galen coming?" Clair asked.

Ian shrugged. "He probably arrived at Wolverton Manor several hours ago, since he was on horseback."

Clair smiled. "I am glad your cousin could attend," she said.

Ian nodded, noting that Clair's aunt was wearing a smile of pure satisfaction, looking quite like the cat that swallowed the canary. He wondered at her smugness.

Lady Mary had been clandestinely watching the two youngsters all the way from London. She knew two lovebirds when she saw them. She smiled a secret smile. Oh, yes! Wedding bells would be ringing if she had her way. And it would be soon. She didn't want her niece to have a seven-month baby, something upon which gossipmongers would be sure to expound. She smiled her secret little smile again. She knew beyond a shadow of a doubt that Ian was too honorable to take Clair's virtue and not do right by her. And despite her niece's scientific bent and vows to remain single and pursue her supernatural studies, Clair was head over heels in love with the handsome baron. It was a coup de grâce.

How the other matchmaking mothers would turn pea green with envy! Yes, Lady Mary knew, her Plan A, *To Catch a Baron*, was running full steam ahead. She would definitely use her stuffed doves for an altarpiece at the wedding.

Stifling the urge to pat herself on the back, she addressed herself to the couple. "Yes, Ian is such a big man. I am sure you need fear no wolf at his door."

Clair's frown deepened at her aunt's comment. She placed a hand on Ian's arm. "You must let me handle the situation if danger appears. I have come quite prepared."

Ian didn't like the sound of that. He liked it even less when she pulled a small derringer out of her valise.

"Silver bullets," she confided proudly.

"Bloody hell, Clair! Have you got a maggot in your head? Give me that thing before you hurt someone." He glowered as he reached for the gun.

Stubbornly, she shook her head. "I am an expert shot."

"That's what I'm afraid of." Ian held out his hand, but Clair ignored him. The situation was farcical, ludicrous, and downright scary. Clair with a gun!

Clair's eyebrows raised in question.

"You'll shoot somebody accidentally," he explained. "And being the fine markswoman you are, it could be fatal."

She slipped the derringer back into her valise. "I promise to keep it hidden away, unless there is an emergency."

Ian threw up his hands in disgust. "Heaven help us from females carrying guns and driving buggies. What is the world coming to?" His question had both ladies glaring at him and giving him the silent treatment until they were shown to their respective rooms in the earl's home.

Clair stopped outside the second-floor room assigned

to her and her aunt. Mary excused herself and went inside, while Clair stood outside with Ian.

Bowing, he demanded, "You are going to rest after our journey. No snooping, spying, or sneaking around until I can go with you."

Crossing her fingers behind her back, Clair gave him a sweet smile. "Of course."

"Of course you'll rest, or of course you'll snoop?"

"Rest," she replied pettishly.

Kissing her forehead, he turned and headed toward the third-floor stairs. Looking over his shoulder he called, "It's almost dusk. I'll be back in a couple of hours to escort you to supper."

Clair slipped inside her room, quickly brushing the travel dust off her clothes. She sighed as she glanced at her aunt, who had already taken off her cloak and bonnet. "I wish either my maid or yours could have made the trip with us."

"You know Karla had that nasty toothache and Pam's baby was running a fever," Lady Mary replied.

Removing her bonnet, Clair dropped it on a delicate chair with pale pink flowers. "The earl's butler told me he would send a maid up later to help us dress." Unlatching her valise, she pulled her silver comb and brush set out and began brushing the tangles in her waist-length hair. "I thought it odd that the earl wasn't here to greet us," she said.

"His butler said he would return shortly. Some emergency with one of the tenants."

Hmm, Clair mused. "Nonetheless, I guess I shouldn't look a gift wolf in the mouth."

"What was that, dear?" Lady Mary asked, straightening from taking off her boots.

"Nothing much. Just a thought." Clair finished brushing her hair.

Lady Mary surveyed her niece with a critical eye. There was no doubt about it: Clair looked different, more confident, and unfortunately more secretive. "Is there anything you would like to talk to me about?" she probed, hoping Clair would confide in her about a relationship with the baron.

Clair shook her head, setting out her toilette articles. "No." She couldn't tell her aunt about Ian yet. It was too new, too personal—and besides, she knew exactly what her aunt would do. She would be married before she could say, "In a pig's eye."

Although Clair longed to talk with her aunt, she knew deep down that she could not take the bridal veil just yet. She and Ian had to resolve their differences concerning her research and studies. Ian had to accept her as she was and would always be: as a scientific Frankenstein to the blissful end, even after marriage. Though she knew many women lost their identities when entering the married state, Clair would not allow that to happen.

She grimaced and tied her hair back in a long braid. She loved Ian Huntsley with all her heart. She just had to bring him around to her way of thinking. He was only a man. They weren't as astute as females. They weren't as determined as women, and they certainly weren't as smart. Still, he was *her* man. She sighed. That part of her body, which had truly been untouched until a few nights before, was throbbing. Her blood was on fire. Her breasts were aching. She was looking forward in a totally unladylike manner to discovering more of Ian's expertise in lovemaking.

Glancing out the corner of her eye at her aunt, who was slipping into her bedrobe, Clair mused that she and Ian stood little chance of being alone together. Not with everything working against them.

Sensing her niece's restlessness, Lady Mary asked, "I take it you are undertaking your search now?"

Clair nodded.

"Be careful. Remember the story about that silly young girl who was always running around in that dreadful red cloak."

"Red Riding Hood?"

"Yes, dear. That's the one."

"Your point, Auntie?" Clair questioned, her hand on the doorknob.

"Well, dear, she got eaten!"

Clair kissed her aunt's cheek. "I'll be fine." Then she slipped out the door.

In the hall outside she checked to see if anyone was about. Good, she thought cheerfully. She was alone. Hurrying down three doors, she came to the earl's chamber, a fact that she had learned earlier by questioning the footman. Since Asher wasn't in at the moment, it seemed the perfect time to search his room.

Slipping inside, Clair took note of the deep burgundy hues in which the chamber was decorated. They surprised her. She thought a werewolf would be more comfortable in earth tones such as brown and green. Meticulously she made her search, finding nothing, and was just about to slip out the door when she heard the sound of the earl's voice in the hall.

Stifling a curse, Clair hurried over to the large plush drapes. She slid behind them just as the door opened and someone stepped inside.

Asher walked into his bedchamber, giving it a quick glance as Wilder trailed behind him. He swore as he noticed the pair of delicate green shoes barely visible under the drapes. She's at it again, he thought with wry amusement. Clair was on the hunt, and she hadn't been in his home for more than an hour.

Asher started unbuttoning his coat, while Wilder lounged against the wardrobe. "Asher, it's just a speck of dirt on your sleeve. I don't see why you have to change the jacket," the second vampire complained.

"I want to look my best for Clair," Asher answered with a sly smile. Here was a chance to advance his cause, the sinful seduction of Clair Frankenstein.

Wilder stared at him, stunned. "You truly care for that freakish woman?"

Asher slid his jacket off and reached for another. "Of course. Clair is a lovely lady. She's a special lady who has quite taken my heart."

Wilder scowled. "You're insane, that's what you are. She's a Frankenstein and would tell—"

Asher interrupted and hurried him out of the room before Wilder could reveal who and what they were. Still, all in all, Asher patted himself on the back. He would have scored quite a few points in pursuit of Clair's seduction.

Intrigued by what she'd heard Asher reveal, Clair nevertheless breathed a great sigh of relief when he left. Hurrying out of the room, Clair thanked her lucky stars. How embarrassing it would have been if Wilder had spotted her in the earl's boudoir. It would have been another humiliating scene to haunt her. The Honorable Christopher Wilder would have thought her a reprehensible Peeping Tom. Of course, he would have been wrong. She was merely a dedicated, hardworking scientist with an inquisitive mind.

Still, Ian would have killed her if she'd been caught in Asher's room. No, she thought sarcastically, Asher would have killed her. Or it would have been a toss-up between the three men.

And what was she supposed to do about Asher's feelings for her?

Thirty minutes later, with the clock ticking, Clair finished her search of the earl's library. She knew Ian would be coming to her room soon. She barely had time to go back upstairs and get dressed.

Shutting the desk drawer, Clair sighed with disappointment. So far her search had come up empty. She had found nothing but an old portrait of an ancestor of Asher's dressed in an outdated coat and floppy black pirate hat. He really was a handsome wolf. If she hadn't been in love with Ian, Clair really would be tempted to take a chance on the Wolfman. After all, she did love puppies.

Just as she shut the drawer with a snap, Clair once again heard the unmistakable sound of Asher's voice. Panicking, she slipped underneath the huge cherry desk.

Asher escorted Lady Montcrief inside his library, his sharp eye searching the room. Wearily, he shook his head. There. He'd spotted a flash of green peeking out from underneath his desk. Clair, again.

"Asher, you are not paying attention to me," Lady Montcrief complained. She pressed herself against him, running her hands through his burnished chestnut locks. "Come, darling, let's play a bit."

Yanking her hands from his hair, he forcefully turned

231

the lusty lady around and escorted her back out the door. He gave no explanations, only shook his head at Lady Montcrief's antics. But outside he grinned, his white fangs sharp. Clair Frankenstein was like a dog with a very big bone. And she could chew on him anytime.

Rhymes of the Ancient Predator

"Humans, humans everywhere, and nary a drop to drink," Asher commented dryly to Ian as he surveyed the assembly of houseguests for his two-day party. The guests were scattered throughout the large music room, each in some variety of activity. Some were playing cards at the far end of the chamber, some were gossiping in small groups, and a few of the ladies read while one played a soft tune on the pianoforte.

The room was elaborately decorated in shades of pale wine and creamy white, with glistening wood paneling. Paintings done by Rubens and Rembrandt were interspersed among the bronze wall sconces. A thick Persian carpet was centered on the floor.

Ian scanned the room with a quick glance. There were twenty-one guests, thirteen of them male and four married couples. "I see a few supernaturals interspersed."

Asher waved a hand elegantly. "Too few. The humans here tonight are definitely in the majority."

"It's lucky that the vampire high council put severe fines on those vampires who drain their victims dry."

Asher nodded, his blue eyes frosty. "Yes. Discretion has saved us from being hunted down and destroyed like in the old days. Those were not pleasant for my kind." His eyes took on a faraway look. "To be hunted like rabid dogs by unwashed rabble . . ."

"If the coffin fits," Ian suggested. Suddenly his attention was drawn by the lovely vision of Clair entering the room. His heart rate sped up and his breathing quickened.

"You know far too much about us," Asher said, his tone irritated. Then, noticing the physical changes in Ian, Asher turned toward the door. He noted Clair. "Ah. So it's like that, is it? You've bedded her."

Though his tone was politely contemptuous, his feelings were anything but. Asher was incensed at the thought of Clair in Ian's grip. Ian touching all that soft, white flesh, those pale graceful arms holding him. Ian being loved by Clair. A pang shot through Asher's heart and he felt a blood-red tear begin to form. Quickly he blinked, showing Ian no weakness. Clair was truly lost to him now. He wanted to lie down and die, except he was already dead.

Asher's words had captured his attention, so with a glower Ian turned to face him. "Careful, Asher. I don't care what you are, but talk rudely about Clair and I will personally stake that black heart of yours."

Asher raised his upper lip in scorn. "Calm yourself, Huntsley. I concede the point and the game. You have won the fair Clair, although you do not deserve her. She is too special for you. Or, for that matter, for even my grand personage. But it appears she has made her choice," the vampire went on his voice husky with an unrequited longing that would never be satisfied.

He watched the way Clair was looking at Ian, love shining in her stormy gray eyes, and said, "Yes, you are a lucky man. But if you hurt her, you will answer to me!"

Cocking his head, Ian studied his opponent. "A conscience, at this late date?"

"It happens every hundred years or so. It seems we live not as we wish, but as we must."

"I intend to marry her," Ian admitted.

Asher looked surprised. "I heard you say once that you wouldn't get married until hell freezes over."

"I guess I owe the devil a winter coat."

Asher nodded, his eyes a glacial blue. "Has she said yes?" he asked. He felt morbidly curious as he observed Clair speaking with the Duke of Ghent and her aunt. She was a vision in her deep bronze gown of pale silk with tiny satin roses of green interspersed among the bodice and sleeves. Her hair was pulled into a sleek topknot with only a few curls left down to grace her face. The style showed off not only her delicate features but also the elegant lines of her neck. Asher felt his pulse quicken and the fiery rush of hunger.

Ian snorted. "Not exactly." Then he smiled at Clair, his features fierce with pride and possession. "But she will."

This time, Asher was the one who snorted. "You have your work cut out for you, Huntsley. That woman has a mind of her own."

Ian shook his head. "What's mine, I keep. And make no mistake, come heaven or hell, Clair Frankenstein is mine."

"A threat?" Asher's tone held both amusement and contempt.

"You concede graciously?" Ian was shocked.

Asher nodded. "I am many things, but not blind. She loves you. Not a particularly bright choice, I am thinking. Especially since she could have had my superior personage."

"Well, I'll be bloody deuced and damned! You're in love with her too." Ian felt flabbergasted.

"An unfortunate occurrence, I can assure you. It certainly wasn't in my plan."

His mind spinning, his fists clenched, Ian glared at the master vampire who stood so tall, elegant, and handsome. He was furious that Asher loved Clair. Clair was *his* true love and his territory. But at the same time, Ian's common sense told him that Clair was safe from any threat from Asher or his nest. Asher would fight to the death to protect Clair, just as Ian himself would. "Then she is safe from all threats," he muttered, speaking his thoughts aloud.

Arching an eyebrow, Asher glanced at Clair. "She is safe from all threats," he repeated. "However, I do reserve the right to wring her pretty neck if she doesn't stop snooping about the place. I have had a bloody hard time not stepping on her while she searched my house on her spy mission. She's like an albatross about my neck."

Ian chuckled. "That's my girl. But have no fear. After she attends your ball tomorrow night and sees you hale and hearty on two legs—not on four and snarling at her—your problem is solved. She will admit she has been wrong in her deductions and leave you alone."

"Alas, both a pleasure and a penance."

Before Asher could say more, Lady Montcrief arrived, escorted by a reluctant Galen. Ian's cousin had seen Ian's stiff stance and realized by the tense expression on Asher's face that the conversation was one filled with danger. Galen had also deduced that the conversation was about Clair.

Lady Montcrief, ignoring the volatile atmosphere, tapped her fan on Galen's arm and stopped before the earl and Ian. Her beauty was like that of a coral snake—shiny and colorful, but deadly to the touch, Galen saw. He watched her bat her eyes at both men, interrupting their conversation, and smiled greedily.

"Such a luscious contrast. Night and day. Sin and sinful," she remarked, licking her lips and looking them both over like horses at Tattersalls. Then, turning toward Galen, she added, "And noon. You are the midday sun, all glorious in its splendor."

Galen acknowledged her words with a brief tilt of his head, disliking the woman behind the obsequious comment.

Ian stared stonily at her, wondering what he had ever seen in the blowsy brunette. He'd once had a brief affair with her. "If you'll excuse me now," he said, turning and leaving with his cousin at his side. He and Galen quickly crossed the room to where Clair was standing with Ozzie and Lady Mary.

Asher was thinking much along the same lines as Ian and Galen, unbeknownst to Lady Montcrief. On and off, he and Jeanette Montcrief had enjoyed each other's charms for the past five years. A new addition to the nest, she had been a tasty distraction for a time. But the thrill was gone, the flame of attraction burned away to mere ashes.

"I seem to have driven the rakish baron away," Lady

Montcrief said, her eyes glaring with undisguised hatred at Ian.

"Perhaps," Asher commented. He regarded Ian and Clair, Ian's possessive hand on the small of her back. "But I rather think he was running *to* something. In fact, I think he has been unknowingly looking for something to run to for years."

Lady Montcrief sniffed disdainfully. "Whatever can he see in the chit? She's so common. Too pale in her looks and much too mannish in her studies."

"Careful, Jeanette," Asher retorted coolly. "Your claws are showing."

Lady Montcrief turned and placed a well-manicured hand on his arm. "I can scarcely wait for tonight. My body is throbbing for that big, delicious prick of yours to be buried deep inside me."

Asher withdrew his arm from her grasping fingers and gave her a chilly smile. "The night's not done, and my desire is not yet settled on any one *lady*." He emphasized the last word.

Lady Montcrief caught the insult and would have returned his icy contempt with a blistering setdown had the earl not glided so quickly away.

Her face frozen in a mask of polite civility, she hurried over to a small group of men. She motioned to Christopher Wilder with a discreet gesture, then started for the balcony. Wilder followed, a leer on his delicate, cruel features.

He met her outside, his expression curious. "Well?"

"Something must be done about that Frankenstein cow!" Lady Montcrief said without any preface.

"Hmm. Yes, her." He paused deliberately. "Her udders are mouthwatering. I thought to try them myself. I wonder if Frankenstein blood is somehow different from other mortals'."

"What utter rot! She's nothing! A pretentious little nobody who thinks she is smart," Lady Montcrief hissed, her catlike brownish yellow eyes turning a deep cherry red.

Staring into her eyes, Wilder quipped, "And I thought *green* was the color of jealousy."

"I am not jealous, you twit. I am merely concerned. She is dangerous to us all, poking that silly nose of hers into things better left alone. Though I grant she is not totally stupid. She could still stumble onto our secrets. Look how close she came to discovering what you and I were doing that night at your house. A few more minutes and my face would have been quite red."

Studying her, he smiled lasciviously. "Yes. Her timing was most unlucky. I was quite overset about it. In fact, Asher and I have discussed the Frankenstein chit for that reason more than once. He, however, assures me that she will be no problem to our nest or race," he went on, his expression bland. He held his breath, waiting to see what Lady Montcrief would do. If he could get her to commit to the removal of the unwanted Clair, that would be all the better.

"She must be gotten rid of as quickly as possible."

Wilder shook his head, his blond curls jiggling. "Asher would be most displeased. Fatally displeased, I am afraid."

Lady Montcrief drew in a sharp breath. "It hasn't gone that far, has it? He hasn't bedded the bitch yet."

Wilder shrugged. "Who knows? You know how private Asher is when he chooses. But I agree, the girl has got to be disposed of in a manner not leading to our front door."

"Tomorrow night," Lady Montcrief advised, calculating all the problems involved with draining and disposing of Clair's body.

Wilder shook his head. "You're mad. What about Huntsley and his cousin McBain? They won't let anything happen to her."

Lady Montcrief laughed. "Ian will be long gone to his estate in Yorkshire, called away by some emergency, I predict. I feel quite sure Galen will follow like the dutiful cousin he is."

Thinking, Wilder conceded that she was right. At times the grasping Lady Montcrief was quite brilliant. But, "That still leaves Asher."

"I will keep Asher occupied while you do the deed."

"Oh no. That dog won't bite. Asher would suspect me right away. He knows I don't fancy the chit. *You'll* have to get rid of her."

As much as Lady Montcrief wanted Clair gone, she valued her own slender neck too much to expose it to Asher's biting rage. Frustrated, she stamped her tiny foot. "Point conceded." If Wilder wouldn't do her dirty work, she would find someone else who would. Someone she could point the finger at afterward without endangering herself. "The cow will be safe for now."

Her temper momentarily cooled, she reached over and scratched Wilder's chest, tearing his shirt. Her fingernails were needle-sharp, drawing a thin line of blood. Hungrily she lifted up on her tiptoes and began to lick at the midnight snack. "Delicious."

Wilder's body leapt to attention. Regretfully he pushed her away, hearing laughter close by. "You know Asher's rules about eating in front of his guests."

Licking her lips dramatically, she nodded. "I know

only too well. Not in front of humans *or* werewolves. And don't snack on the humans. He can be so frightfully stiff-necked at times."

"True," Wilder agreed, fixing his coat over the tear in his shirt as he led her back into the music room. His quick eyes noted Asher talking with Mrs. Walling, a striking older woman who was a widow, if Wilder remembered correctly.

His gaze settled next on his nemesis Clair and on Huntsley. They were standing in a corner, chatting cozily with the aunt and the Duke of Ghent, who also appeared totally intent upon one another. Wilder shuddered. Birds of a sodding feather, he thought grimly.

Across the room, Ian caught Christopher Wilder's look of revulsion, but he dismissed it as Clair gently touched his shoulder.

"It has been a delightful evening with the most enchanting company. A memory to cherish," Ozzie, the Duke of Ghent, pronounced gallantly as he gazed in fascination at Lady Mary.

Again Clair nudged Ian, her smile blinding as she nodded to Ozzie. Her plan to place her aunt and the duke together was working perfectly. The elder couple were cooing at each other like lovebirds.

"Yes, it has," Mary replied softly, her pink cheeks becoming crimson. "But I think it is time for us to retire." She directed the last words to Clair, her look indicating several other ladies who were taking their leave.

Glancing around, Clair quickly assessed the diminishing number of guests. She acquiesced with a quick movement of her chin.

"I know the hour is late, but if you please, Lady Mary, I would like a few more minutes of Clair's time," Ian requested as he smiled charmingly at Clair's aunt. "I'll see her to your rooms."

Lady Mary nodded and turned to Ozzie, who proudly escorted her from the room.

Clair's eyes were bright with unshed tears as she watched them leave. "Oh, Ian. Isn't it wonderful? I do believe there is a touch of May in the winter air."

"You said they were in love once. I believe it's a flame that never died," Ian observed. "How would you feel if your aunt married?"

Clair laughed merrily and clasped his hands, the sound like the tinkling of bells. "Like it was Christmas. I love her so much. From the time I can first remember, Mary has been mother, friend, and teacher all rolled into one. She deserves to be happy."

Thinking over her words, she corrected her statement. "Actually, we have been very happy in the Frankenstein household. But Ozzie would give my aunt a joy beyond that." She frowned, trying to refine her thoughts. "Like with fresh strawberries, my favorite. I so love them. But when I add cream, fresh strawberries become even more tasty."

Ian chuckled. "I understand. And what of your own strawberries and cream?" he asked, steering the conversation to a more personal bent. This was the topic dearest to his heart.

"Cream?"

"Marriage."

"Oh, I do believe Ozzie will propose to Aunt Mary."

Ian shook his head. "*Our* marriage, Clair. The marriage that should take place as quickly as I can get you to an altar."

Placing a hand against his chest, she warned, "Ian, we

have been through this. I love you, but I can't believe we should wed unless you embrace my studies and accept that they are as much a part of me as the color of my eyes. I won't give up my research."

"Clair, it's not that I mind your research or work, though heaven knows you would never have to work with my fortune. It's the manner of research you undertake. It's too dangerous. I would worry about you all the time." She started to protest, but he held up a hand, stalling her. "Just like I worry now."

"You are being ridiculous. Nothing irreversible has ever happened to me on my forays into the supernatural. Besides, we can work together on my various projects."

Exasperated, Ian frowned. "I have my estates. Look how busy I've been the past few days on small emergencies that spring up from nowhere. And soon you'll be busy with our children." His frown went away at the thought of making babies with Clair.

The look in his eye shouted, "Let's get naked." Quickly, Clair dropped her hand from his chest, taking a step backward. "It's late. Auntie will be worried. I need to go upstairs to bed."

"Without me," he snapped. Then, seeing the irritated look in her eyes, he added sincerely, "I'm sorry. I just want you so badly. I can't wait until this bloody house party is over and I can get you alone and have my wicked way with you. Let me correct that. My wicked, wicked *ways* with you."

He wanted to tryst the night away in Clair's arms. He was cocksure about it. Yes, he thought grimly, *it* was certainly sure. Roaring and ready to go. All it took these days was for him to think about Clair and her plump white breasts. . . .

Clair stifled a groan as she presented her arm for him to escort her upstairs. She wanted to count every one of those wicked ways with her fingers. She had become a fornicating floozy. What a naughty thought! She arched a brow. Ian definitely had that kind of effect on her. Drat, it was going to be a long and very lonely night.

Ian sighed. So far Plan C was limping along on three legs. And bloody hell if it wasn't going to be a long wait until dawn. He kissed Clair chastely at her door and left, his breeches uncomfortably tight.

Clair went inside her room. Glancing around, she found no sign of movement. No sign of her aunt. She beamed, knowing just what her aunt was doing and with whom.

But . . . she and Ian had had little to no time alone together. Her aunt was probably going to be gone for a bit longer. Clair slipped quietly from her room.

Before she could reach the landing to the third floor, she heard suspicious giggles and the opening of a door. Glancing around her for somewhere to hide, she noticed a darkened nook under the stairwell. She slipped inside only moments before she spied the married Mr. Bear sneaking into Mrs. Walling's room, his chamber robe on, a garish creation of bright red. Next she saw Galen McBain lightly tapping on the newly widowed Lady Harringon's door, who was evidently not very bereaved.

She thought she could move out from her hiding place then, but before she could, Baron Golde with his bright golden locks craftily, like a thief in the night, entered Mrs. Edmonds's bedchamber. Then, as Clair was preparing to step out into the hallway again, she observed Lady Montcrief entering Mr. Wilder's room. Much to her disgust and surprise, the baron's wife, Lady

Golde, soon followed Lady Montcrief into the not-so-honorable Christopher Wilder's chamber.

"A ménage à trois?" Clair was fascinated and affronted at the same time. Soon, however, her scientific little brain was hard at work trying to figure out the angles and acrobatics needed to accomplish such a task. To manage to put one peg into two holes? The visual she constructed made her face turn beet red.

Turning her mind to her own rendezvous, she waited several more moments to make sure the coast was clear. Then she slipped up the staircase, only to nearly be caught by Mrs. Bear. The married lady was engaged in a passionate embrace with the also-married Viscount Edwards. The fact that the embrace was so lusty saved Clair from discovery as she silently darted behind a large Ming vase near the third-floor staircase. After several minutes of heavy petting and embarrassing noises, the couple slipped silently down the hallway and into one of the other guest rooms—probably Mrs. Bear's, Clair reasoned, since Mr. Edwards's room was occupied by Baron Golde and Mr. Edwards's wife.

Clair shook her head at all the bedroom antics. No wonder her aunt had always been so vehemently opposed to her and Arlene attending any house parties in the country. They were virtual dens of iniquity. In fact, she wondered, if she went back to her own room, if she would have to ask, "Who's been sleeping in my bed?"

Her head reeling, she went to step from behind the Ming vase just as her aunt stepped out of Ozzie's room. "Drat! Drat! And double drat!" she shouted silently. There would be none of Ian's loving tonight.

Luckily her aunt was distracted by Ozzie's sizzling kiss and hadn't spotted her. Carefully and quietly, Clair eased from behind the vase and tiptoed back to the stairs. It was lucky that people didn't have eyes in the backs of their heads, she thought. Then she remembered one of Uncle Victor's more dismal experiments. He had once implanted a second set of eyes in the back of an owl's head. The poor thing had gotten dreadfully confused as whether to fly forward or backward, and so the bird kept crashing into chandeliers.

Remembering where she was, Clair took off like greased lightning and slipped down the stairs to her room, barely getting her hair undone before her aunt entered. Both glanced at each other sheepishly. Each lost in their thoughts, they let silence reign.

Much later that night, the stillness was broken by a scream. Both Clair and Lady Mary would find out in the morning that it was Mr. Bear, who had found three to a bed more than a little uncomfortable. Yes, Mr. Bear had found out who was sleeping in his bed: Baron Golde. And it hadn't been, "Just right."

See No Werewolf,
Hear No Werewolf

The day went exceedingly fast for Clair. Breakfast was embarrassing, as Clair sat down next to Baron Golde and his wife, as well as several other participants in the night's bedroom antics. Clair ate quickly, a blush on her face through most of the meal.

At breakfast she was informed that Asher had been called away on estate business, while the Honorable Christopher Wilder, the Bears, Lady Montcrief, and several others were going on some scouting expedition to some old ruins. That left Clair free to search the manor, except Ian kept her busy until late after luncheon, trying to whisk her away to private spots for private moments.

Her aunt, however, had the tenacity of a blood-hound, finding them before anything more than a passionate kiss or two could be shared. Ozzie trailed behind her aunt like a lost puppy. Galen, never one to be left out of any teasing of his cousin, also popped in on them right at any moment the two found themselves alone. The crafty bugger always had a big smirk on his face, and Ian cursed beside her. Clair found it both humorous and frustrating.

Later in the day, Clair finally got to begin her search for proof of the earl's preternatural abilities, for Ian got an urgent message from his Yorkshire estate. Fortunately for Ian, the estate was only four hours away on horseback. Unfortunately for Clair, Ian would have to miss the country ball the earl was holding in his guests' honor.

Ian kissed her goodbye, warned her to be careful, and promised to return as quickly as possible the following morning. He waved as he and Galen left. With both regret and relief, Clair watched him ride away.

Although sad, Ian's departure gave Clair the freedom she needed to explore the downstairs estate, which turned out a disappointment, with the exception of the cellars. Those she was unable to view since they were locked up tighter than a drum.

It turned out entirely a wasted day. She found no werewolf proof. No wolfman footprints, except for the wolfhound prints Clair had discovered earlier. She got no mad, passionate lovemaking. And her chaperone was only a chaperone until Ian left; then Mary went off on her merry way to pave her path to hell with desire. Clair thought all these things as she watched her aunt Mary and Ozzie walking along the terrace. Ozzie was holding her too close, and Mary was cooing at him.

"Traitor," Clair mused out loud. The way Aunt Mary

was gazing at Ozzie with heat in her eyes, and the way Ozzie was looking at her aunt, as though she were a seven-course meal or new recipe, it was more than obvious what the couple had been doing. They'd been frolicking and fornicating, while Clair had been forced to take a nap all by her lonesome.

"You sneaky little coquette," she muttered to herself about her aunt, a half smile on her face. "It's you who need the chaperone, Auntie." Clair stood alone by the balcony entrance, waiting for the earl to be announced. Glancing out the large crystal-cut windowpanes, she could see the soft white glow of the full moon. At least one thing would come from this dismal day. Tonight, when Asher didn't show up, she'd have her proof he was a werewolf. Werewolves had to change on the night of the full moon. It couldn't be helped.

Of course, she knew Asher would make up some lame excuse—like another emergency on the estate—for being absent. But it wouldn't matter. She would have more circumstantial evidence. During the next two full moons she would contrive to be around Asher and note he'd be once again not available. If she were very lucky, she might even get to see him shape-shift. What a thrill that would be, making her scientific day. Clair smiled beguilingly. She was getting closer to the truth. Fulfilling her Frankenstein destiny. She would join the greats such as Galileo, Newton, Darwin and her uncle Victor.

Her smile froze then turned to an open-mouthed O.

Asher grinned wolfishly at her as he walked down the large marble staircase. Gotcha! he thought gleefully as he made his bow to her.

"You're not a . . ." Clair stopped herself before blurting out the *w*-word.

"A what?" Asher's expression was amused. He had never seen Clair so stumped before.

"A . . . a . . . a-afraid of wearing that hue of burgundy for an evening jacket. How refreshing, since most of the men here are dressed in somber black or those garish colors yellow and green," Clair said in a rush.

"Drat! Drat, drat, and triple drat!" she muttered to herself. She had done it again—convinced herself that earls were werewolves and barons vampires, when in reality everyone was human and no one was a supernatural predator at all. What a huge disappointment she was to the Frankenstein name. There would be no prestigious Scientific Discovery of the Decade Award for her. No publication. No lecturing in front of her peers in the scientific halls of academia. What would Uncle Victor say? Bloody hell. What would Ian say? He would probably never let her live it down.

"My, you are fast on your feet," Asher commented. Seeing Clair's confusion, he grinned. "Ah. You were talking about fashion and here I thought you were talking about something else." Dropping her hand politely, he took a step back and glanced down at the deep burgundy of his coat. "I could change. Would you like to see me change?" He hesitated, enjoying Clair's chagrin. "Jackets, that is."

Flustered, she shook her head. "You look divine, as always." Clair's mind was racing, her angst receding somewhat as she tried to find explanations for her abominable lack of investigative skills.

"Humph!" she muttered, vowing to apprentice herself to Mr. Durlock Homes for a time and learn his superior investigation skills. Asher preened a moment, then entered the receiving line to greet his guests.

In a drat-I-can't-believe-he's-not-a-werewolf depression, Clair strolled outside, taking the large stone stairway leading from the terrace down to the gardens. The air was crisp and the soft white orb of the full moon nestled into the velvety black sky. It shone down, highlighting the lush green foliage of the garden.

Strolling down a path at the edge, Clair kept thinking about her mistakes. Ian the vampire was not a vampire. Wilder the vampire was not a vampire. Ozzie the warlock was not a wizard. And Asher the werewolf was not a wolf. How could she have been so wrong? Where had her hypotheses gone awry? What fatal steps had she taken in her research that led her to this once-again humiliating moment in time?

And who was making that whimpering sound?

Alert, Clair hurried up the path farther into the deep shadows made by the trees along the side. Someone was in trouble. A female, by the sound of the cry.

Stumbling into a small opening between the hedges, Clair came upon a scene straight from one of those horror novellas, the ones which were much more fictionalized than her uncle Tieck's novel. She blinked, gasped, then blinked again, trying to understand what she was seeing.

The red-haired maid whom Asher's butler had assigned to Clair was draped over one of Christopher Wilder's arms, her bare neck exposed. Blood was flowing from a wound on her neck. The maid was crying, her arms beating to no avail against Wilder's chest.

Turning, his gaze malevolent, Wilder bared his fangs, and his eyes glowed with an otherworldly light.

"Bloody hell!" Clair cursed, unconsciously using one of Ian's favorite phrases. "You *are* a vampire. I was right! Right!"

For one small second Clair wanted to dance with joy, until the reality of her situation came crashing down upon her. She was alone with a fang-baring, blood-drinking killer!

The maid's cry interrupted her thoughts. No, Clair wasn't alone, and she had to do something to save the maid. She reached up to touch her silver cross, only to remember she hadn't worn it to the house party, since she had been hunting werewolves and not the walking dead.

Quickly discarding her plan to back the vampire away from the maid by clutching a cross, Clair settled on another scheme. Grabbing a thick fallen branch, she charged Wilder and swung it at the vampire's head. As plans went, she would later realize, this was doomed to failure.

Wilder grabbed the branch with one hand, still holding on to the maid. Behind her, Clair heard a hiss that made the blood curdle in her veins.

"Well, bloody hell," she muttered. She had wanted to find a nest of them, and she had. Leaping away from Wilder, she turned to find herself face to face with an enraged Lady Montcrief. Her face Clair would long remember, with its glistening incisors smiling in satisfaction.

"You're mine, bitch," Lady Montcrief laughed, her tone sharp as nails. "Tonight, you die!"

"You won't get away with murdering me, you blood-sucking witch! Ian will hunt you down and stake you like you deserve," Clair vowed, her face pale with fear. Lady Montcrief was evil incarnate, and Wilder wasn't much better. She had been right, in a manner of speaking. She supposed they could write that on her tombstone: *She got most of the facts wrong, but she was right at least once. It killed her.*

"You can't kill her. Asher will be livid," Mr. Bear said, appearing, slurring slightly due to the length of his fangs. They were extremely long, Clair noted in an abstractly terrified, rational manner.

She agreed with him wholeheartedly. Meeting Mr. Bear last night at the dinner party, she had found him rather insipid and stupid. Tonight, he was a genius. "He's right! Asher will be upset!"

Lady Montcrief snarled, her fangs lengthening even more. As Clair stared in fascination, she realized fearfully that there were many ways to die. And half of those were here in the garden with her, where death was sitting on his pale horse in the guise of Lady Montcrief and her nasty friends.

A thump to Clair's left caught her attention. Wilder had dropped the unconscious maid on the ground, coming to stand next to Mr. Bear. His canny eyes watched Clair hungrily. "We have no choice, Bear. She knows too much now. But I want to play with her first."

Clair shuddered. Revulsion was thick in her voice when she challenged him. "In a pig's eye!"

Mr. Bear looked worried as he glanced from Wilder to Clair and then back again. "You're drunk on blood lust, Christopher. You're not thinking clearly. Asher will be very angry if you kill his honey pot." Pointing a finger at Lady Montcrief, Mr. Bear added, "And you're just jealous of the chit."

"And you're afraid of Asher," Lady Montcrief hissed scathingly. "You want to be master of our little nest, but you're too afraid to challenge him."

Bear shrugged. "Asher's too strong. I won't beat a dead pony, Jeanette. I still think it's a grave mistake to kill her. Mesmerize her instead."

Lady Montcrief turned her fiery red eyes on Mr. Bear. Their heat was almost physical as she growled, "She knows too much. We can't take the chance. Asher will understand. Besides, the Frankensteins are a queer lot. None of their descendants can be mesmerized. We have no choice. Humans are a devious race, and this one," she added with loathing, "this one is more devious than most. She alone knew of our nest. She knows what Wilder is. She even accused me, the accursed bitch!"

Seeing the vampires concentrating on each other, Clair began backing away, wishing she had her lucky rabbit's foot. Wishing Ian were there. Wishing she had told him she would marry him. Wishing Frederick were around. Her uncle. Brandon Van Helsing with his Van Helsing stakes. What a horrendous night! She was all dressed up and waiting to be bitten and sucked to death by a pack of vicious, immoral vampires.

As Clair moved, Lady Montcrief grabbed her and jerked her up close and personal. Using all her strength, Clair shoved back and screamed for everything she was worth. It was a long shot, but it was the only shot she had: the vampires' strength was much greater than hers.

Lady Montcrief quickly yanked Clair back by the roots of her hair. "I'm going to so enjoy draining all your pretty blood. Then, when I'm finished, I'm going to chop you into little pieces and feed them to Asher's wolfhounds."

Clair jammed her thumbs into Lady Montcrief's eyes, a diversionary tactic she'd read about that actually worked.

"Damn you to hell, you stupid vixen!" Lady Montcrief screeched. "You'll pay," she glowered as she slapped at Clair blindly, a blow which sent Clair reeling.

Through the roaring in her head, Clair heard Asher's voice. "Jeanette, how many times have I told you not to play with your food?" His sounded like the voice of doom.

Clair lifted her head and then quickly had to lay it back down. She felt as if she had a concussion. She blinked and turned her head to the side just as Asher knocked Lady Montcrief a good five feet across the clearing.

Clair blinked, then blinked again as Asher snarled, exposing long white fangs, hissing at Wilder, who was now crouched and ready to attack. She wanted to sink into unconsciousness. She was an idiot. Asher was not a werewolf pretending to be a man. No, he was a *vampire* pretending to be a man. The master vampire. The leader of the London nest. And she, Clair Frankenstein, was a bona fide idiot. She'd had it all so right and all so wrong.

A scream of pain caught her attention. It was Wilder. Despite the pain in her head, Clair raised herself to her elbows, lifting her head. She had to help Asher, since he was fighting to save her life.

Wilder was pinned to the ground, and Asher had the younger vampire by the throat. "Look out," Clair managed, as she helplessly watched Lady Montcrief hit her protector with a piece of iron fencing.

Out of the corner of her eye, she saw Mr. Bear and managed to whisper, "Help him."

To her despair, Mrs. Bear appeared, fangs long and wicked-looking. Together Mrs. Bear and her husband also attacked Asher.

"No!" Clair shrieked before she began sinking into darkness. Snarling, hissing and growling sounds swarmed all around her.

Suddenly, from a great dark distance, she heard Lady Montcrief and Mrs. Bear scream, and then Wilder's curses turned to awful gurgling sounds. Then Clair knew no more, for the world went utterly black.

Clair and Mary, Quite Contrary, How Does the Vampire Go?

"My head aches," Clair muttered. "Too much port after dinner." Her head nestled on the downy pillow, she struggled to come fully awake. "No. I was attacked by a vampire." With a gasp, she recalled that it was two vampires, to be exact.

She moaned, slowly opening her eyes. It was still night. Candles lit the bedchamber, casting shadows on the wall. One silhouette was of her aunt Mary, sitting with her head against the back of an armchair, and her gentle snores were a quiet comfort to Clair. The next silhouette was Asher's. He was seated on her left. Reflecting a weariness of both soul and body, his face was scratched in several places and his left arm was in a sling.

"You're awake," he said quietly.

"You saved my life." Clair's eyes showed her gratitude.

He nodded solemnly.

"The maid?"

"I imagine she's a trifle anemic, but she'll live. I had to erase her memory of the night, however," he replied, watching Clair closely, his pale eyes grim.

"You're a vampire," Clair whispered, wonder in her voice. "And all this time I thought you were a werewolf. What a bacon-brain I am."

"The Wolverton name can be misleading," he said with a smile.

"Yes. It can." She didn't know whether to be embarrassed by her faux pas of mistaken supernatural identities or excited by this, the start of her great scientific discovery. "What happened to Mr. and Mrs. Bear, Mr. Wilder, and Lady Montcrief?"

"Wilder and the Bears are dead," Asher said, a hint of regret in his voice. "Not just undead, but really dead."

"You killed them to save me?" Clair's expression was both solemn and grateful. She smiled sadly. "My vampire in shining armor."

Asher shook his head. "I had help."

"Who?"

"Ian and Galen," the vampire answered reluctantly.

"Where is he? Is he hurt? Was Galen? Oh no! Ian must be dreadfully hurt to not be here with me." Clair weakly tried to rise from the bed, but she fell back with a soft moan as dizziness engulfed her. If Ian died, a part of her would go with him. And she would *kill* him.

Asher patted her hand. "Calm down, Clair. Huntsley's not badly hurt. Neither is his cousin." Asher ached to hear the worry in her voice and to see the tears of relief in her eyes when she realized Ian was all right. "He's cleaning up the mess. Wouldn't do for the other guests to find dead vampires—truly dead vampires—lying around the place." He wiped a tear from her cheek. "It will be dawn in a few hours. I have much to tell you before I leave."

Clair reached up and held his hand. "You're going away?"

"Yes. The high council will need to hear about the details. It is forbidden by vampire law for those of our species to kill one another."

"Will you have to go before a judge and jury like a human trial?" she asked, concerned. "You shouldn't get in trouble for helping me."

He explained gently, "I will most probably only be fined, due to the circumstances. Lady Montcrief and Wilder were both hunting in my territory against my express wish, and they both intended to kill their meal."

"What happened to Lady Montcrief?"

"She's being punished."

Hearing the tone of Asher's voice, Clair, though curious as always, decided not to ask any more about her.

"When will you be back?"

"After the meetings with the council I have decided to take a brief trip to Paris. I have a friend there, a Mr. Bufet. I'm seeking answers to questions which have bothered me for some time."

"And I imagine you will drink fine wine, visit with old friends, and kiss a few pretty maids all in a row."

Asher chuckled. "Something like that. Now, listen. I need to tell you a few things."

And he did just that, patiently explaining why Clair's research couldn't be made public. He presented her with all the facts in a concise manner—solid reasons such as wide-spread panic, vampire hunts, and human deaths that could range in the thousands.

He told Clair how the high council had been formed over two hundred years earlier, a council which had required that vampires go virtually underground in the seventeenth century and forbade them to drain their victims dry in the eighteenth century. And that had all been in an effort to stop the vampire-human wars.

Asher explained how vampires, werewolves, warlocks, and other supernatural creatures were very territorial and clannish. They didn't mix much from species to species, except in desperate situations. Vampires, he explained haughtily, were at the top of the food chain, while werewolves were earthier and lacking in refinement. He informed her that aging warlocks had a tendency to go crazy due to all their researching of spells, but that they were regarded by vampires as necessary evils since they could work a bit of magic on a nest's enemies. And lastly, Asher reminded Clair that vampires needed to stay a myth, a scary story to tell late at night.

Through this entire astonishing tale, Aunt Mary slept the sleep of the innocent.

Reluctantly Clair agreed to Asher's request, giving her sworn vow to not publish her findings or talk of them with anyone outside her immediate family. It was a hard decision. The scientist in her was screaming "no," and the compassionate part of her was whispering "yes." She had no choice but to agree, she reflected thoughtfully. For her life, she owed Asher a debt of gratitude she could never repay.

As Asher stood to leave, he handed her a folded piece of paper. Then, tenderly, like the soft brush of a butterfly's wings, he kissed her lips for the last time. It was a kiss of love, she recognized sadly.

"If Huntsley doesn't treat you well, let me know. I'll

come, Clair. Wherever you are." And with one more lingering glance, he left on silent feet.

Clair opened his note, tilting it to see in the candlelight:

Every Night and every Morn
Some to Misery are born.
Every Morn and every Night
Some are born to Sweet Delight;
Some are born to Sweet Delight
Some are born to Endless Night.

Clair fell asleep before she could wipe away the single tear that rolled down her cheek.

The next time she awoke, night had faded. The early morning sun filtered in through the window. Clair felt the warmth of someone's hand squeezing hers tightly, like a lifeline. That warmth gave her a sense of peace. It was Ian, and he was gazing at her with all the love in his heart. His fortress of solitude had crumbled and to his island there was a bridge.

Ever so tenderly, he leaned close and rested his forehead against hers. "Oh God, Clair. I was so worried."

Galen leaned against the far wall, a weary smile on his face. His arm was in a sling.

Clair smiled briefly at Galen; then she tenderly stroked Ian's cheek with her hand. "Asher said you got hurt. How badly?"

"Some bruising, and I took a deep cut to my thigh. But I'll be fine in a day or two."

"Asher said you and Galen helped rescue me." Clair cradled his cheek in her hand. "Thank you, Ian. Galen."

Ian's cousin nodded briefly, embarrassed by the warm sincerity of her praise. "Now that Sleeping Beauty is awake, I think I will go and have a spot of breakfast," he said.

"Thanks, Galen," Ian replied, adding his own heart-felt gratitude.

Galen shrugged and left the room.

Clair turned her attention back to her true love. "I'm sorry I don't remember what happened after Lady Mont-crief slapped me. I can't believe a lady can hit that hard."

"The bitch is a vampire. She could have killed you with that slap."

Ian's features were grim, his eyes burning with a fierce light. Clair had never seen such raw rage.

"When I saw you there . . . God, Clair, I thought you were dead. I felt like somebody reached inside my chest and ripped out my heart." He gathered her into his arms. "Don't ever do that to me again," he scolded. "You can't die on me. Promise."

Studying his beloved face, his deep green eyes glistening with unshed tears, she nodded, awed. "My darling," she said, hugging him back, "I love you too."

He released her, sitting back down in his chair. "Asher was your vampire."

"I know."

Glancing at the open note on the end table by her bed, he added solemnly, "He's in love with you."

"I realize that too."

"And?" Ian asked, his fists clenching and unclenching.

"I respect Asher. But I respect and *love* you. Forever." It made her feel good to know that Ian was so concerned about her well-being. He was part of her destiny. And that was a miracle.

Ian brought her hand to his lips, gently turning it over and kissing her palm. "Marry me, Clair. Now. Today. I can't bear to lose you. I don't care anymore about your research. If you want to work on your paranormal theories, I won't complain as long as you're with me."

"About the research . . ." Clair tried to explain.

"I'll support whatever you do."

"About the vampire study—I got most of it wrong," she admitted, looking forlorn.

Ian took pity on her. "You were right about Wilder from the start," he reminded her.

"Yes, I was. But then I decided I wasn't. And Asher wasn't a werewolf. And I didn't even suspect Lady Montcrief or those horrible Bears—although I did think Mr. Bear had terrible taste in whom he let into his bed," she added thoughtfully.

Ian gave her a hug. "Clair, anyone can make a mistake. I'm sure that on your next project, your spectacular research will astonish us all."

"You're trying to placate me," she accused.

"Is it working?" Ian asked with an incorrigible grin.

She touched his hand, needing to tell him that she had promised Asher to give up her vampire thesis. And after seeing injuries to both herself and Ian, she'd decided vampire sleuthing was just too dangerous. Wisely, she decided to add werewolves to the mix of what to avoid. "Ian, about my research—"

He interrupted. "I told you it was fine with me. Do whatever you want, as long as you'll be my wife."

Regretfully she explained, "I can't reveal what I know about vampires. Asher revealed much to me. But it's too dangerous letting the human world know that theirs and the supernatural world coexist side by side."

Ian nodded. "No prestigious award?" he asked.

"I guess not. All my big dreams," Clair said. She hesitated, gazing at Ian, wondering why she didn't feel worse. Then, suddenly, a big grin split her face as she realized a fundamental truth. "*You* are my award, the only prestigious and precious award I need."

Ian could scarcely believe her words, but the truth was there for him to see, shining in Clair's eyes. "I love you, Clair Frankenstein," he repeated. "Marry me."

On the other side of the bed, Clair's aunt, who had slept through Asher's confessions and Ian's vow of love, awakened at the word "marry."

"Marriage!" Lady Mary trilled. "How perfectly divine, and such a surprise! Truly, a marvelous surprise. We'll have the wedding at St. George's Cathedral in three months. That will give me long enough to plan the wedding." Giving Ian a hard look, the woman added, "And you, young man, stay out of my niece's bed. I'll have no six-month wonder baby to present to my friends."

Clair choked as Ian matched her aunt look for look.

"I hate to disappoint you, Lady Mary, but I am getting a special license. Clair and I will be married in three days."

His statement got Lady Mary's back up. She puffed out like a bantam rooster. "That cock won't crow, young man. You'll be married in two months with four hundred of our closest friends invited to the wedding."

No, Ian thought, this cock won't crow, but it will stand to attention. There was no way he was waiting two months to have Clair back in his bed. "One week," he bartered.

"I haven't said yes," Clair interjected. Neither Ian nor her aunt paid her any attention.

Lady Mary ran on like a train on a one-way track, butting heads with the equally stubborn baron. "Seven weeks and not a day sooner. Victor and Frederick must come to London, and Frederick must get some new clothes. He takes forever to outfit, you know."

Ian rolled his eyes. Just what he needed, a monster and a quack at his wedding. "They can wear what they have on," he grumped.

"Poppycock." Lady Mary snorted indelicately. "Pure poppycock. Whoever heard of the bride having no one to give her away? And a Frankenstein bride at that!" She was indomitable, her family stubbornness rising to the occasion. "Clair will need a dress befitting the grand occasion," she went on, "and she will, of course, wear the Frankenstein veil. It has been handed down from bride to bride for over two hundred years."

Ian heard Clair moan. Surprised, he patted her hand.

Clair's moan wasn't from pain, but from disbelief. The Frankenstein veil was a curse. It was so ugly, no self-respecting bride could possibly want to wear the hideous thing.

Oblivious to all but her wedding plans, Lady Mary continued. "I, of course, will wear a light shade of blue, I believe. It will take the dressmaker quite a while to sew all the little flowers I will need on my gown."

Ian was not to be outmatched by the feisty little Tartar, even if he was surprised by her suddenly crotchety attitude. She was actually quite contrary when crossed. He wondered if Ozzie knew this less-than-attractive side to Lady Mary's character. "Ten days," he offered.

Tugging on Ian's arm, Clair once again tried to gain his attention. "I haven't said yes."

Lady Mary was just as determined as Ian, and she intended to gain the time she needed to plan the wedding of the century. Her plan had worked out, after all; she deserved to benefit from it. "Six weeks," she suggested.

Clair yanked on Ian's arm again. "I haven't said yes!" she shouted.

However, no one was paying the least attention.

"*Two* weeks," Ian bargained, his expression blank. It was his poker face. And though these stakes were high, he wasn't bluffing. And he was sure he would win. Though his Plans A and B had failed miserably, his Plan C had been a success. He was finally marrying Clair.

"Five weeks."

Ian shook his head. Clair's aunt was a Trojan, standing firmly against his formidable Huntsley will.

"One month. It is my last offer," Lady Mary said. Inside, she was beaming. She had the crafty baron cornered. One month was what she had wanted all along. One month to plan the wedding. It was enough time for her to get everything ready, and also a short enough spell in case Clair was already with child.

Ian nodded, shrewdly judging his opponent's joy. "You win, Lady Mary. One month."

"I haven't said I'd marry anyone!" Clair shouted for the umpteenth time.

In perfect unison, both Ian and her aunt turned to stare at her, both arching their aristocratic brows and making her feel like a child. Then, without further ado, they went back to discussing the wedding plans.

Clair would have stomped her foot if she could have gotten out of bed. She would have yelled some more, but she was so tired. She would just sleep a little and then argue with these two impossible idiots afterward. She had to admit, they were idiots she loved.

She fell asleep before Ian's tender kiss, and so she missed all the discussion of her wedding. Thus she ended up wearing the Frankenstein veil, that veil guaranteed to make any bride cranky. When she woke, she would put it all in an update to her friend:

Dear Jane,

I wasn't speaking to Ian, but now I am again. In fact, I am in love with him! We went to a house party at the Earl of Wolverton's where I had hoped to get the evidence I needed to prove my hypotheses. Unfortunately, I almost got myself and Ian killed. The Honorable Christopher Wilder—who was not so honorable—is now quite dead. Truly dead and not just undead, for he was a vampire. So were Mr. Bear and his wife, along with Lady Montcrief. Aren't you glad you weren't at this house party with all these vampires? Imagine the stakings your father would have required!

Anyway, the Earl of Wolverton is not a werewolf and Ian is wonderful. Have I told you that before? I am in love, and we are to be married.

Oh, and the Duke of Ghent is really a chef, not a warlock, and he wishes he wasn't a duke. He is courting Aunt Mary. Isn't that marvelous? He was once a suitor for my aunt, before he had to marry into a great deal of money. Well, he didn't actually marry the money, he married the heiress who had the money.

I wish you to attend the wedding—my wedding to Ian, not Aunt Mary to the duke. Although they may marry in the not-so-distant future. The wedding is in four weeks. (My wedding.)

With fondest affection,
Clair

P.S. Great-aunt Abby is giving me the city of Alexandria as my wedding gift. Yes, I knew you'd understand.

P.P.S. I am also being forced to wear the Frankenstein family wedding veil. Each night I am leaving it in the attic unwrapped, in hope that large rats will take a liking to the hideous thing and eat it. Wish me luck!

The Wedding Bell Blues

Today was the day! Her greatest triumph. Her niece would be getting married in a matter of five hours, and Lady Mary rejoiced as she hurried down the staircase. Her bouncy steps made a pattering sound on the marbled stairs.

Today of all days, all things must go according to plan. Mentally checking her list, Lady Mary noted that Clair's wedding gown was ready, as was Abby's French gown, since Abby believed herself to be Marie Antoinette, the deceased queen of Louis the Sixteenth, this week.

The church was decorated with stuffed doves and lovebirds, courtesy of Lady Mary, of course. And the chapel was fair to overflowing with orange blossoms, jasmine, and gardenias. It was a visual as well as olfactory feast.

Now all she had to do, Lady Mary knew, was get Victor out of his lab—a major feat in itself—and find Frederick, who had been celebrating rather heavily the previous night with the groom's cronies. Shaking her head, Lady Mary hoped that Frederick was getting his required eight hours of beauty sleep, which he most certainly needed.

On her way to her brother's lab, she ran into Brooks. The butler politely handed her an envelope from Jane Van Helsing.

Opening the envelope and reading the brief letter inside, Lady Mary frowned. Jane was not going to be able to make the ceremony. Poor girl, Lady Mary commiserated. Going to Holland to care for her injured aunt and then coming down with the measles—as if Jane didn't have enough on her plate already, being one of those eccentric Van Helsings. How Jane survived in that family of vampire-hunting lunatics, Lady Mary would never understand. Fortunately, she herself was a Frankenstein and removed from such things.

Glancing back up at Brooks, she asked, "Do you know where Frederick is?"

"In the library, asleep on the floor," Brooks replied, stonefaced.

"He's bosky, is he?" Lady Mary asked, shaking her head. "Well, I suppose boys will be boys—or in this case, monsters will be boys."

Brooks looked heavenward, beseeching. Employed for over thirty years with the Frankensteins, he often wondered how he had remained sane.

"How late was he out?" Mary asked. "And can he be made to sober up before the wedding?"

Brooks replied, "He arrived home around four this morning, singing about graveyards and monster balls."

Lady Mary raised her hands to her eyes. Of all the days for Frederick to be nursing a hangover! He would be very cranky when he awoke, and a cranky monster was usually one to avoid.

Brooks leaned in closer to her, confiding, "Master Frederick was with that bell-ringing fellow from Notre Dame last evening."

"Heavens," Lady Mary exclaimed. "That fellow is mad as a hatter. Running around bell towers and swinging on ropes!"

Suitably satisfied that Lady Mary would put the blame square on the humpbacked shoulder where it belonged, Brooks sniffed disdainfully and added, "That bell-ringer fellow took your nephew to one of those places for Frederick impersonators who like to play cards. Unfortunately, one of the young gentlemen decided to try and attain Master Frederick's height with a pair of stilts, and he fell onto a stage where a person of suspect repute was singing. This enraged the singer, who threw a bottle of wine at the young gentleman and hit him on the head. Which upset that bell-ringing fellow, who grabbed up the singer and threw her over his shoulder, fleeing off into the night. Naturally Frederick and his impersonators were all asked to leave."

Brooks leaned in even closer, almost whispering to Lady Mary as if the walls had ears—which of course in the Frankenstein manor could well be true. "You know how Master Frederick feels about rejection."

Lady Mary patted the butler on the arm. "I know. Poor dear boy."

At the first appearance of the Frederick impersonators, Lady Mary had worried that her adoptive nephew would get a swelled head from all the attention being focused upon him. And that wouldn't do at all, since Frederick already wore a size-eleven hat. Instead, her nephew had grown more and more upset until Victor finally explained that the young gentlemen were seeking his approval. Victor's words had finally settled Frederick down, which was a good thing. A three-hundred-pound monster throwing a temper tantrum was not a pretty sight.

Brooks nodded regretfully.

"Well, there's nothing to be done for it now, Brooks. Let us leave him to sleep two hours more. Then please wake him up and be sure to give him my tisane for overindulgence," Lady Mary commanded. She peeped into the library. Inside, Frederick was sleeping as peacefully as a baby—well, as much of a baby as a six foot eight man with feet the size of Derbyshire could sleep. Mary smiled sweetly, noting that Brooks had gone to the stable and brought a horse blanket back to cover her nephew.

Studying Frederick, Lady Mary worried that he looked a tad greener then usual this morning. Her nephew really must have tied one on last evening.

She quietly closed the library door and, shaking her head, she headed in the direction of her brother's lab. Victor too would be behaving inappropriately, working on the morning of his sister's greatest achievement.

"Men," she mumbled as she made her way down the basement steps to Victor's laboratory. You couldn't live with them and you couldn't live with them. Of course, Ozzie might be the exception to the rule. Mary was certainly willing to find out.

Opening the door, she entered the lab to find her brother scribbling something in his large maroon journal. It was a book Victor Frankenstein was never without.

"Victor, Victor, do you know what day this is?" she asked pettishly.

"The eighteenth," her brother answered absentmindedly, continuing with his writing.

"Good. Now that we know the date, can you tell me what is *important* about this date?" Lady Mary jibed, her eyes narrowing as Victor continued scribbling.

"It should have worked perfectly," he grumbled. "Just perfectly. I used the right-sized corneas for the eyes. All the muscles and nerves were attached precisely. The patient could see just as clearly in the day as in the night," he muttered to himself.

Lady Mary sighed. Her brother was talking about his latest scientific work. He had taken the eyes of a jaguar and transplanted them into a blind man's eye sockets. The results had been remarkable. The blind man had not only been able to see perfectly well in the daytime, but he had gained uncanny night vision as well. But it appeared a glitch had been thrown into the wheels of the experiment, and Victor never handled glitches very well. In fact, Frederick had learned his temper-tantrumming from Victor, his adopted father.

"The last time we spoke, your patient was doing incredibly well. What has happened, Victor?" Lady Mary asked worriedly. Her brother's transplant operations could give hope to so many.

Her brother raised his head wearily. "Side effects. Who would have thought a jaguar's genes would be so similar to those of an ordinary house cat? Every time my patient sees a mouse, he chases it about the room, then tries to scale the drapes."

"Oh, dear. That is unfortunate."

"It gets worse. He wants milk for every meal and has

the unfortunate tendency to groom himself by licking his arms and hands."

"Yes," Lady Mary conceded, "I can see how that would be a great disadvantage at a dinner party. You can't have your guests licking themselves at the table."

"Quite," Victor agreed morosely.

Lady Mary leaned over and patted her brother's arm. "You'll correct the problem. Perhaps you can give your blind patients the eyes of owls. They have remarkably clear sight."

"Hmm?" Victor managed, his forehead creased in thought. "Hmm," he said again. "It might just work." He thought some more, looked momentarily hopeful, but that look was soon replaced with a crestfallen expression. "Owls wouldn't groom themselves at dinner parties, true, but there is still the mousing side effect."

"Oh dear, you're quite right." Lady Mary paused; then, leaning over to look her brother in the eye, she asked archly, "Victor—besides the eighteenth, do you know what day this is?"

Her brother focused, truly focused, on her words, and his eyes widened in recognition. "Good grief. It's Clair's wedding day to that baron fellow!"

Good! Lady Mary rejoiced. She had finally gotten through to her brother. "Yes. And you need to prepare yourself for the ceremony. After all, you are giving the bride away." And with those words, Lady Mary burst into tears. She had just realized for the first time that her niece would be leaving the Frankenstein home—the niece whom she had loved like a daughter, whom she had raised since Clair was four.

Mary remembered the first frog Clair had tried to make fly after attaching paper wings to its back. Gri-

macing slightly, she also recalled the frog's rather igno-
minious landing, after it was dropped from the top of
the house. Clair had been in tears and never again tried
to get any creature to fly unless its wings were already
built in by nature. Lady Mary would never forget her
niece's horrified expression as the frog fell thirty feet
and made a terrible splat.

What if the baron didn't treat her beloved Clair
right? Mary wondered. What if he was the type to sip
brandy all night long? What if he had warts?

And would the baron leave Clair free to be her wonderful, inquisitive self after they were wed? Would he
cherish her forever? Would Clair ever come visit her old
aunt again? Would she ever see Clair's children? What
had she done by succeeding in her stupid Plan A, *To
Catch a Baron*?

Awkwardly, Victor patted his sister's shoulder. "Come
now, Mary. All chicks leave their nest."

"My darling girl is leaving me!" Lady Mary said. And
she cried harder.

Embarrassed, Victor prodded her. "Come, my dear,
you are a Frankenstein. Buck up." He did so hate seeing
women cry. It made him feel helpless, especially when
his aid merely made his sister grab a handkerchief from
her pocket and sob harder.

Growing desperate, he hit upon a grand idea. A brilliant Frankensteinian plan. "Eureka! I know, Mary. I
will *make* you another niece," he stated grandly.

The Bride Is a Frankenstein

Six figures dressed all in black entered St. George's Cathedral and joined the congregation. The oldest of the group marched to the front of the altar and bellowed in a voice at odds with the size of her diminutive figure, "Where's the funeral?"

Lady Mary, clad in her blue wedding finery, hurried to the old woman's side and explained, "Lady Vandeover, you have your days confused. Tomorrow is the funeral for Mr. Pugsley. Today is my niece's wedding."

"Wedding, did you say?" Mrs. Vandeover asked, lifting her hearing horn.

Lady Mary nodded, motioning for one of the ushers to come and escort the wizened woman to a seat. "Here, let Mr. Sleet help you and your party to the pews."

Beside her, Ozzie asked, "Is Mr. Pugsley a relative?"

"No, her pug."

"She's using St. George's Cathedral for a *dog's* funeral?" the duke questioned, amazed.

"She's very well off, you know." Lady Mary told him all about the woman as he escorted her back to her seat.

Glancing about, she felt her spirits revive. The church was still like one in a fairy tale, decorated beautifully with gardenias and orange blossoms. The smell was heavenly. White stuffed turtledoves and lovebirds were placed strategically all around.

Over a hundred and fifty guests—Mary's compromise with Ian—sat in the pews. The Frankensteins and their friends sat on the left; Ian's family and friends were seated to the right, staring over at Frederick. Lady Mary decided their awe must be due to such august company.

As Ozzie seated then took his seat beside her, Lady Mary proudly surveyed the assemblage. Frederick was dressed in a rust-colored jacket, which toned down the greenish cast of his skin. He looked remarkably fine, Lady Mary decided, studying him, for a man who was wearing someone else's face.

Next to Frederick sat Victor and Professor Whutson, both talking shop. Beside them, Clair's uncle Tieck busily scribbled more notes, having confided earlier to Lady Mary that he was writing a sequel to his last novel.

Lady Mary frowned. She'd had enough of all this vampire business. It had almost gotten her beloved niece killed. And if it weren't for the fact that Clair had met Ian through the whole nasty business, she would be quite put out.

"Let them eat cake!" Lady Abby cried from next to Lady Mary. She was dressed to suit her role as Louis XVI's queen.

Mary patted the woman's hand. "We will, Marie. Soon. And it will be delicious. Ozzie made it, you know." She smiled fondly at her lover.

"That's 'Your Highness' to you," Lady Abby huffed.

"Yes, dear," Mary replied.

At the back of the massive church, another famous figure entered. Dr. Durlock Homes. He stood for a moment surveying the scene, stifling a smile. It wasn't something he did very often. His work was so serious and grave that he had a hard time finding humor in anything but the most absurd.

Beside him, the tall, mustachioed Artie Doyle appeared and asked, "Which side is the bride's?"

Holmes lifted an eyebrow. "Rudimentary, my dear chap. Rudimentary." He pointed, then went and seated himself beside Professor Whutson in the seat vacated by Victor, since it was time for Victor to escort his niece to the altar.

The church grew quiet as the wedding march sounded, and the bridal procession began their walk down the aisle. A collective gasp came from the assemblage upon seeing the bride standing in the entrance. She was indeed a vision, dressed in yards of creamy satin with pearl inlays. Clair carried orange blossoms in her hand, and on her head was the Frankenstein wedding veil—a monstrous creation of lace, feathers, and flowers, with a towering crown topped by a tiara.

Yes, what a vision I am, Clair thought glumly. How could she have let them talk her into this hideous costume? She knew it was custom. All Frankenstein brides were married in this nasty veil. It was said to bring good luck.

"In a pig's eye!" she muttered.

"What's that?" her uncle asked, leaning as close as he could with the offensive veil. "You aren't regretting your decision to marry Ian, are you? Even though he is not in a scientific profession, I find myself rather liking him."

In fact, Victor had been estatic over Clair wedding Ian. So much so that he had gotten drunk and fallen into one of the graves he was robbing. Luckily, Frederick had come along and rescued him.

"No. No doubts whatsoever," Clair said.

Her uncle Victor smiled and patted her hand on his arm. "Stiff upper back, my dear. Let's give them the old Frankenstein show."

Clair smiled bravely, even though her knees were shaking, and she began her triumphant walk down the aisle. Soon the festive mood caught her spirit and she forgot about her hideous veil, reveling in her good fortune.

On this day of all days, Clair felt only love for Ian, her family, and her friends. It was a very special day, one she would remember when she grew old and gray. Yes, this was a very special day. Like the day she had discovered sodium sulfate could make exploding gas. Her uncle had shown her, and he had been so proud when she repeated the experiment all by herself, even though she blew up his favorite beaker.

Glancing to her side, she took in her uncle's proud visage. He had always encouraged her to fly to the stars, in spite of the fact that she was only a female. And when she had fallen, both he and Clair's aunts had been there to pick her back up.

As she made her way down the long carpeted aisle strewn with flowers, Clair passed Lady Delia and Delia's mother. The pair wore matching scowls. Clair grinned.

This reminded her of the time Delia fell into the mud at a picnic after Clair showed around her collection of spiders.

She passed Frederick, who had tears running down his cheeks like after the great electrical storm of 1819, when he had first drawn breath at the grand old age of thirty, twenty-one, thirty-five, etcetera.

Clair passed Lady Mary and Ozzie, both crying quietly, which reminded her of all the times her aunt had been present to dry her tears. It reminded her of all the times her aunt had encouraged her explorations and her curiosity, enriching her life with soft laughter and love.

Next Clair walked past Great-aunt Abby, who majestically held up her quizzing glass, nodding. The gesture took Clair back to the time her great-aunt knighted her, when she'd been Henry II. At least today, her aunt was impersonating an appropriate queen. For when she said, "Let them eat cake," they could.

Finally, Clair's attention was drawn to Ian, and her heart melted. He was so handsome, standing tall and kingly at the front of the church. She knew with an instinct as old as time that he and she had found a grand love that would transcend borders and lift winged souls to flight.

She paused longer to study him. He looked magnificent in his dark gray velvet jacket, and his long black hair was tied back in a queue. He wore a green vest underneath his coat, and it matched the color of his eyes. Those eyes were filled with unconditional love for his bride, even in her hideous veil.

Victor placed Clair's hand in Ian's when they arrived at the end of the aisle; then he stepped away as Ian lifted the veil from her face and flipped it back. "Now I can see you," Ian said softly. "You are the most beautiful thing I have ever beheld in my life." His tone comple- mented his serious expression, for his eyes glistened with unshed tears.

"Thank you." She grinned, joyful tears of her own spilling down her cheeks. "For the compliment, but more for getting that beastly veil out of my face."

Ian chortled.

"Who gives this woman?" the bishop asked, frowning at the levity of the wedding service.

"I do," Victor answered after a slight pause, sounding a bit choked up.

"Do you, Harold Ian Huntsley, take Clair Elizabeth Frankenstein to be your lawfully wedded wife?" the bishop asked.

Giggling, Clair nudged Ian. "Harold?"

"Hush, Clair. Now is not the time." Ian felt a blush travel up his face. He truly despised his first name. It had been a curse throughout his life.

"Harold." Clair giggled again. She couldn't imagine such a whimsical name for such a formidable man. But all that mattered was that they were to be wed.

Despite Clair's giggles and the oddity of the bride's side of the family, the wedding turned out to be the usual, tra- ditional, emotional affair. Afterward in the receiving line, Ian stood with his arm wrapped around his bride's waist. He proudly introduced her for the first time as his wife to his family and friends. His life was now complete in a way that he had never known. He felt a sense of complete well-being. Clair was his. He had found his one true mate.

"Take care of her, young man. She has been a daugh- ter to me," Victor warned kindly. "My Clair is special."

Ian nodded. "Yes, they broke the mold when they made her."

"No. That was Frederick, not Clair," Victor replied. He looked mildly confused as he moved aside to let other well-wishers congratulate the bride and groom.

Ian shook his head. He would have to get used to this. But as Clair smiled up at him, her eyes shining with pure joy, he decided she was well worth putting up with living around a nest of odd ducks and a few quacks. He'd mostly only see them at family gatherings, anyway. "I love you, Clair Huntsley," he said.

Clair grinned mischievously. "I love you too, Harold."

Hmm. Perhaps he would have to rethink the matter. Playfully, he swatted his wife on her nicely rounded behind. *Harold?* Just wait until he got her alone tonight.

Haunted Honeymoon

Clair came out of the water closet and glanced toward the balcony, where Ian stood in all his naked splendor. He was watching the last rays of the golden sunset give up the ghost and blend into shades of purplish gray, soon to be black. He wore a smug, satisfied leer on his handsome face.

"Thank you, God," she whispered. *Thank you for listening to children's prayers, for creating the human heart and spirit which can survive against all odds. Which can love in spite of fear. Which can, despite loneliness and by your great grace, find love. And thank you most of all, God, for creating two people so right for each other and bringing us together.*

Staring at her handsome husband, Clair was awed that he'd been able to create such a perfect person. "God," she said, "you've still got Uncle Victor beat in my book."

She walked past the lovely old four-poster bed and

mussed linen sheets where she and Ian had made love earlier. Their joining had held a raw, primitive passion, each of them claiming the other in the ancient rites of love and lust, and Clair blushed at the memory. Reaching Ian, she tenderly wrapped her arms around his hard, muscular back, heated in spite of his nudity. He reached behind himself and pulled her into his arms, his chin coming to rest on the top of her head.

Clair sniffled, holding back her tears. In Ian's arms, she had found completion. It was a place so miraculous she would never leave it willingly. She hugged him more tightly, glancing out at the darkening sky.

"It will be a full moon tonight," she said and shivered.

Ian tucked his wife closer, his legs pressed to the outsides of hers. He leaned his head back and breathed deeply. He smelled sex, orange blossoms, and the scent of the coming evening. "I love the way the night smells and sounds," he said.

Clair tilted her head, leaning back to look at him.

He went on, "The night has its own music, the stars their own melody. The moon has a song which sings to me."

"So there *is* a poet buried inside you," she teased. "I thought that was only Asher."

"Hmph. Asher and his 'She walks in beauty,'" Ian sneered good-naturedly. "Poppycock."

"Poppycock? So, I'm not a beauty who walks in the night?" She loved teasing Ian.

He gently lifted her chin, pretending to study it with haughty thoroughness. "Some men might find you lovely. I find your jaw a bit too stubborn." That was for calling him Harold, he thought.

"Some men might find your gray eyes mesmerizing. I

find them full of obstinate challenge." That was for bringing up the top-lofty Asher on their honeymoon. He didn't want to be haunted by a vampire's ghost.

"Some men might find your graceful manners most pleasing. I find them sadly lacking in decorum—a trifle hoydenish." That was for giggling in church at his first name.

"Some men might find you a handful." He grinned wolfishly, a predatory gleam to his eye as he cupped both breasts tenderly. "I find you . . . a handful."

So saying, he scooped her up and carried her inside, depositing her upon the rumpled sheets. He came down atop her, his nostrils flaring. "All in all, Clair Frankenstein Huntsley, I find you to be quite remarkable."

Lovingly, Clair gazed upon her husband's face. "And I find you to be more interesting than any supernatural species I have ever investigated. In point of fact, you are supernaturally magnificent all by yourself."

Ian grinned deviously and stripped off her robe. Clair was soon to be greatly surprised, he knew. He licked and nipped every inch of her flesh.

Squirming, Clair felt as if her skin were on fire. That area between her thighs began to tingle as Ian licked his way up her body. She looked down at his dark head buried between her legs and gasped. What was this? Did men and women really do *this* on their wedding nights? As Ian glanced up at her, a wicked grin on his face, Clair's thoughts all came tumbling out. "My, what big teeth you have."

The look he gave her would have melted a glacier.

"The better to eat you with, my dear." And he proceeded to do just that, nuzzling the honey-gold curls between her thighs. He sucked and bit, gently bringing on a climax that had Clair touching the stars. She screamed in delight.

Ian's grin was one of pure male arrogance in knowing that his mate was well satisfied, and soon he would be too. His erection was so stiff and heavy that he was afraid he would burst before he could savor her lush, tight warmth. Seconds later he was buried in her hot, pulsating heat.

Hungrily he attacked her mouth, feeding on its sweetness as he thrust into her with a savage rhythm. With indomitable spirit, Clair met him thrust for thrust, her body bucking wildly as he sucked on her generous white breasts. Again she screamed.

He was killing her with a pleasure so pure, Clair thought it must be tied to infinity and the creation of the cosmos. "I love you, I love you," she chanted over and over.

Ian could feel Clair's tremors beginning, and knowing she was about to climax he reared back and plunged deep one last time. She screamed again. He shouted, her loving words as well as her fulfillment bringing on his own. He found release in a hot burst, his seed flooding her warm dark depths.

Moments later he was supporting his weight on his elbows as he bowed his head to hers, his thick hair damp with sweat. "I love you, wife." He would never get tired of saying those words. He would never get tired of seeing her all pink and flushed with his lovemaking, her eyes glazed over with spent passion.

Rolling over, he pulled Clair to him, her tawny hair cascading over his chest. He kissed the top of her head. "I have two wedding gifts for you that you haven't yet received."

Clair's sleepy eyes lit up. "I love surprises," she said.

He grinned. "I know. You'll get one now and one later on tonight."

She sighed. "You know I want them both now. I'd argue about it, but I'm just too tired. So . . . how about that second surprise?" she coaxed seductively, running her fingers through the curly hair of his chest. Oh, how she loved the feel of her husband. Oh, how she loved this man. He was her miracle.

"Later," he promised. He hugged her tightly, savoring the feel of her naked body so close to him. "I know that bloody vampire Asher is always spouting poetry, so I decided on something special. On expressing myself in words the way you like but I haven't been able to do."

Clair propped herself on his chest, her eyes wide with surprise. "This is a gift indeed. I know poetry is not your forte."

"Hush, Clair, and let me get this said before I lose my blasted nerve." He pushed her head back onto his chest and began the poem, which eloquently told the feelings of his soul:

"How many have loved your moment of glad grace,
and loved your beauty with love false and true.
But one man loved the pilgrim soul in you
and loved the sorrows of your changing face."

Clair's tears wet his chest, and Ian thought it a fitting end for that man who had once kept his heart encased in iron. "I will always love you, Harold Ian Huntsley," she said.

Then she was asleep, before he could scold her about using his first name. She looked so adorable in slumber, and he couldn't really blame her—after all, this was the third time they had made love in less than two hours. He always had such tremendous energy on nights of the full moon.

As Ian watched his wife sleeping in his bed, in his home in Wales, he felt his cup run over with love. Clair was his mate. She was in his territory. The two things gave him such a primitive sense of possession he wanted to howl with joy.

Tenderly, he lifted one of her long burnished golden curls that came nearly to her waist, and he inhaled the wintry scent of Clair. She was so beautiful, inside and out. She had awakened a hunger in him that only her companionship could sate.

In sleep, her remarkable curiosity and indomitable determination didn't show. Still, her smile held a hint of the minx. Yes, Ian knew, Clair Frankenstein Huntsley would always lead him a merry, merry chase.

Restless, he rose and prowled the room, then gave up and stepped out onto the balcony. He was so happy, he ached. Clair had broken the tower walls of his heart with her wit, compassion, energy, and humor. He loved her so much, and he wanted to make her happy. He knew she was forlorn about giving up her supernatural studies, but he had a big surprise for her. Though she wouldn't be able to publish these findings, she would be able to study deeply in private. And the deeper the investigation, the better. She wouldn't even have to leave home for her research. She could eye him here all she wanted.

Oh yes, he could hardly wait to see the look on Clair's face when she discovered his second surprise. He realized that she would be mad at first for his sin of omission. But he also knew her scientific curiosity would get the better of her bad temper—if she didn't kill him first.

He looked up into the night sky. The full moon had risen. Ian's body thrummed with energy and white-hot heat—the call of the wild. Ian laughed, the sound husky and deep as fur rippled out along his skin.

The transformation began. He threw back his head and howled.

Jerked awake from her sated slumber in the bedroom, Clair could swear that she'd just heard a wolf howl. On her wedding night, no less. Another spine-tingling howl convinced her that she wasn't having a delightful nightmare of werewolves and vampires. There *was* a wolf howling and, from the sounds, it was at the foot of her bed.

Peeking from under the covers, Clair gasped. Out on the balcony, her husband of less than a full day was transforming into a wolf before her very eyes. He was down on all fours, with fur covering every part of his body, with the exception of one part, which grew even longer and more rigid—if that was possible. Now *that* she'd expected on her wedding night. But not with all the fur.

Her eyes round, her fists clenched, Clair gasped, "I'm married to the Werewolf of London and he never told me!"

She turned to deal with him.

The Trouble with Hairy

Clair would never forget last night as long as she lived. The trouble with Harold Ian Huntsley was that he was a werewolf as well as her husband of one night. He was her lying, big-fanged, hairy husband. Call her an odd duck, but the werewolf part hardly threw Clair for a loop; it was the lying part she couldn't tolerate. Her husband had said he had a big surprise for her on her wedding night. He wasn't kidding. From mortal to wolf in less than five minutes. It would have been awe-inspiring if she hadn't been so mad about being deceived.

Clair had, of course, tried to talk to Ian about her anger. But how could you have an intelligent conversation when the person you're arguing with was howling at the moon? So Clair made the grown-up decision, packed her bags, and left her bridegroom of less than two days to go home to her family.

Now that Clair was almost home, she faced several

dilemmas. How could she break the news to her family? *Should* she break the news to them? How could she tell them that the perfect nobleman she had just married was furry and fanged once a month. She, the brilliant and eccentric scientist who was never going to get married, had fallen in love hard, fast, and forever with a four-footed liar.

Remembering how thrilled her family had been at the ceremony, Clair dreaded telling them the bad news. She hadn't married beneath her; she had married into a whole new species!

"I've left my husband on our wedding night because, you see, the trouble with Harry Ian is that he's hairy Ian," Clair mumbled to herself, testing it out. "Well, you didn't actually see, but I did." Shaking her head intently, she decided that wouldn't work. Uncle Victor would just want to watch the transformation and take notes. She would get no sympathy from him.

"Ian is the Wolfman of London," Clair tried. No, Frederick would just pat him on the back and welcome another monster into the family, she surmised. Desperate, she glanced outside the carriage window. They were pulling up to the Frankenstein family townhouse.

Irritated, she pulled on the red cloak her devious husband had given her for a wedding gift. He had kissed her soundly, then begun calling her his Little Red Riding Hood. A red cloak! How appropriate, since he was the big, bad, lying wolf.

To think, he had kept his werewolfism a secret when she was in the midst of the biggest supernatural investigation of her career. It was unforgivable. She would never see him again. Well, it was mostly unforgiveable. Damn his big furry head!

Knocking on the front door to the townhouse, Clair stamped her foot. Ian was going to pay for his deceit. She just hadn't figured out how. But being the Frankenstein she was, she would figure a way. The Frankenstein family butler interrupted her thoughts of revenge.

"Why, Miss Clair, what are you doing here?" Brooks asked curiously. "What have you gotten yourself into now?"

"Brooks, what a horrid thing to say to me! You make it sound as though I go around courting trouble," Clair retorted.

Brooks put on his long-suffering expression. "Trouble is your middle name," he said.

"No, it's Elizabeth. And this time everything is my husband's fault. The baron is a . . ." She cleared her throat and tried again. "Ian is a . . ." She trailed off in a fit of coughing, unable to denounce her husband for the werewolf that he was. She didn't understand it, but somehow the words lodged in her throat.

Brooks raised a brow. "Yes?"

"Oh, never mind. Where is Aunt Mary?"

"Lady Mary is in the Blue Salon. She is going over a funeral service for the hamster, Stedman." Brooks gestured the way politely, his curiosity running rampant. Why was Clair home from her honeymoon minus one groom? He started to follow her, but she pointed to the stairs and her baggage. "I can find them myself, Brooks."

He picked up her portmanteau and sniffed. "I can take a hint," he groused.

Clair shook her head, following the hallway toward the Blue Salon. She knew Brooks was curious, but she had other things on her mind right now—like the sight of her naked husband growing extremely long claws and fangs.

Entering the Blue Salon, Clair spied her aunt immediately. Lady Mary was talking to a thin older woman with red eyes and nose. The woman was dressed all in black. Clair recalled her briefly. She was a widow by the name of Bonni . . . something or another. Clair moved to the receiving table and waited as the older woman spoke.

"Yes, I think I like the relaxed pose that frog is wearing," the woman said, pointing to one of her aunt's favorite specimens, a large green frog wearing a red ascot and reclining on a lily pad. The frog's legs were crossed. "Yes, give Stedman that pose. He was always so busy in life, scurrying here and there, biting at his cage. I think he deserves a rest in the afterlife."

Glancing around, Clair noted the small box on the receiving table. Stunned, she blinked her eyes and looked again. Still stunned, she closed her eyes and counted to ten. Opening them, she found that she hadn't been wrong; the box held a very large, very ugly rat.

Brooks walked up beside her and noticed her expression. He smiled slyly.

"I thought you said this was a hamster. This isn't a hamster. It's a big fat rat," Clair whispered. *A big fat rat just like my husband.*

"Lady Bonfield thinks it's a hamster," Brooks replied, unruffled.

"But it's a rat," Clair argued.

"To you and me, yes. But Lady Bonfield has bad eyesight. And she is too vain to wear spectacles."

In spite of her troubles, Clair had to stifle a chuckle. This was a first for her aunt: stuffing a rat and giving said rat a funeral service.

She shook her head. "Brooks, tell my aunt I'll meet her in the library when she's finished here."

The butler nodded.

Clair made her way to the library, and there she sank down wearily onto the rose brocade sofa. Why hadn't Ian told her the truth about his supernatural lineage? All those weeks of running around and worrying over her research, and everything could have been greatly eased by the knowledge that Ian was a wolfman. It would have also helped in those first days, when she was trying to track the London nest of vampires, if she had known Ian had otherworldly powers. But rather than studying the supernatural, she had been the victim of a super hoax! It was not to be borne!

Face clasped in her hands, Clair wrinkled her brow. She needed to formulate a plan, something where Ian got down on his knees and crawled to her—in human form, of course, preferably through hard gravel and pleading for mercy. Mercy which she would not grant. Mercy which she would absolutely, positively not grant.

The picture of Ian clear in her mind, Clair added more. Maybe he should crawl naked to her, his broad shoulders and arms rippling, his thick thighs bulging with muscles, and just above his thighs, standing at full attention . . .

Clair fanned herself. No, not naked. Ian should definitely not crawl naked to her.

Her thoughts were interrupted by her aunt entering the room. Glancing up, Clair noted vaguely that Lady Mary's expression was worried.

"Clair, what are you doing here? This is your honeymoon."

"I've left Ian," Clair replied, her eyes sparkling with gray fire.

"But it's been less than two days," Lady Mary remarked, shocked to her gentle soul.

"I know. But I had no choice. He's a wolf." This time, the words came clear and free. Odd, Clair thought. *I can reveal Ian's werewolfism to my aunt, but not to my butler.*

"Dear, you knew that when you married him. Ian is a handsome rake, and the ladies have always found him attractive. Besides, they say reformed rakes make the best husbands."

Clair rolled her eyes. She loved her aunt, but sometimes the dear lady could be a tad dense. "Not *that* kind of wolf, but a *real* wolf. A furry, big-toothed werewolf." Her words hung in the air rather like a big stink.

Lady Mary's eyes became as round as saucers. Then, after several seconds of silent contemplation, she remarked, "Clair, nobody's perfect."

Clair's eyes widened with disbelief. "He's a *liar* and a werewolf. He is so far from perfect as to be completely imperfect."

"They say love is blind," her aunt retorted.

"It would also have to be deaf in this instance, Aunt. Ian actually howls at the moon."

"Well, dear . . . that's what wolves do. I guess even wolfish husbands," Lady Mary replied, her brow furrowed. "I was going to ask you if you were sure about this, but I can see that you are."

"Yes. Ian transformed into a wolf for my wedding gift."

"Well, dear, you have to admit that is an original wedding gift. Won't your uncle be thrilled? Think of all the scientific questions he'll get to ask."

It had been a stupendous sight, Clair recalled. So awe-inspiring that she had cried soft tears of wonder. But she was not about to let her aunt know that. Ian deserved no defense from her.

Instead she said, "Ha! He lied to me. All that time I was investigating the vampire nest here in London, and he was one of the supernatural creatures I was looking for. You know I thought he was a vampire pretending to be a man. Instead he is a werewolf pretending to be a man, wooing me with those hungry green eyes." Clair was furious. She hated being lied to about anything. It went against her grain and of course the family motto: The truth at all costs.

"He knew how important my work was to me, and that prestigious award. Yet Ian straight-up lied when I asked if he was a vampire."

"But he isn't a vampire, dear. He's a werewolf," Lady Mary reminded her.

"But he knew that I thought that he was a supernatural creature, and he is a supernatural creature—just not a vampire."

"But you didn't ask him if he was a werewolf, only a vampire. You thought the Earl of Wolverton was a werewolf."

"Don't remind me. Yes, I was the girl who cried wolf. But Ian was aware that I thought the earl was a were. When I needed to know where the weres were, Ian knew the whereabouts of the weres, because he *is* the were," Clair finished dramatically.

Lady Mary's head was spinning. Her niece was a genius at times, but this wasn't one of those times. "Ian didn't lie. He just didn't explain his ancestry. I admit it is an unusual heritage. But think how lucky you are. You needn't ever run out of fresh meat."

Clair crossed her eyes. Leave her aunt to find something positive in this situation.

Seeing her niece's annoyance, Lady Mary added, "Besides, now you have your supernatural subject right at your front door. In point of fact, your research of preternatural predators can take place in your very own home. And may I remind you what a nice home it is, the ancestral Huntsley baronial estate."

Clair shrugged. "I will admit I am a tiny bit excited about having my own personal specimen to study at leisure. But that is the only point in Ian's favor."

Her aunt raised her eyebrows. "The only point?"

Clair blushed, remembering the fiercely passionate lovemaking of her wedding night, before the groom had got down on four legs and run off after the cat.

A loud knocking could be heard down the hall. Lady Mary glanced in that direction, remarking astutely, "I think I hear the wolf at the door."

Clair scowled. "Well, I am not one of the three little pigs." Moving closer to the hallway, she called out loudly, "Brooks, if that is the treacherous, lying dog Baron Huntsley, don't let him in."

"Clair, remember you are a lady," her aunt admonished.

"Too late," Ian warned, his green eyes glowing with anger as he stalked into the room. "The wolf's not only at your door, he's in the house. Run, piggy, run."

He stood tall and formidable, glaring at Clair, dark circles under his eyes marring the perfection of his handsome face. Clair's leaving had devastated him.

Stealthily he approached, halting only when his boots touched the hem of her dress.

Angrily, Clair kicked him. "You know I hate piggy jokes."

Ian reacted to the attack by grabbing Clair and pulling her into his arms. His lips smashed down on hers. It was an angry kiss, the kiss of man who had woken up the morning after his wedding to discover his mate had fled his lair. In other words, he was not a happy wolf. He was a big mad wolf with big white gritted teeth.

Clair's body responded, her love for Ian filling her, reminding her of how he made her feel. Heart aching—as well as other regions of her anatomy—she reminded herself of his deceit. Fiercely, she pushed him away.

"You beast!"

Ian's eyes flashed angrily. "I won't deny it. I am what I am."

Dramatically, she pointed a finger at him and continued, her words fueled by anger. "You four-footed bounder! You lying lycanthrope."

He grabbed her finger, put it between his lips, and bit gently.

"You whopper-telling werewolf."

Uncomfortably, Lady Mary cleared her throat. "I have to go and see to your great-aunt Abby, who is hosting tea for Louis today." She exited the room.

Ian glanced briefly at the departing woman, then switched his attention back to his angry wife. Clair's gray eyes were sparking a deep flinty color. Her cheeks were flushed and her bosom was heaving. He wanted to make mad, passionate love with her. But seeing her expression, he knew it would only be mad love right now.

He had known Clair would be a tad upset that he hadn't

revealed his werewolfism sooner. He also knew she hated liars. But he had foolishly thought her excitement, her unrelentingly curious scientific mind, her Frankensteinian lust for exploring the unknown, would overrule her female nature. He had gambled big and gambled wrong.

Worse, he had never thought that Clair would leave him. It was humiliating. It was maddening. It was something he had become acquainted with more frequently since falling in love with a Frankenstein, this impossible mix of frustration and feeling as if he were stuck on another continent, not knowing the native language. Did anyone speak Clairese?

"I thought you would be thrilled to continue your research up close and personal . . . on me," he remarked, waggling his eyebrows. "I told you long ago that I would be honored to be your lab experiment. Think of all the research you can do late at night. On my body." He smiled wolfishly.

Clair shivered. He was playing dirty. She had only tasted a tiny amount of Ian's lovemaking, and it was better than any scientific discovery she had ever made. Now her body craved his, the fiend. He'd probably expected that when he first made love to her. Now she was an Ian addict, addicted to werewolf love. The cad!

She narrowed her eyes, her mouth a firm straight line. All she said was, "Ha!"

"You can explore to your heart's content. Run your fingers over my body. Feel my muscles. Feel how they stretch, like how I feel you stretch when I fill you with . . ." He took her fingers and ran them over his chest.

"Harold Ian Huntsley, behave yourself. Brooks is probably listening at the door," Clair admonished sternly, her cheeks bright red. But her mind was reeling with the possibilities. She would count all the hairs on Ian when he transformed, then compare that to the number of hairs on a natural wolf. Of course, Ian would have to find her the natural wolf. She could measure his fangs and all sorts of other things.

He chuckled. "I love it when you get embarrassed," he said. He began stalking her, and Clair backed away, shaking her head, her tawny curls bouncing.

"I love it when you kiss me," he continued. "I love it when you get a new idea and your eyes sparkle. I even love it when you drag me into trouble on one of your investigations." Ian paused, watching the pulse in his wife's throat as she circled behind the settee.

He smiled wickedly. He could hunt Clair forever, predator that he was, and never tire of it. She was the most wonderful thing that had ever happened to him, and she was most definitely *his*.

"Most of all," he finished, "I love it when you scream my name when you reach climax."

Clair's blush spread to her chest, and she glared at him, waving her finger back and forth. "You . . . you dog!"

"Wrong species," he said. He jumped over the couch and grabbed Clair, enfolding her in his arms. "Clair, I love you. Wolves mate for life, and you're mine."

He pulled her around to the front of the settee and settled her in his lap. At first she put up a token resistance, but his kisses weakened her. Who was she fooling? She loved Harold Ian Huntsley to the depths of her soul. He was her other half. She was a fool for this handsome wolf.

She held him close, then regretfully pushed herself

away from the comfort of his warm chest. She had questions to ask. He had answers he needed to give to her.

"You lied to me, Ian," she said.

He tipped her chin up and looked into her eyes. "I never lied."

She started to protest. He put his finger on her lips and shook his head. "I didn't tell you what I was at first because I have my family to protect, plus a whole clan of other werewolves. We let few humans into our circle because of the danger. It's the same as with Asher and the vampires."

"But you could have told me about yourself later," Clair protested. "And what about when I thought the Earl of Wolverton was a werewolf? You knew he was a vampire. Why didn't you tell me?"

Ian shook his head solemnly. "Clair, all supernatural creatures protect one another. We have to. It is our blood bond and our blood duty. The preternatural world is a small one."

"That's why you threw me off the scent with Ozzie, telling me he was a practitioner of the black arts when he only studies the culinary arts."

Ian nodded.

"What about when we made love for the first time? You could have told me then."

"Clair, I was so concerned about getting you to marry me that night, I didn't think revealing I was a werewolf was the correct courting procedure."

She turned her face away, but Ian continued, "Clair, we shapeshifters share a pact. We can't reveal what we are to humans unless they are related by blood or marriage. I couldn't tell you what I was until you were my wife."

She searched his eyes and saw he spoke the truth.

"I told you as soon as I could. If you had waited around long enough for me to transform back, I would have explained. Instead you chose to run home," he scolded gently. "We can't solve our marital problems like that."

She leaned her head against his chest, slipping her arms around his waist. "I guess not. But I was so angry at you." She understood family loyalty.

"I know," he teased, "you were yelling at me like a fishwife."

"Hmm. Your bark is worse than your bite. All you did was howl and growl back."

"I wasn't in a position to do anything else." He kissed the top of her head, her golden curls shining in the light from the large bay window. "Are you truly upset that I'm a werewolf?"

Clair leaned back and gazed up at him. "Can I be turned into one?"

"No, Clair, that is an old wives' tale. Werewolves can only be born, not made by being bitten."

The thought momentarily shocked Clair. She glanced down at her stomach. "Our children will be shapeshifters?" she asked.

She didn't know how she felt about that.

Ian studied his wife, his expression intense, his dark green eyes glittering with emotion. He was proud of his ancestry. He wanted and needed his wife to be proud of it as well. "Would you mind?"

She thought for a moment. "I don't think so. I love you and would love any child you gave me. But still, I don't have enough data to completely support a declaration at this time," she answered honestly. A sudden image of herself feeding a cute furry wolf cub flashed in her mind, and she smiled with happiness.

Ian nodded, seemingly satisfied. He then gave her more information: "When two weres mate, they produce were-children. When a were and a human mate, their children are human, although the child sometimes has extraordinary hearing and eyesight. But if the were and human mate two days after the full moon, if the female conceives then, the child *will* be born a were."

Clair was fascinated and thrilled. This was having her werewolf and eating him too. She had a thousand questions. She had Ian, her own personal lab rat to study— correction, lab wolf. She started to ask more, but Ian shook his head. "I need to speak with your aunt Mary to swear her to secrecy. Have you told anyone else?"

"No. I began to tell Brooks, but I couldn't get the words out."

"You wouldn't be able to."

"Why not?" she questioned, her eyes full of that indomitable Frankenstein curiosity.

Ian smiled. Many women would have fainted if they knew they were married to a card-carrying werewolf; his Clair was exhilarated. He was a lucky man, if he could only keep her out of trouble.

"We're protected by an ancient spell. Humans that know about us can't tell unless they tell someone with a strong blood link to them."

"So Uncle Victor can know, and Great-aunt Abby," Clair surmised. She frowned. "But not Frederick?"

Ian shook his head. "Frederick is an exception. He can be told."

"How strange," she muttered, her mind reeling.

"Every newly wedded couple has a learning period," Ian suggested.

"Yes, like, do you like orange marmalade with your toast? Not, what did you eat last night—or better, whom?"

Ian arched a brow, his expression affronted. "I don't eat humans! My clan never does. We are extremely civilized, Clair," he said stiffly. "If shape-shifters ate humans, we would be discovered, and we haven't lived this long by doing stupid things. Only a few rogue clans attack humans for food, and they are far, far away."

Clair cocked her head, chewing on her lips. "Just how old are you, Ian? How long do weres live? For centuries, like vampires? I know Asher is over four hundred years old."

The earl's name brought an instant scowl to Ian's face. He didn't like the fact that Asher had fallen in love with Clair. She was his, and the handsome master vampire had better never forget that. Still, Asher had saved Clair's life.

"Ian?" his wife prompted, her eyes round with concern. She feared she would grow old and gray while Ian remained handsome and vigorous. She would be on a cane, and he would be running circles around her.

"We can live to be a hundred and thirty. I'm forty-three in werewolf years. We age more slowly."

Clair shook her head sorrowfully. "Drat. I'll be an old woman when you're still a spring chicken. Will you still love me when I'm sixty-four?" She tried to make her voice light, but inside she was hurting. She would have wrinkles, and he would have trollops winking at him.

"Of course I will, darling. You are my mate for life. I won't mate again," he answered truthfully. "By the time you're fifty, I'll be fifty-nine in werewolf years, so we'll both have a gray hair or two," he assured her. He held her close and let her feel his love. "Like I said, all new couples have to make adjustments."

His answer soothed her, just like his hand, which was rubbing circles on her back. Yes, Clair supposed she had a few adjustments to make, marrying a werewolf. But how hard could it be? The bed linens would probably have paw prints on the full moons when it rained. But, then, as a child she had slept with her dog, a large collie, and that had been both warm and comforting.

Ian would probably need to shave twice a day. Clair wondered briefly about fleas, and if she might sometimes join him baying at the moon. It had actually looked rather fun.

Yes, she decided, she would be fine. The adjustments would probably be few and far between. She would tackle them with her usual Frankensteinian fortitude. Besides, how many women had a real wolf in their bed?

"You do know, Ian, that I am still going to be competing for the prestigious Scientist of the Decade Award. Instead of werewolves and vampires, I'll go back to my ghost research."

Ian nipped her ear. "I had hoped to have you started on motherhood as soon as possible," he urged, his large, capable hands caressing her stomach.

"As soon as I win the Award, we can have all the children you want."

Ian started to argue, but Clair placed her finger over his lips. "You have no room to complain about my working for the Award, not when you are moonlighting as a werewolf."

He arched an eyebrow, then nodded and grinned. "I

think I'll like having the Scientist of the Decade for a wife."

Clair laughed. "You know the trouble with you, Harry Ian?"

He leaned back and studied her. "What?"

"Absolutely nothing."

Tall, Dark & Hungry

LYNSAY SANDS

It bites: New York hotels cost an arm and a leg, and Terri has flown from England to help plan her cousin's wedding. The new in-laws offered lodging. But they're a weird bunch! There is the sometimes-chipper-sometimes-silent Lucern, and the wacky stage-actor Vincent: she can't imagine Broadway casting a hungrier singing-and-dancing Dracula. And then there is Bastien. Just looking into his eyes, Terri has to admit she's falling for someone even taller, darker, and hungrier. She's feeling a mite peckish herself. And if she stays with him, those blood-sucking hotel owners won't get her!

Nina Bangs
Master of Ecstasy

Her trip back in time to 1785 Scotland is supposed to be a vacation, so why does Blythe feel that her stay at the MacKenzie castle will be anything but? The gloomy old pile of stones has her imagination working overtime.

The first hunk she meets turns out to be Mr. Dark-Evil-and-Deadly himself, an honest-to-goodness vampire. His voice is a tempting slide of sin, and his body raises her temperature, but when Darach whispers, "To waste a neck such as yours would be a terrible thing," she decides his pillow talk leaves a lot to be desired.

Dangerous? You bet. To die for? Definitely. Soul mate? Just wait and see.

CHRISTINE FEEHAN
DARK DESTINY

Her childhood had been a nightmare of violence and pain until she heard his voice calling out to her. Golden and seductive. The voice of an angel.

He has shown her how to survive, taught her to use her unique gifts, trained her in the ancient art of hunting the vampire. Yet he cannot bend her to his will. He cannot summon her to him, no matter how great his power.

As she battles centuries-old evil in a glittering labyrinth of caverns and crystals, he whispers in her mind, forging an unbreakable bond of trust and need. Only with him can she find the courage to embrace the seductive promise of her . . . *Dark Destiny*.

Dorchester Publishing Co., Inc.
P.O. Box 6640
Wayne, PA 19087-8640

____5050-1
$7.99 US/$9.99 CAN